THE PRINCE WITH SIX FACES

by Anna Holmes

©2024

Cover art copyright Jason Holmes 2024.
Published by Elyssia Books.

First Edition, 2024

ISBN-13: 978-1-954732-26-1

For all of us who didn't fit (yes, even you)

Trigger warnings: homophobia, transphobia, eugenics, inappro-
priate teacher-student relationships, unethical medical practices

Part One

–

Clockbridge

Chapter One
An Inconvenient Reunion

Max hurried through the streets of an unfamiliar city with his coat drawn up. He'd taken Flora's address from an old letter and hoped desperately she still lived there. These houses were charming little things with window boxes and painted shutters—stark opposition to much of the city, which seemed to carry a layer of dirt. He counted the house numbers until he found the one she'd noted on the letter. He practically flew up to the landing, knocked at the door, and prayed.

It opened, and there was Flora, her black hair pulled back into a sensible braid as always. "Max!" she chirped, equal parts shock and delight. "What are you doing here?"

He smiled wearily. "Hello, Flora. May I come in?"

"Yes, yes, yes," she said, pulling him by the arm and shutting the door behind him. "I'm just so—you never get to leave."

Get to was doing a lot of heavy lifting. As the only heir to the throne of Saltrush, Max spent most of his time being droned at by advisors or snapped at by his mother. Travel, particularly undiplomatic travel, had long been off the table. "It's…well… something's happened."

Her dark face went sallow with dread. "Oh no. A coup? A plot? *Assassination?*"

"No, no, nothing like that."

"Oh, thank goodness." She turned to light a lamp. "Sorry about the dim, it's for the—"

"Experiments," he said. "I remember."

She smiled brighter than the lamp. "So, what is it?"

Max hesitated. It would be one of two times he'd spoken it out loud. Flora watched him carefully, then pulled him a little more gently toward a plumply-stuffed couch. He sat and took stock of his words. "Flora, do you know anything about curses?"

She sat down next to him and wrapped her hands around a knee. "Some. What happened?"

What happened. His stomach knotted itself, and he hunched his lanky body to try to relieve some of the pressure. "There was this fey visitor."

"*Max.*"

"Missteps were made. She was unhappy."

"And now you're cursed?"

"It wasn't completely my doing—Mother had a hand. But the long and short of it is I'm being *taught a lesson.*"

They sat in quiet for a moment. He could tell by her pursed lips that she was trying to think of what to say. She opened them and said gently, "What lesson is that?"

He laughed mirthlessly. "If I knew, I wouldn't be in this spot.

I can have a guess, based on what's happening, but even that is so...."

Flora looked like she wanted to ask but was holding in her words. She turned her head toward Max and waited patiently, as she always had done. Something in his chest eased. This was why he'd sought her out, not simply to have somewhere to go. He took a breath. "Every morning at dawn, I wake up...different."

"What do you mean?"

"Changed."

"Like...?"

"I wake up in a different body. There are six of them, including this one."

"Six." Flora pursed her lips together. "How long has this been happening?"

"Almost a month?" he said.

"Oh, Max."

"Mother decided she'd had enough and sent me out into the world to get it fixed. But I haven't the faintest idea how to actually *do* that. So I came here, to you."

"I don't think I do, either." He knew he shouldn't be disappointed by that: it was just that he'd always felt that Flora knew everything, even when he knew that wasn't true. She brightened. "Don't worry, though. I'm sure we can find someone to help."

"What makes you so sure?"

"We're in Clockbridge," she said. "There are experts on everything here. It's no Solarian University, but there has to be someone here who knows about curse removal. In the meantime, stay with me. I'll keep you safe."

"You're sure?" he said. "The way this will look…."

"What? I have visitors," she said with a sprightly laugh. He raised an eyebrow. "As far as people know, I could have six of 'em at a time."

"Surely people would have some thoughts about that."

"I'm already the woman with the dim house full of science experiments," she said. "Besides, a dinged reputation is a small cost to help you."

"Thank you, Flora," he said, bowing his head.

She looked up at a large clock against the wall. "Look at the time. Are you hungry?"

His stomach turned over. In truth, he hadn't had much to eat in days. Trail rations only got him so far. "I…."

"Be honest."

"I could eat your house."

"Let's make sure you don't, then."

Flora talked to him over her shoulder as she cooked, chipper and thoughtful as ever, though he caught her studying him in a way he didn't quite understand yet. Maybe she was looking for hints of the next version of him to come, or maybe she started to doubt his story. He was certainly in disbelief, day in and day out.

"How are my parents?" she wanted to know.

"Haven't you been writing?"

"Hrrmm…." She squirmed.

"They're well," he assured her. "Very little has changed."

"That's why I don't really write," she said with a little shrug. "There are only so many ways to say 'things are exactly the way you left them'."

"Oh, I wouldn't say that," he said.

"At home? Absolutely. Maybe not with you. Definitely not with you."

"Until recently? No, not much changed.But not with you," he said, leaning forward. "Last I heard, you got some sort of consulting appointment."

"Yes, the Solarian University has me working on a few pieces of research," she said enthusiastically. "I'll show you."

"Flora, I'm not a cryptobiologist. I would have no idea what I'd be looking at."

"Well, no, but they're fun to look at."

He nodded with a little smile. Very little *had* changed, even if she had been away for five years. Life marched on, though. She collected accolades while he rusted away in a castle. He wasn't jealous, exactly, just acutely aware. He and Flora had been compared so many times over their childhoods that it was just a fact of life now.

She turned with her pan of boiling something. "You all right?" she asked, tilting her head.

"Just thinking."

"I know," she said with a smile.

"How did you learn to cook?" he wondered. "Going from never allowed to *touch* a cooking pan to making food for visitors."

"I forced myself to learn at the university." She drained her pan, a giant cloud of steam fogging up her spectacles. "It got a little embarrassing, you know? Being that noble girl who doesn't know how to do squat for herself."

He did know, or he thought he did. Being on the road had been a jarring introduction to reality, realizing he didn't even know how to rent a room in an inn. "You daring girl."

"Small acts of resistance, Maximillian."

That had always been his trouble. When he protested, he did it whole-chested, and everything from the rights of laypeople to his own personal freedoms became mistaken for immature acts of rebellion. "I ought to have you run my life."

"Careful now," she said, waving her wooden spoon. "Say that around the wrong people and I will be forced to do just that."

"Not here."

"No, not here." And, unspoken, it seemed like that's why she liked it here.

They ate at Flora's cozy table with its lace tablecloth and little flower vase and for the first time in over a week, Max felt full. She watched him finish his second helping and murmured, "You've really been through it, haven't you?"

"No, of course not," he said with a laugh. "Princes don't experience hardship."

She didn't laugh. "Did your mum really kick you out?"

"Told me not to come back until the *issue* is resolved," he confirmed wearily.

"Oh, Max. I'm sorry." Hernose scrunched up. "But why?"

He shrugged uncomfortably. "I heard a dozen different answers, you can take your pick. 'It makes people uncomfortable.' 'It's bad for diplomacy'—but that's a catch-all, isn't it? 'I'm evidence we don't get along with everybody.' That's a good one."

"No, Max, I'm asking—"

"Hiding me away is inconvenient, and showing me off would be crude," he said, barreling on. "Oh, plus there's the fact that Mother's precious son is sometimes a daughter."

"*Max*, listen to me—wait, really?"

"Six different bodies and you didn't think some of them might be a different gender?"

"I guess I just thought…well, I don't know. That's got to be…."

Disorienting, disconcerting, forcing him to question himself and everyone else. He just nodded gruffly. Max wasn't used to being gruff, but what *was* he used to these days? Flora's hand found his arm. "Hey," she said. "We'll figure it out."

He lifted his eyes. He'd come here because he had nowhere else to go, but he'd also come here to feel less alone. He didn't know why it was such a surprise when she said *we*, but something he'd been clutching very tightly loosened a little. "Thank you," he managed.

Her smile did a good job hiding her pity, but he could still see it. "I was trying to ask why? Why did you leave?"

"Flora, I just explained—"

"No, not why did she throw you out?—why did you go? That

just doesn't seem like you. You would fight tooth-and-nail, you would dig your heels in. What happened?"

What had happened? He wasn't ready to talk about *that* at all. "I just couldn't fight anymore," he said.

Flora showed him to the guest room, then hastily scooped glass dishes and dripping columns into her arms and shuffled out with them. "Don't worry, these are just cultures," she said. They looked like fuzz growing on gelatin.

She came back to fluff the pillows and test the oil in the lamps, then left him to it.

Max ranged the room restlessly. He was exhausted, but something in him wouldn't let him lay down and sleep just yet. He found himself looking in the small brass mirror on the dresser. Dour pale, long elven features, shaggy silver hair just this side of needing a haircut, pointed ears. The face that looked back at him all his life until about a month ago. Now this face was desperate, wan, as though it knew that it was going to be forced away in the morning. There were never repeats, never a chance to get comfortable.

He pushed the mirror away. The last thing he needed was his own countenance to remind him. He was acutely aware his body was on a timer, and he had no idea what was coming. He'd been prepared to wait to approach Flora until he was himself again, but it had been a relief this morning when he'd woken up himself. A fleeting relief, because there was always something else lurking around the next dawn to surprise him.

He sat on the bed, which squeaked a little. All right, so Flora didn't know about curses, but she'd promised to help him find someone who did. That would be good. He rubbed at the back of his neck, trying to relieve a little of the stiffness he always seemed to carry now. The potentiality of transformation, Aubric called it. To Max it just felt like mild cramping.

He carefully removed his clothes and folded them, not knowing when he'd need them next. His bag was stuffed to the gills with fabric just to keep him covered, because of course none of these six bodies could be the same size.

He paused and breathed out. He'd been running on sheer adrenaline these past few days. It was time to slow down.

He'd be safer here. No one to wonder why a different person was coming out of the inn rooms, with someone to help him cover if he needed it. He could rest here.

He needed to rest.

Max wasn't sure why dawn always came as such a surprise. It was always there, and every day now, stretching or scrunching came with it.

He rolled over onto his stomach and braced himself on his arms as his limbs lengthened. He watched his skin change from pale porcelain to a dark red and tried not to think too hard about the tail slipping down between his legs. His fiendish form was his least favorite. He never felt right, like his elbows and knees and horns were constantly jamming into things and he was always tripping over his own hooves. He laid his head down on his forearm and waited for the tearing feeling to subside, then slid back into sleep, exhausted.

When he woke again, he wasn't sure exactly what time it was, but the sun shone bright in between the white lace curtains. He unfolded his lengthy body and smoothed down the long white hair before tying it back. He went to the washbasin and splashed at his face while avoiding the mirror, still turned away. Even if he didn't avoid it, most of what he'd see would be neck, this form was so tall.

He dressed as quickly as he could and made his way out to the living area, where Flora sat perusing a book. He was about to speak, but she glanced up and promptly started to shriek.

He put out his hands. "Flora, it's me, it's Max."

She was halfway into a lunge to snatch a sword off the wall when she stopped, put her hand to her chest, and breathed out quickly. "Max? You're…sure that's you?"

He nodded, a little chagrined. "I always wear a blue scarf," he said, pulling at the soft blue silk. "That's how you can tell."

Flora patted her chest and nodded. She bent to pick up her book, which she'd flung. "I'm—sorry, I shouldn't have panicked."

"No, no, it's my fault for not warning you."

She tilted her head. "You…sound different."

"Do I?" He supposed that this form—the third to present itself, and therefore labeled number three—had a voice that echoed deeper in his chest than his original. "I hadn't noticed. Then again, I haven't much been speaking to people."

"You haven't?"

He laughed. "Gods, no. I'm just trying to get through without being spotted."

"What? It's not like anyone can tell you're cursed."

"Anyone who tries to talk to me the next day can."

"Oh," she said. "What happens if you're spotted?"

"Surely you've noticed the superstition around curses."

"Yeah, but that's just unscientific nonsense. Unless it's specifically made to propagate, it's not going to affect other people."

"Is that the prevailing attitude here?" he wondered.

"This is Clockbridge," she exclaimed. "Science is everywhere. Why do you think I'm here?"

"Well…that's good, then," Max said. "In little villages along the road, probably less so."

"No, you're right. It's good that you kept yourself safe." She shifted on the sofa. "In the meantime, I have an idea for you. Speaking of science. There's a maker's guild office in the Clock District. If you post there, I bet you'll draw some attention."

"A maker's guild?"

"Alchemists, magical item crafters, mage's apprentices, all that. It's the closest thing to a mage circle as you're going to get here."

"Really? A city this big and there's no circle?"

"Nope," she said. "I guess there aren't really any mages here, now that I think about it."

"You've never thought about it before?"

"Hey, I'm not a mage!"

"Well, *I* am," he said. On the one hand, it would have been nice to get a second magical opinion on his curse; but on the other hand, any mages this close to Saltrush would be known to Aubric.

"I hear that they tried to establish a circle, but independent mages wanted nothing to do with it." She gave him a sly look. "You've been keeping up with your magic?"

"Flora, please."

"I'm proud, that's all." She turned her book over in her hands. "In the Guild here, lots of people have multiple specialities, or dabble in different fields. I'm willing to guess that you'd find somebody who knows something. If you want to try."

"Well, yes," he said gratefully. "Let's go."

"Breakfast first," she said. "You're not getting anywhere running around on an empty stomach." Max's stomach grumbled. She stood and patted his shoulder. "You sit down. I'll get something started."

He eased to the sofa and looked around the little living room. The grandfather clock against the wall read eleven. He hoped she hadn't waited for him to eat. Along the walls sat more dishes of things on ever more tables, all shrouded in the dim. Perhaps it was his imagination, but he thought he heard something move. He stood and hurried to the kitchen to sit at the table again. "So tell me of your research," he said. "What are you working on?"

Without turning around, she said, "There's a particular hormone secreted by several toad hybrids that looks suspiciously like what allows fey, fiends, and celestials to cast magic without learning. If I can prove that Solasthalas didn't create innate magic out of nothing, someday we may be able to replicate it in humans, elves, and underkin."

"Wow. That would…upend a lot of things."

"Yep," she answered brightly. "But what's the fun in thinking small?"

Flora was his first and oldest friend, but sometimes she frightened him. "You're not thinking of doing it to yourself, are you?"

"Oh, no, experimenting on yourself never ends well. Don't worry. Volunteers only. And that is a long ways off. First we have to understand what it is and whether that makes the toads magic or not, then whether it's a byproduct or the catalyst for innate magic. Then we ask, 'Is it safe?' and, 'Is it a good idea?'"

Max was relieved to hear the latter part. He nodded as though he could do any more than try to wrap his head around the idea. He'd studied magic, along with many other subjects, and the mere concept of being able to do some magic without learning it boggled his mind. He'd had to learn to observe the flow of ether throughout the world and himself to channel it.

"Wait," Flora said. Her eye wandered over to him. "You're a fiend right now. Can you…?"

"No," he answered. "I don't think it works that way."

"That's interesting," she mused. "That to me suggests that the hormone isn't present in your body—any of your bodies. You say there are six—is there one of each lineage?"

"You are correct." He leaned on his arm. "Flora, I'm sorry, but can I ask you not to study me? I've had quite enough of that from home."

"What? Who studied you?"

"Guess," he said, grimacing.

"That seems cruel."

"It was."

"Nothing to fear from me," she promised. "Only idle curiosity."

He nodded. Even that could be difficult, but he was staying in her home. Flora finished up breakfast and put it in front of him. "You've really been through it," she said softly.

"I really shouldn't complain."

"You could."

"I have money, a place to go, prospects. There are plenty who don't get that."

"And how many of them are cursed in the first place?" she asked.

"I'm not sure. I've never given it much thought until now."

"Probably not many. I think, if you wanted to, you could feel a little badly about it."

He smiled a little. "Should I?"

"I think maybe."

"I'll consider it."

Flora held her fists to her hips, spoon still held. She looked like she had something to say, but as so many did around him, she held her tongue. Max wished she wouldn't, but neither would he make her uncomfortable. So he ate his breakfast gratefully and prepared to journey into the wider world of Clockbridge.

It was called Clockbridge, it turned out, because spanning between the residential district and the mercantile Clock District was a bridge that was raised and lowered by the turning of massive, massive cogs. At the top of the central bridge tower sat a stately clock whose innards were outside, the workings climbing up the tower. Max stared up and ran his hand over his long white hair. "The maintenance for that must be ridiculous."

"Oh, yeah, they're out here all the time, fine-tuning and re-pairing," Flora said, sweeping her stray hair from her eyes and holding down her skirt. The sea wind whipped cold, and Max wished he wasn't too big for his coat. "But that's part of the interesting thing about it. The Guild makes this place unique."

"And that's where we're going?"

"One better, actually. There's a dive bar kind of next to the Guild Hall. They have a message board there that's busy with people looking for or selling things."

"What makes it a dive bar? Is there a swimming pool?"

"No, no," she laughed. "It means it's dingy. Kind of run down. But in a charming way. Things are usually a bit sticky."

"And that's a good thing?"

She considered. "Yes," she decided.

They crossed the bridge to the mound of land that housed the mercantile district, and Max couldn't help but crane his neck and look at the brick buildings that rose tall on either side of the street. "Are there really so many people here?"

"Yes," she answered. "It's kind of hard to comprehend some-times."

Saltrush was not small, but this made it seem like a quaint village in comparison. There were people behind the windows, in the streets, even more places he couldn't see. "And who rules it?"

"No one. The Guild is in charge."

"Who rules the Guild?"

"There are directors, I guess, but they're supposed to defer to the will of the Guild members."

"Several people can agree enough to run an entire city?" He marveled.

"Apparently. It's not like we can see it working."

"That seems…at least back home, anyone can attend a legislation session."

"And anyone can join the Guild. If you've a craft."

"And if not?"

"Well, you can apprentice."

Hmm. Max folded his long arms out of habit, trying to keep them under control. They kept on over cobbled streets lined with gas lamps, past more buildings and shops—so many shops—until they came to a pockmarked gray facade with a swinging sign with a goat painted on it.

"This is it," she said.

He shook out his shoulders. "All right," he said. "Let's see what a dive bar is."

Inside, it was relatively quiet. A few people sat at round tables, hunched over early drinks. It smelled of wood and vaguely stale drink, and a pretty underkin barmaid looked across the bar. "Be right with you," she said.

Flora nodded brightly and went to the far wall, where a bulletin board practically feathered with slips of paper hung. She pulled out a notepad and a pen and handed both to Max. "Go on."

He thought for a length, trying to come up with the words. In the end he wrote:

Seeking magical expert on curses. Please reply via bulletin board.

-a visitor

Flora nodded her approval, and Max, not knowing how it would change his life, pinned the slip to the board.

Chapter Two
The Answer

Max woke the next morning as he usually did: twice. Once for the change at dawn, once for the day. It was always hard transitioning from number three to any of the other forms since he was so tall, but this morning, cramping seemed to stick around. He slept miserably and woke up again feeling as though he were swimming. He opened his eyes.

The first thing he noticed was that number three had given way to number five, a celestial woman with close-shaved golden hair on one side and shoulder length waves on the other. The next thing he noted was that he was crushing his wings by lying on his back. He rolled forward with a groan and then felt it. A horrible pressure in his abdomen, and a wetness underneath him. He rolled out of bed and clutched the top sheet to him and found a bright red spot on the bed. "Flora," he called, his light voice rising in panic.

The door swung open almost immediately. "What, what—Max?"

Max pointed at the bed. "I'm—wounded."

Flora looked at the bed and then down at Max, blinking slowly. At length, she started to giggle. Indignantly, Max said, "Nothing about this is funny! I have never been *injured* by the curse before!"

"And you still haven't," she said.

"What do you mean—I'm *bleeding!*"

"Oh, Max," she said a little fondly. "It's your first period."

"My—"

"Didn't you ever learn about the birds and the bees?"

"Of course I did—" He deflated. "You mean this is normal?"

"So normal." Flora patted Max's shoulder.

"You do this every month?" he asked, horrified.

"Yes, of course," she said, struggling and failing to contain a smile. "Not so easy, is it?"

"It's *horrible,*" he gasped, curling his arm around his abdomen. "How can you…how do you *live,* losing this much blood…?"

"Max. It's okay. It's totally normal." Flora patted his shoulder.

"And to be in this much pain?"

"Also normal."

"That seems…."

"Unfair?"

Max nodded, swiping his longer hair from his face.

Flora smiled. "You're not the first to say so, nor will you be the last."

He wilted a little. "You must think I'm a great fool."

"No, I don't," she said consolingly. "I think you're going

through something you've never experienced before. Come on, let's get you clean and dressed."

Max let her help him to his feet, his wings flapping pitifully. Flora drew a bath, then showed him what to do with a pad. "Thank you," he said.

"Oh, there's no need for that."

"There is," he insisted, leaning his arms on the edge of the tub and resting his chin on those. "I've come into your home, disrupted it, asked much of you…"

"You really haven't," she said. "You barely let me feed you. Even if we hadn't been friends from the cradle, you're going to be my king someday. I'd like to be able to say I did my best for you."

"More than. But I hope you know you don't *have to* do any of this."

"I want to." She patted Max's head. "This one is pretty."

"Thank you, I suppose," he said with a little smile.

"Do you want her gone?"

"At the moment? More than I can say. I'd like to go to bed knowing what I'll be the next morning. A privilege I never knew I had until it was lost."

"That's as close to a complaint as you've gotten," she said. "It must really bother you."

"Imagine not being able to plan more than half a day ahead because you may or may not be able to do business wearing a different face. People on the road really don't care for yesterday's."

She murmured, "Yes, there's an unfair prejudice against fiends. I've noticed it a lot in the area. Fey aren't far behind. Celestials only get in good because of the angel connection."

Max looked back at the small golden wings he was attempting to keep out of the water. "Even so, people are…strange about it. But not quite as strange as they would be if they knew about the curse at all."

Flora filled the sink with water and began soaking the sheet. "Superstition and nonsense, all of it. Solasthalas made us all afraid of each other."

"Oh, I think we would have found ways even without him."

"Most likely," she said, disgruntled. "Do you want to check the message board at the Gray Goat today?"

"I think so, although it might be too much to hope for that someone answered it on the first day."

"Oh, be a little hopeful. It's good for you."

"I'm not interrupting your assignment, am I?"

"No, no," she said. "This work is slow, sporadic."

"Are you thinking you'll stay here?"

"For a while longer, at least," she said, shrugging a shoulder. "It's either that or go dusty at home dressed like one of Mother's doilies."

"I can see the appeal of this place in comparison."

"What about you?"

"I have to get home," he said. "As soon as I can break this damned thing."

"You don't want to stay out a bit, see the world?"

"It doesn't matter," he said with a skewed smile. "I have responsibilities."

Flora nodded slowly. "I suppose I will too, one day."

"Enjoy this," he advised. "Once they start having talks with you that include the words 'it's high time you…', it's over."

"Oh, we've had those," she said with a breezy laugh. "I've just ignored them."

Max had often admired Flora's ability to choose what she cared about. It seemed so easy for her to absorb herself in her studies and shut out the rest. He'd never been able to do that. The disappointment of his parents, his people, all mattered too much. Sometimes overwhelmingly so. Flora knew one day she'd inherit the Nythera estate and she'd be bound to the same set of rules he was. He truly hoped she enjoyed the freedom her studies gave her for the time being. For him, it was too late.

The hot water of the bath helped ease the horrible aching, and Max managed to walk without regretting every step. Yesterday he'd drawn attention for his height and his horns, and the people in the street couldn't avoid eye contact fast enough. Today, street vendors fell over themselves to offer him samples, compliment him, try to start conversations. Number five was pretty, objectively so. Her symmetrical features and shapely figure caught many an eye along the road, and Max abhorred it. It was as though his thoughts ceased to matter when they came from a pretty mouth. "Is this what it's like?" he asked, keeping his voice hushed.

"What do you mean?" Flora said.

"For you. Do you feel this objectified?"

"Oh," she said, bewildered. "Sometimes. I'm not as pretty as you are now, though."

"That's nonsense." Max didn't consider himself the best judge of a woman's beauty, but Flora was lovely. Her inquisitive features were compelling, and the rich warm brown of her skin and high cheekbones had entranced many a gentleman caller before she left. "You're very pretty."

"Oh, well, thanks," she said. "But not everyone thinks so. You're more…classically beautiful."

"I don't—" Frustrated, he considered his words carefully. "I don't know how to feel about it. People are so strange to her."

"Her?"

"Sorry. I tend to refer to the forms as separate people. Helps me keep them straight. She's number five."

"No, that makes sense. How did you come up with the numbering system?"

"The order they appeared. My original shape is number one, and the underkin woman is number two, and so on."

"Who did I have yesterday?"

"Number three."

"So they don't repeat in a pattern," she mused.

Uneasily, Max said, "I'd rather not talk about it. At least, not in public."

"Oh. Right. Sorry."

"No, it's all right," he said, dodging another salesman. "Relentless."

"You should see them at night," Flora said. "It's a whole different place."

He already felt like this massive city might swallow him up. The idea of walking past the shops at night seemed daunting, not to mention all the rumors of criminals skulking in the dark.

They made it back to the Gray Goat mostly without getting accosted, and Flora talked to the barmaid while Max made his way back to the bulletin board. He found his brief listing amongst the other fliers papering the board and stared. In a severe hand under his own writingread, *Come to the Brass Hall at midnight. Fourth chamber. -C*

His heart jumped. Someone had answered him. Someone might know something. He went up to Flora and handed her the paper. "Look! Where's the Brass Hall?"

The barmaid whom he had forgotten was there, an underkin woman with strangely pointed ears like an elf's, took note. "What could a pretty thing like you want at the Brass Hall?"

Max's wings flapped indignantly of their own accord. He was about to launch into a diatribe that seemed to come terribly easily today, but Flora cut him off. "We're looking for someone," she said.

"Well, the Hall's one place to find people. Can I see that?" Flora slid the paper across the bar. The barmaid read it, and Max could have sworn that she held a blink for a second too long. "I wish you luck finding your person," she said, handing the slip back.

"Thank you," Flora said, steering Max away from the bar by the elbows. Once they were outside, she said, "You good now? I thought you were going to burst a blood vessel."

"I'm…fine," he said, breathing out. "What's the Brass Hall?"

"It's a spoof of the Gilded Hall," she said. "That's a gathering place inside the Guild building for the upper echelon of the Guild to rub elbows. The Brass Hall is where the workers go. It's got a rough reputation. She was probably just looking out for you."

"Shouldn't it be my decision, whether or not I go?" he asked.

"It is," she assured him. "But if you're going, you're not going alone."

Max held his breath and let the irritation pass over him. Flora meant well. She always did.

The clock on the bridge was lit up brilliantly at night, both above and below. Max wanted to stop and marvel at it, but midnight drew closer. Flora walked alongside, her short legs trotting to keep up with Max's brisk pace. They said little to one another as they went.

True to Flora's description, the vendors became even more adamant by night. Max didn't like the way they leered as he and Flora avoided being sold bottles of wine or books or a substance that people kept talking around but not naming.

As they turned down a side street not lit by the gas lamps, Max was sure they were about to be grabbed. Instead, Flora opened a hatch alongside a building and gestured. "In, in."

"How'd you know where this is?" he wondered.

"It may surprise you, but it's not always easy to come by magical toads," she said wryly.

"There's a black market down here, isn't there."

"It's more of a murky gray. As long as nobody looks too hard at where things are coming from, it's fine."

"Flora, you never cease to amaze me."

"Research waits for no one," she said.

Max considered the open hatch for a moment. Now that he was more removed from the barmaid's comment about a pretty girl going to the Brass Hall, he was starting to wonder if it was a bad idea after all. He took a breath. No, he wanted to know. He steeled himself and went down the short drop from the hatch.

He emerged into a long, dark hallway, lit by torches in braziers along the stone walls. Brass plaques glinted next to dark arched doorways. The hall was conspicuously empty of other people. Flora dropped down behind him, closing the hatch with her. She took one of the torches off the wall. "All right, chamber four should be the fourth doorway. Makes a certain amount of sense, doesn't it?"

He felt like he should mute his footsteps, like he was somewhere he wasn't meant to be. Flora kept quiet, too, and together they found the fourth room. Max pulled open the large door and went inside.

It was dim and dank inside, and Max could hear something dripping in the far corner. "Well. This is lovely."

Flora lit another torch off the weak flame of hers, and the room brightened enough to reveal a figure standing in the back. Max tried not to jump. "C, I presume?" he said hesitantly.

The figure stepped forward, and Max's breath arrested in his chest. He was a handsome man, with the pale pearlescent, almost purple skin and eyes of the underkin and the long limbs and pointed ears of the elves. He wore a cap over long white hair tied back, and a white shirt whose rolled-up sleeves showed off well-muscled forearms. "That's me. And who're you?"

"Max," he said, tentative.

"Max. You must be new in town."

"That's right."

C finally stepped completely into the light, folding his muscular arms against his barrel chest. "Then you should know that magic is a big no-no."

"What?" Flora said, frowning.

"Yeah. Guild doesn't want any finger-wiggling."

"Then they should make that clear," Flora said with the same light peevishness of someone finding out the bar was out of their favorite drink.

"They are," C said firmly. "Right now."

Max's hair began to stand on end. "You're not here to help me," he accused.

"Oh, I am. This is a warning. And if magic is a no-go, curses are much worse."

He stepped forward again, looming over Flora and Max both. Panic rose in Max's throat, and instead of thinking, he acted. He half-formed a spell and flung it, then shouted to Flora, "Go. Run."

His panicked magic didn't take. C was unaffected and well

within reach of Max. He closed in behind Max and snared him, strong arms crossing his body and pinning him, wings and all, to C's chest. He saw Flora freeze in the doorway.

C leaned down to Max. "Whatever that was, you shouldn't have done it."

Max gritted his teeth. He couldn't move his hands to cast or even to ineffectually slap at him. And yet he couldn't help but notice that C's hands were closed fists, not grabbing. "And you shouldn't be holding me like this."

"Shouldn't I? You're the one bringing dangerous magic into the city."

"It wasn't dangerous. It was just a charm."

"And I'll just take you at your word, shall I?"

"You could."

"That would be foolish," C said. "But all right, let's say I'm a fool. Let's start over. Hello, I'm Cormac."

"Max," he got out.

"So that wasn't a lie." The way he couldn't see Cormac but could hear his low voice, could feel it on his ear, sent a shiver from Max's collar all the way down his body and made it difficult to form words.

"No. I came ready to negotiate in good faith. You seem to be the duplicitous one."

"Oh, now, that's hurtful," Cormac said with a tsk.

"You're answering an advertisement from someone looking for help with violence!"

"I *am* answering it to help," he said. "This warning is better than you'd get from a lot of others. I wasn't looking for a fight. You're the one that brought it."

"I did not—for gods' sakes!" Max sputtered. "This—this I didn't need. It's bad enough, being cursed, disoriented, hated, turned out by your own parents, but then there's people on the road who'd rather see me in the ground than cured. Then I finally get here, and there's a bit of hope for the first time in *weeks,* and you came in to stomp all over it! I *hate* this!"

His voice echoed, an unbridled shriek that shook his whole body. Flora blinked, and Cormac's arms loosened just a touch. "Hey, listen, I'm sorry—"

"Are you?" Max demanded. "Are you really? Because you were about to turn me out of the city. Back onto the road with the people who want me dead for something I can't help."

"I wasn't," he said quietly. "All I meant was keep quiet."

"Oh, right. I'll just hide myself, make myself small for the large group in power. That will work out *splendidly.*"

"Plenty of people do it. You think you're the only mage in town?"

"And what is the problem with magic?" He asked. "Half the population does it naturally. Are they banned, too?"

"As long as they keep their spells to themselves, everything's fine." He let Max loose. "I am sorry. You're not going to find anyone here to help you. Really, I am. That's a tough swallow."

Max's shoulders came down. "Don't you worry," he said. "I will leave and take my magic with me."

"Before you do...." His face softened into a smile. "Come by the Gray Goat. I work there nights."

"When you're not giving people very courteous warnings."

"Right. Drinks are on me."

Max tilted his head. "Are you saying that because you feel sorry for me?"

"I'd like to hear your stories."

"Well." He looked down. The skin along his chest still prickled. "There are many I shouldn't tell."

"Those are the best. Might tell a few myself."

He stared hard. "Is this because I'm pretty? Because you should know that can turn very quickly."

Cormac burst out laughing. "I—I'm sorry. You're threatening me, and it's adorable."

"And you're condescending."

"I am lots of things, but condescending isn't one of them." He leaned back and put his hands in the pockets of his vest. "And weak to a pretty face isn't another. Don't worry. You're safe from me."

Something about the way he said this…there was a touch of something sad. Max couldn't help but wonder. Quickly, he reminded himself that this was a thug who had just held threatened him.

And yet. His heart quickened a little. "Let me walk you home," Cormac said.

"No, thank you."

"I *have* to walk you home," he clarified.

"So you know where to find me if I make trouble."

"Something like that." He gestured to the back of the room. "Shall we be going?"

Flora looked at Max helplessly. For her sake, Max let the last of his ire cool. "All right," he acquiesced. "But you swear to me you'll leave the house and its occupant alone."

Cormac put his hand to his chest. "My hand to the gods," he said.

Max followed him into the dark. There was a secondary door there; one that led to a different dark hallway. Cormac navigated with ease, either due to his experience or his underkin eyes. Perhaps both. He led them to a platform with a pulley and winch, and he said, "Hop on."

Flora looked incredulous. "Both of us?"

"It's easier than it looks."

She didn't look convinced, but, for lack of options, stepped onto it anyway. Max followed, and Cormac grasped the rope and started to haul them up. Flora openly stared at his arms, and Max politely tried not to.

They came to a back room of some sort, with stacked crates and some large items covered by burlap. Cormac led them through to the front of a shop, where clock dials and enamel music boxes glinted in the moonlight coming through the store window. He ushered Max and Flora out, then locked the door behind him. Max lifted an eyebrow. "Why do you have a key to a place like this?"

"That's one of those stories I shouldn't tell. Maybe after a few drinks."

"That's awfully presumptuous, thinking I'll be there for a few."

"That's a five gold word."

"I know a lot of them."

He laughed. "And you're humble, too."

"I've never been accused of that before."

Cormac pocketed his key ring and gestured to the cobbled streets. "After you, ladies."

Flora looped her arm protectively through Max's and walked stiffly on. Cormac said little, but Max caught his eyes darting into the alleys and around corners as they went. Max kept his back straight and his wings taut against his shoulders. The vendors in the streets all seemed to note Cormac and kept quiet as they walked on. This made for an uneventful walk home, which Max was thankful for, at least.

At length, they came to Flora's door. Max had only just gotten here, but the idea of leaving the city made him want to collapse. It was the right choice. It was the *only* choice. And yet, he knew that Flora would try to get him to stay.

Cormac took a cursory look at Flora's door, then made a little bow. "I hope I'll see you again," he said, catching Max's eyes. "Ladies, goodnight."

Max nodded once and watched him vanish into the dark. Flora unlocked the door and urged Max inside before shutting it with a massive exhale of breath. "Whew," she said. "You really saved us with the flirting there."

"Flirting?"

"I...thought you were doing it on purpose. He definitely was."

"He should know that's the least appropriate way to get a person's attention," he grumbled.

"I don't know, it seemed to work pretty well on you," she chuckled.

"What?"

"You're thinking about it, aren't you?"

"He's interested in number five. Not me."

"You're the one inside number five."

"I suppose," he grumbled. "Not that anyone else has seemed to care."

She patted his shoulder. "You're having a rough day. Why don't I get you a hot water bottle and we can call it a night?"

At this point, he'd like nothing more.

Chapter Three
One For the Road

Number six was a human girl with red hair and freckles just about everywhere, and number six carried on what number five had started the day before. Max groaned and held onto his abdomen as the sun streamed in, unwelcome.

After breakfast, Flora fidgeted while she watched Max pack. "You're sure you're going to leave today?"

"After last night?" he said. "There's very little that could make me stay."

"What if I say please?"

"That…might just do it." He sighed, pulling the buckle taut on his bulging bag.

"I don't like the thought of you traveling the road. It's not safe for anybody, let alone…"

Him. He knew. And yet, he saw very few other options. If magic was verboten here, there was very little chance of him getting what he needed. Flora tilted her head, braid spilling over her shoulder. "At least rest a few more days before heading back out there."

He felt the weight of the bag dragging down his arms.

"Please?" Flora said.

He let go of his bag and sat back. There was no guarantee he'd turn into a man tomorrow, and if he was going to continue to feel this nauseous and explosive, traveling would be even less fun than it usually was. "All right," he said.

He sat in Flora's living room and read a book while she flitted around, checking on her experiments. She hummed to herself. He set the open book in his lap. "You really think he was flirting?"

"Oh, definitely," she answered.

Flora had more experiences being flirted with than he did, certainly, so he was inclined to trust her. But she was usually the naive one, so this sat funny. "Huh."

"Do you want to see him?" she said.

"Do I want to see the man who threatened me?"

"It was a warning."

"Flora."

"He did apologize."

"Hmm." He leaned his chin on his hand and attempted to go back to the book. If he was being completely honest with himself, he was interested in Cormac and his breathy brogue and those stories he'd only tell over a few drinks. There was something about him, a gravity that pulled him in. Or maybe that was just his arms. He looked up again. "I don't even know if he's interested in men."

"Maybe you can find out," she said, raising her eyebrows. "Will you stay long enough to find out? When number—which one was it? Five? When number five comes back, you *have* to go see him."

"I...could go see him tonight."

Flora brightened. "Yes! But—wait, how? You aren't going to tell him the whole thing, are you? You'd have to get to drinks first."

"I can get to drinks," he said, "with just a little duplicity."

"Five gold word. What do you mean?"

He waffled. "I can use magic to disguise myself."

Flora's eyes shot wide open. "You can *what?*"

He blushed what he was sure was a bright tomato-red on number six's face. "I'm not very good at this kind of magic. Hopefully he didn't get too good of a look at me."

Flora nodded encouragement. "Why didn't you use this when you were in danger?"

"I did, now and then, but it's especially hard to create an effective disguise while fearing for one's life." He shuddered. "I'd rather not talk about it."

"Okay," she said. "Let's talk about tonight."

"To...night?"

"You said you could see him tonight!"

"*Could.* I was just saying I could."

"Come on. You're not staying long. What's the harm in having a little fun?"

"Is this the same Flora? My innocent, sweet Flora who thought we were married just because we spent time together as children?"

She laughed. "It's been a while since I thought boys and girls automatically got married to their best friends, Max. I know a little better these days."

"Still! To suggest *I* of all people sow wild oats…"

"You are exactly the person whom I'd encourage to do just that, given you're never going to get another chance."

"Oh, don't say it like I live in a convent."

"I know clerics in convents who get more freedom than you do."

"Of course you do," he said fondly.

Flora droppered something into a glass dish. "I'm just saying. It's an opportunity."

"I will…think about it."

Max wrestled with himself for a while, turning pages without really comprehending what he'd read. As the sun sank lower in the sky, his leg bobbled nervously.

He could go and leave if it felt bad. Or he could stay and not throw his lot in with the lout who'd grabbed him. Or he could leave the city altogether. The choices swirled together and over-whelmed him.

At long last, without really thinking about it, he stood up and summoned his magic. Then, without really thinking about it, he used it to make himself look like number five again, for as long as that would remain. Before leaving, he checked himself in the mirror. He had until the spell slipped away from him to either get out of there or make the fool's choice and tell Cormac about the curse.

"You're going?" Flora asked.

"Yes, yes," he answered a little hotly.

"Good," she said mildly. "Don't come back too early now."

"Flora."

"What? I'm just excited for you."

He pushed out a breath, smiled and shook his head, and left.

Today he dodged the street vendors a little better, keeping his head turned from their stalls and walking quickly across town. The large Guild building loomed in the distance, and he felt like it was watching somehow. Like it would know he'd done magic.

What else was he supposed to do, show up and claim he was Max? There was a reason changing shape every day was a curse. Consistency was important to people. And with all respect to number six, her features didn't quite have the same *volume* as number five's. Max still wasn't convinced it wasn't those features that interested Cormac, but, well…

He supposed he would find out.

The Gray Goat was much livelier in the evening, with patrons chatting and laughing instead of staring miserably into their ales. The barmaid was busy shuttling drinks back and forth, but she still smiled and made surprised eye contact on seeing him. "You're back," she said.

"I am," he answered with a barely suppressed little smile. "Is, um…is Cormac about?"

She raised her eyebrows. "Cormac? Sure. He just got back, actually. Good timing."

"Oh, look at that."

"Look at that indeed." She leaned her arms across the bar and spoke conspiratorially. "And what might you want with my brother, exactly?"

Brother. He supposed that made sense. They both looked a unique blend of lineages, though the barmaid was more round of feature than most elves. "He invited me for a drink."

"Did he? That's…um—"

The door opened, and Cormac came out from the back room, his shirt and vest covered with a green cloth apron as he hefted a barrel to the bar. "Brenna, the delivery's in—oh. Max."

Brenna patted Cormac's shoulder. "Why don't you let me handle it? You've got a visitor. A *lady* caller."

He rolled his eyes and elbowed her gently. "Oh, get off. Sorry, Max. She's incorrigible."

"A five gold word," Max said with a nervous laugh.

"I don't know too many of those, so I hang onto the ones I do." He slung his apron off and over a hook behind the bar, then came to the little half-door that separated the bar area from the seating and opened it. "Come on back. I figured we could talk somewhere a little less public."

"Have fuuuuuun," Brenna called.

"You're terrible," he said with a fond smile. He led the way up a small wooden staircase to a narrow second floor, essentially an open hallway with two doors. He went to the one on the right and opened it for Max.

It was a small room with a bed made of a ticked mattress stacked on a pile of pallets, with crates for seats at one battered table. Prominently against one wall stood a workbench, full of wood shavings and cut pieces of wood. "Sorry, it's not much," he said, a little embarrassed, as he tossed his hat to the workbench.

"It's cozy," Max said, and he meant it. The furniture may have been ramshackle, but there were cheap market prints in handmade wooden frames on the walls, and someone was tending some flowers in the flower box.

"Well, sit anywhere you like," he said, smoothing down his hair. "Can I get you that drink?"

"Please."

"What'll it be?"

"Have you got any wine?"

"Sure, but it's shitty. If you're a wine drinker, though, you'll probably like one of Brenna's drinks. It's got fruit in it."

"I'll take one of those, then, please. Thank you."

"So polite," he said with a smile.

"I can be less so if it's more comfortable."

"No, I'm just not used to it. Usually it's more of a slam on the bar and a grunted 'whiskey'. I could get used to polite. Be right back."

Max perched on one of the crates and folded his hands between his knees. He looked around the room at the hand-sewn blue curtains, the single pansy in a bud vase on the windowsill, and at the clock on the wall. Unlike everything else, the clock was pristine, polished brass and silver with a swinging pendulum behind glass. Over the murmur of the bar still audible through the floor, it chimed the hour, and the blue enamel skies shifted over the dial, with the moon just coming into view.

Max stood to admire the clock, folding his hands behind his back. Footsteps heralded Cormac's return, and Max turned. "This is beautiful."

"Oh, thanks," he answered, setting a pair of drinks on the table. "I made the case."

"You didn't."

"I did. I apprenticed at that shop we went through last night."

"And you work nights at the bar, and late nights doing…other work?"

"It's a busy life," he said with a weary-sounding laugh.

"When do you sleep?" Max wanted to know.

"Rarely and briefly."

He returned to the table and tried a bit of the drink. It was sweet, but not overwhelmingly so. "This is good."

"Brenna is good at making do with what we get," he said.

"Doesn't she own the bar?"

"Oh. Oh, no," he laughed. "The Guild owns the bar. We just work here."

"I guess that makes sense." Even though he couldn't see it, he could practically feel the looming gray building through the walls. "Is there anything this Guild doesn't touch?"

"Not really," Cormac answered somberly. "It either owns

things and you pay your dues to it, or it regulates them. I get that it must seem weird, coming from out of town.”

“It just…makes everything about work.” No wonder the vendors were so aggressive.

“Isn’t life like that, though?”

It wasn’t in Saltrush. People’s professions were how they made a living, and then they…lived. Perhaps he was a little too credulous, or naive, believing it would be that way everywhere. Perhaps it was good that he was getting out into the world.

Cormac leaned forward. “You all right?”

“Yes, sorry, just thinking.”

“You’re feeling sorry for me.”

“No, I—admire you very much for being able to juggle all these things.”

“But you think I shouldn’t.”

“You’re going to burn yourself out.”

He laughed. “Burning out is for rich folks. Guild elites, merchants. The rest of us just work.”

Max supposed it was a fair point. He was coming at it from the perspective of someone who’d never had to worry about money and whose work was a very advanced form of bookkeeping. A privileged position. He tried very hard to be aware of when he was out of touch. “Still. That’s hardly safe, is it? You must be so tired.”

“I get along all right. But what do you do?”

“Right now? I hunt for a solution to my curse.”

“Right, that’s got to take precedent,” he said ruefully. “How long's it been?"

"A month."

He pulled air in between his teeth. "That's…tough."

"I can feel you not asking," Max said, smiling over his drink before taking a big swallow.

"I'll admit it's hard not to. It must be enough of a pain that you'd go hunting in a place like this for answers, though, so it must be hard to talk about."

"You're…strangely empathetic about it."

"Is it so strange?"

"People keep trying to kill me or run me out of town, so yes."

Seriously, he said, "And that won't be much different here. Maybe they won't assemble a mob, but the elites will find a way to get you off the street."

"Another reason to go."

"But maybe there's a little bit of a reason to stay," Cormac said. "I found something for you."

"What?"

"I had a little ask-around earlier today. Turns out there's an alchemist in town who specializes in purging curses. A real old school witch type. That's as far as I've gotten, but my source is credible. I can keep working the Hall for more."

Max's heart leapt. "You'd do that?"

He rubbed at his neck. "Look. I feel bad about the way last night went. I didn't use my words the best."

"You don't have to stick your neck out because of that," Max insisted.

"It's not that big a deal. Folks just assume I'm asking in my *professional* capacity."

"Which is working for the Guild?"

Cormac flinched. "I guess that wasn't very hard to figure out." He added hastily, "I won't tell them about you. No one else should've seen the notice you posted, either."

"Thank you. How—?" He hesitated. "How did you get started doing that?"

Cormac looked down into his lap. "That's a three-drink story. Just know that it wasn't my choice, and I did a lot of fool shit when I was desperate."

Max nodded. "Desperation can do a lot to a person."

"Especially kids, like we were. Brenna and I. We came here when…well, it wasn't a good time." He drank the rest of his cup and set it down. "Think I'll get another. Can I tempt you?"

Max hesitated. Ordinarily he was measured in his drinking, especially now that his body's tolerances changed by the day, but he'd already thrown caution to the wind just in coming here. "What the hells," he said, passing his glass over. "Why not."

"That's the spirit. Just a moment."

Max sat and listened to the pleasant ticking of the clock and the general drone of the bar. Cormac returned with fresh drinks and sat back down. "So, where're you from? This all seems like a surprise to you, so it can't be too close by."

"No. I'm from Saltrush." Cormac squinted in thought, and Max leaned forward. "Don't worry. Most people don't know about us. We're in the Great Forest."

"With all the fey?"

"That's the one. There's one clearing, and that's us."

"A lot of celestials there?"

"Elves, mostly. Some humans." He froze as he realized his mistake.

"I can't help but notice you're not an elf or a human."

Something about Cormac's face tightened, his gaze sharpening like he could look right through Max, through the illusion and through number six's skin to see the real Max underneath. And that made Max acutely aware of how loose his hold on his spell had become.

He had to leave. Now.

He scooted up to the edge of his seat, put his feet flat on the floor, and hesitated.

Then again, Cormac had been accepting so far. He'd promised he wouldn't turn Max over to the Guild. He wasn't staying long; what was the harm in having a little fun? A little fun with a tremendous risk attached.

"Max?"

Max settled back into his seat. "You're right, I'm not an elf. Not right now."

"Not right—when are you an elf? When the full moon hits?"

Max made a face, chagrined. "I change shape. Every morning I wake up different."

Cormac sat back and folded his arms with that same pointed, assessing look. "You...sure, all right."

"You don't believe me. That's fair." He let the spell dissipate and revealed number six. "Here's what I look like today."

Cormac stared. "What the fuck," he managed.

Max's cheeks burned. It was worse than Flora's reaction. Why had he thought a virtual stranger would be as understanding as his best friend? This was a bad idea after all. He shot to his feet and took a step toward the door, not even able to form words.

Cormac didn't get up or try to block him, but Max felt a light touch on his wrist as he passed. "There's no need for that," he said softly.

"You're—"

"I'm just wondering who the fuck does that to someone. I don't know a lot about curses, but this had to come from someone, right? You didn't go and open up a forbidden crypt or something?"

The heat hadn't left Max's cheeks, but he found he could laugh now. "No, I'm not *that* big of a fool."

"You can go if you want," Cormac said. Hesitantly, he followed with, "I'd rather you stayed a little longer."

Max looked at the remaining half of his drink on the simple table. Even though he'd just been wearing a magical disguise, he felt almost naked now, revealed. Cormac had never seen this face before. That made it a little more difficult to shuffle back over and sit down, but he found himself smiling.

"Some curses, I get," Cormac said. "But this one...." He shook his head. "What good does it do?"

"So far, I've expanded my wardrobe and learned how to sneak out the back doors of inns so no one questions why a completely different person is staying in the room."

Cormac winced. "Yeah, this must be horrible for traveling."

"Not to mention painful."

"It hurts, too?"

"Growing pains. All the time."

He whistled low. "I don't envy you, Max. That's a bad hand."

"You can see why I want it gone."

"Can't you just use your magic disguise like you did coming in here?"

"Only for a little while at a time," Max said. "And the longer it's up, the more people can tell, usually."

"I thought there was something a little off. But it's the way you sound."

"Every body has a different voice, that's another thing I've learned," he said with a rueful smile. "You met number five yesterday. This is number six of six. You can tell it's me by the blue scarf."

"You were wearing that yesterday, weren't you."

"Hardly take it off," he answered. "The thing has kept me alive on occasion."

Cormac smiled a little. "How so?"

Whoops, he was getting a little too loose-lipped. He set his drink down and said, "A three-drink story."

"Now, you can't just allude to something like that." And they were closing in on that third drink. It would have to stop there.

"I shouldn't have," Max said with a little laugh. "Let's just say Flora was 'startled' the first morning after I arrived."

"She'd've hurt you?"

"If she thought I was an intruder? Certainly. Otherwise, goodness, no."

"She seemed a little timid."

"Don't let that fool you. She's a fighter when she needs to be; she just keeps her sword on the wall rather than at her side."

"I'll bear that in mind," Cormac said. He tilted his head. "Another drink?"

"That would put us in three-drink territory. I think I'll decline respectfully this time."

He smiled. "All right. It's been a pleasure, Max."

"And to you as well."

"Are you leaving town, then?"

"I...." He hesitated. Inhospitable as it might be, this city had his only friend—*and* his only lead to a cure, thanks to Cormac. "I might stay. For a while."

"Good. I'll see what I can find out about this alchemist. Come back sometime."

"Thank you. Truly. You don't know how much that means."

"Come on. I'll show you out the back way. You won't have to magic yourself again."

"I appreciate that." And, he hoped, he wouldn't be in sight of that Guild monolith.

He followed Cormac back down the stairs and around to a small back door, which led into a complex of alleyways. Cormac took them as though he'd done it thousands of times, and Max didn't doubt he had. At length, they popped out somewhere beyond the vendor's row, near to the mouth of the bridge.

Max looked back at all the vendors they'd dodged. "A handy circumnavigation," he mused.

"That word has got to be at least nine gold."

Max just laughed. "Sorry."

"Think I can figure out what it means," Cormac said. "Can I see you home?"

"Thank you, but I'm all right," he answered. "We've gotten past the worst of it."

Cormac nodded. "A handy…shortcut. And safe to use for the future, should you need it."

Max bobbed his head once. "Thank you for this evening. I had a good time."

"You sound surprised."

"Honestly? A little."

"Well, thank you for coming. I didn't think you would."

"Well, we weren't off to the best start."

"Here's to a better continuation. Good night, Max."

He started away, and Max watched him go for a moment, then went on his own way.

When he got back to Flora's house, it was dark and the door unlocked. Flora must have gone to bed and realized Max didn't have a key. He decided not to disturb her, locked the door behind him, then repaired to the guest room for the night.

Morning came, though not as bright. Rain had come to Clockbridge. Max awoke to the telltale stretching and broadening, but this time, he wasn't quite as miserable. Number six into number one wasn't the worst jump. He felt for his face—his original face—and breathed out a slight sigh of relief. Any time he got to be himself was a load off his shoulders. He cleaned up and dressed and went to go find Flora. He was sure she would be bouncing with questions about last night.

The house was still dark. Strange.

Flora wasn't in the kitchen or the living room. Max looked at the clock. It was early yet, perhaps she was still asleep. He sat and read for a while, until the clock chimed nine. That was very strange. Flora preferred to be up bright and early, tending to her experiments, which dripped on without her to guide them.

He set his book down and went to her bedroom door. "Flora," he said, knocking quietly. "Are you well?"

Silence answered.

He frowned. It wasn't like her to leave without saying anything, and really wasn't like her to sleep this late. "Flora, I'm coming in."

He tried the doorknob, and the door creaked open to an empty room utterly torn apart. The sheets hung off the bed, the curtains torn from the walls, drawers thrown aside. He put his hand to his mouth, his heart pounding.

On top of the tossed bed, there was a single sheet of paper.

Prince Maximillian—

We have Lady Nythera. If you want to see her alive, come to the sewer join.

Max shut his eyes and breathed out. He was no stranger to

threats, but Flora....

He strapped on his knives and ran out the door.

Chapter Four
The Plot

The Gray Goat wasn't yet open for business, but Max went to the back door and knocked hard. A confused-looking Brenna opened the door. "Hello?"

"Is Cormac here?" he asked breathlessly.

"Who's asking?"

"I'm—" He hadn't thought to put on the celestial disguise before getting here. "I'm someone he saw yesterday," Max said.

"Is he in trouble?"

"No, no."

"Are *you?*"

"I just—I need to talk to him. Please."

"All right," she said slowly. "You found the back door, so that's something. Come in."

All the chairs were up on the tables, the stools upside down on the bar. That was okay. He didn't feel he could sit down anyway, bristling with nervous energy.

Brenna went to the stairs. "Cormac," she yelled.

"What," he yelled back.

"There's someone here for you."

"Tell them I already paid."

"I don't think he's from the Guild," she said. Then she looked over at Max. "You're not from the Guild, are you?"

"No."

"He's not from the Guild."

Max heard grumbling from upstairs, and then footsteps on the stairs. Cormac appeared and Brenna whispered, "You're so popular this week."

"Shut it, will you?" He took a look at Max. "Hey, can I help —?" His eyes caught the scarf, surprised. "Max?"

"Max," Brenna repeated, confused. "Wasn't that your celestial—?"

Max launched into a stream of nervous words. "Please, Cormac, I know I have no right to ask this, but I need your help. They've got her."

"Slow down. Who's got who?."

"Flora. She's not at home, she's not anywhere…"

Cormac stepped closer. "Maybe she stepped out to the market."

"No, there was a fight."

"Was her sword still on the wall?"

Damn it, it hadn't occurred to Max to check. "I found this." He held up the note.

Cormac read it quickly. "*Prince?*"

"*That's* what you want to focus on?" Max snapped. "Her life is in danger."

"I just—I had no idea. I thought you spoke pretty fancy, but
—"

"*Later.* We can deal with all that later. Where's the sewer
join?"

"Don't know." Max deflated, and he said, "But I can find out.
Come on."

He pulled a coat off a hook by the door, and Brenna said,
"Now where are you going?"

"The Brass Hall. Look, I'll owe you one."

"You'll owe me two," she grumbled.

"I'll owe you two," he conceded, placing a kiss to her forehead.

"Don't you get yourself killed," she cautioned.

"Wouldn't dream of it." He gestured for Max to follow out
the back, and they stepped out into the alleys. As they worked
their way through the labyrinth, he looked to Max. "She must
mean a great deal to you."

"She's…my Brenna," was all he managed.

Cormac nodded, then thought. "How do I refer to you?" He
asked.

"What do you mean?"

"Do I use 'he' or 'she'? Or maybe 'His Royal Highness'?"

Max laughed, a clipped sound. "Just Max, and whatever I
look like that day is fine. Please, don't think anything of the
prince thing. I'm in exile anyway."

"That's even more fucked," Cormac said, indignant-sounding.
"A King and Queen—they could *send* for people to fix you."

"Oh, they tried," he said, looking skyward. "It went *badly*. That's a five-drink story."

Cormac checked left and right then led Max across the thoroughfare to the shop he'd taken them through two nights ago. It wasn't all that different by day—still enchanted-feeling, still kind of dark inside—but warm, and this time attended by an older human man with a jeweler's glass over his eye as he worked through a pile of cogs. He glanced up. "Cormac, my boy, I thought I gave you the day off."

"You did, sir," he said. "I have an important question for you."

He took the jeweler's glass off and affixed a small pair of spectacles to his nose instead. "What makes you think I know the answer?"

"You know everything."

"Ah, if only that were true." He folded his grease-stained hands in front of him. "And who is this?"

"This is Max," Cormac said.

"Estien Fletcher," the man said. "How do you do?"

"Well, thank you, and yourself?" Max said by rote.

"Not bad. Still a little curious at what brings Cormac here." He looked over his spectacles expectantly.

"Where's the sewer join?" Cormac said.

"Now why would you need to know a thing like that?"

"It's important."

He frowned. "Is this for your 'other job'?"

"No, nothing like that."

"Right, good." Fletcher blew out a breath and leaned back in his chair, scratching at his bald head. "Outside town a good few miles to the northwest, along the coast. There's a small stone building."

Max said, "Thank you, sir. You've helped more than you could possibly know."

Cormac patted his desk. "I knew you know everything."

"Why are you going to the sewer join?" Fletcher persisted.

"There's someone there who needs help, and the Guild's not sending it."

"Since when are you a hero, lad?"

Cormac scoffed. "I'm no such thing. I'm a thug, remember?"

"Sure you are." He put on a second pair of spectacles and started filing at a part. "See you Friday. Oh, and Cormac." They paused at the door, and he said, "It's good to see you making friends instead of enemies."

"Bah," Cormac said fondly, and exited the shop, Max trotting alongside. "Still treats me like the kid I was when I came here. But I owe him."

"Which way?" Max asked, pointing.

Cormac just turned, and Max followed. He could feel his pace quicken with each moment of silence, the tension in his chest ratcheting with every thought of Flora.

"A long while ago, the Guild sent me to chat with Estien about his dues," Cormac said. "He sat me down for a cup of tea and started talking to *me*. Found out I'm handy with wood, and from then on, I was his case maker."

Max let out a small laugh. "He doesn't intimidate easily, does he?"

"Never did, still doesn't."

"And he doesn't like that you still work for the Guild."

"Picked up on that?" Cormac laughed. "Like you said, he doesn't intimidate easily. He hasn't had much love for the Guild since that day I walked into his shop."

They weaved through people on thestreet, and Cormac took them through a few narrow alleyways. When they were back out in the open and Max felt like he could breathe again, there was a question trying to pry its way out of him. Hells, talking to Cormac was better than stewing in his nerves. He asked it. "Why do you still work for the Guild? You seem to know that it's not...."

"Finish that sentence, Highness," Cormac said, amused.

Max bristled a little. "Well, not particularly wholesome."

"That's a way to put it." He sighed. "Life's hard."

"That's all? You have talents enough to get a better third job than that."

Cormac looked surprised. "I—"

"You shouldn't need a *third* job. For anything."

"That's...a nice thing to say. I just want to give Brenna a better life than we had."

Max thought of the way her eyes had closed when she read the note with Cormac's handwriting on the bottom. "I think she'd rather you safe and your hands clean."

"I know she'd rather that," Cormac said tightly. Max didn't push it any further, but after a dozen more steps, Cormac went on, "That tavern isn't going to buy itself."

"Really?"

"It would be…well, if she can stop paying the Guild, she could fix up the place. Make it hers." He sighed. "She's never had anything that was hers."

"Have you?"

Cormac looked startled by the question. He brushed it off and didn't answer.

"You two are very close," Max said.

"We're the only family we have, and there's very little I wouldn't do for her." He pointed. "The way out is that way. Past the Guild hall and up a ways."

"Thank gods." Max felt suddenly even more afraid. "Will you come with me?"

"To the sewer join?" It was asking a lot, he knew, but he didn't know if he could handle this on his own. Cormac stopped him with a hand to his shoulder. "I'm not letting you go alone."

"Thank you."

"But," Cormac said, holding up a finger, "you owe me a three-drink story."

"Done."

They closed distance on a small stone building. Cormac held his finger to his lips and crept forward, gesturing for Max to stay back. Cormac inched up to the door and tried the knob. When it didn't budge, he pulled out a small leather case and set to work on the lock. The windows were covered by planks of wood. At length, Cormac managed to wriggle the lock open, and he let the door swing open. There was nothing in the building aside from shelves of what looked like bound sheaves of records and a set of stairs leading downward.

Cormac pointed down and tilted his head at Max. Max nodded. Cormac went first, his natural ability to see in the dark an advantage. Max stumbled on the stairs, so Cormac grasped his hand and led him close to the wall so he could feel for it on his way down. The darkness was cold and overwhelming. The rush of water grew louder the further down they got.

They passed under a very large pipe, and the rushing sound softened. Cormac tensed and blocked Max from going forward. Max strained, but in the darkness he made out at least two figures standing as well as one tied to a chair. Flora.

"You'd best hope your friend comes soon, dear," one of the standing figures commented to her. "I'm not a patient person."

"He'll come," she said, voice shaking.

"You sure? Maybe he's saving his own skin this time."

"You don't know Max."

The silhouette of a person—big, broad, armed with a knife—passed in front of the chair and tipped it back abruptly. Cormac tensed as Flora yelped and Max pulled to be let loose. Cormac grasped for Max's hand in the dark, but Max couldn't let this continue. He made a ball of light in his hand and held it up. "I'm here," he said. "Let her go."

The person who'd been toying with her let the chair tilt back upright and turned toward the light. "Prince Maximillian," he said, a grin splitting his red-bearded human face. He made a sweeping bow. "It's an honor."

Max did not know this man's face, nor the face of the grunt along with him, but that didn't surprise him. People hired other people to do their dirty work. He held his chin level. "If you want me, you'll let her go unharmed. Now."

"You don't waste time, do you, Your Highness?" He withdrew a large knife from inside his vest and flipped it in his hand. "What makes you so sure we want *you?*"

"You called me her friend," Max said. "Most people would mistake our relationship for something else. You've been hired by someone who knows me. Now, let's cut the nonsense and talk like adults."

The man looked a little rattled for the briefest of moments, but quickly grinned again. "His Highness is clever. But you've overlooked something quite serious."

"And what is that?"

"I'm not here to talk." He flipped his knife into his hand and brought it down towards Max.

Cormac shouted and rushed out of the dark, his fist cocked. Max dodged backwards at the same time that Cormac struck the man square across the jaw. In the dark, the other figure shuffled themself around, their own blade flashing. "Get the sample," the red-bearded man spat around a mouthful of blood.

Max fumbled for his knives. When he had one drawn, he slashed Flora's bonds. She jumped to her feet and put her fists up. "They stole my work!"

"Well, we're about to have a serious word with them," Max answered.

"No, I mean it's here somewhere. Just—careful not to throw any fire around. It'll combust."

Max's stomach sank. He happened to rely more on throwing fire than on his knives, if he could. "Noted."

"Max!"

It was hard to see if there were more in the dark, but the one he *could* see rushed at them.

Flora kicked out at him. He twisted out of the way and swiped at her with his sword. With a yelp, Flora ducked away.

Well, that sword had to go. Max sent the ball of light in his palm high into the air, where it burned brightly. Fragments of that light strafed across the assailant's eyes. He yelled and shirked back. Flora swept her leg underneath his knee and hooked it, sending him toppling.

He rolled up again ably, like an acrobat parsing a tumble. Max had hoped to get the blade away from him. When he popped up again, it was with blade raised. Flora squeaked and put her hands up. She was not used to being without a length of steel between her and her opponent. As the blade came down, she moved to the side and struck at the man's hand. It didn't knock the weapon away, but it did startle him enough for Max to step in.

This little bit of movement changed the whole situation. The fellow turned his sights on Max. Cormac and the red-bearded man grappled, knocked over Flora's chair, and took turns bashing each other into the wall. "The stairs," Max told Flora. "Go."

"But—"

Max dodged a swipe and cast a sharp look in her direction. "You're unarmed. Don't be a target."

She took a breath and nodded, gathering her skirt in her fists and ducking around the wall to the staircase. Max's chest eased and he gripped his dagger. Rather than slashing at the attacker, he held the blade up and called on the enchantment to bolster his power.

A blast issued forth, but before it knocked the man back, he snatched hold of Max and pulled him along, too.

They smashed into the wall with a ferocity that winded them both. Max pulled for air and tried to rise. His assailant was on him too fast. He'd dropped the sword and instead went for Max's arm and twisted the dagger out of his grip. Smart, Max had to concede. His ball of light suspended in the air went out, and with a great lunge, the man rolled on top of him.

On his back, Max wrestled with the man. He seemed absolutely determined to drive the dagger into Max's eye. Max grabbed his wrist and wrenched it to the side. The edge of the blade caught Max's eyebrow and his cheekbone, but missed the eye altogether. Past the stinging, he gritted his teeth and loosed his other dagger. He jabbed upward with it, clumsily scoring a cut across the man's side. It bought him an opening, though not much of one. Max scrambled backward.

Max's assailant was slow to get to his feet. He seemed to be scooping something off the floor and into his pocket. In the incredibly dim light, Max saw a red smear across the man's fingers and a few silvery shreds of hair stuck to the outside of his pocket. The man turned to run. Max snared his ankle with his foot and brought him down once more, then hurried to stand over him and placed the point of his second dagger to his throat. "Who hired you?"

The man paled.

Over his shoulder, Max saw Cormac heave the bearded man off the ground and toss him crashing into a stack crates, where he lay. Dusting himself off, he stepped into view. "I suggest you answer that question."

The man held up his hands. "Mercy. Mercy."

Max pressed the flat of the blade against the man's neck. "Tell me. Whose bidding are you doing?"

He was afraid he already knew, with the focus on the eye and the blood and the bit of hair, but he wanted to hear it for himself.

"A man named Aubric," the man pronounced fearfully.

The bearded man climbed up from the pile of splintered wood and drew back his arm, a blade in hand about to be thrown. Cormac crouched, grabbed Max, and pulled him in. Max just tensed.

There was a scrape of metal, a shimmering sound through the air, and a glint of steel jabbed against the man's beard. He froze mid-throw, the blade clattering from his hand. Flora held the discarded sword.

"Stop right there," she commanded. If it weren't for the sword, it wouldn't have been intimidating in the slightest.

Cormac's arms were tight around Max, but now he relaxed.

Without a dagger to his neck, the second man scrambled up to his feet and ran away into the dark. Max didn't have any desire to chase him down. He just sagged.

"What do we do about this one?" Flora asked.

Cormac kept both hands on Max's shoulders for a moment, squeezed, then got up and walked over. He waved to Flora to lower the blade. She did. Cormac put all of his weight into a straight kick to the bearded man's sternum. With an *oomph*, he flew back into the pile of broken crates.

"He ought to stay down this time," Cormac said. He went back to Max. Flora watched Max tentatively. Cormac looked at him. "Are you all right?"

"I need—to get out of this place," he managed.

Cormac took Max's hand and pulled him up to his feet. "Yeah. Let's get out of here."

Flora kicked around the things that had been scattered everywhere until she said, "Aha," and picked up a scabbard. She slid the sword back into it. She gathered up her research, too, juggling it all as they went back up the stairs.

"Are you hurt?" Cormac asked Flora.

"No, thank gods. And you two." Somehow, despite being kidnapped and held for nearly twelve hours, she was still chipper. Somehow, Max felt that was for his benefit. "Hey, Max?" she started.

"I don't want to talk about it," Max said dully.

"That's fair," she said quietly.

Cormac looked between the two, but didn't press. Max's hand traveled to the slash on his face, the sting of which was the only thing he could truly feel in that moment.

Cormac led the way back to the city and paid their way past the guards who had since come back from lunch. He regarded Max and Flora carefully. "I'd really recommend against going home. At least until some time has passed. You can stay at the Goat for tonight."

"Thank you," she said.

Max nodded his thanks and kept his quiet until Cormac got him back up in his room. He disappeared for a moment, then came back with a bottle and glass, which he set in front of Max. "You look like you needed it."

Max managed a little smile, toying with the glass. "Flora all settled in?"

"Brenna didn't mind sharing her room for tonight." Cormac sat on one of the crates and looked at Max across the table. "You don't have to tell me if you don't want to, but you seemed…very upset."

"I was. I am." Max sighed, head sagging. "Aubric…is the name of a man I was in love with once."

Cormac's eyes widened. "And he's hiring kidnappers to abduct your friend. Why?"

Max lifted his head. "Believe me when I say, it isn't what you think. It's…not personal."

Now Cormac was flabbergasted. "Not personal? How can

you be so sure?”

“He’s a mage. My mother’s advisor in all things arcane, magical, and strange.”

“Don’t tell me….”

“Oh, he was the first person my mother called.” He found the words caustic, difficult to come by. “He wasn’t able to learn much from me, but it’s just that much more of a *challenge* to him. I used to admire his doggedness.”

“And does your mother know her advisor is—?” Cormac made an empty gesture at the air, like Aubric’s acts defied words. Max supposed they did.

“I think it’s highly unlikely.”

“Do…you mind my asking what happened between the pair of you?”

“I think the full tale is more of a five-and-a-half drink story,” Max said. “And I don’t have that in me.”

“Right. I understand.”

“I found him in bed with one of his students,” Max said. “That’s the short version.”

Cormac’s lip curled. “You couldn’t tell your mum about that? He doesn’t deserve to get away with that.”

“I struggled with it for a long time. I couldn’t even think of it without feeling sick. I resolved to avoid him as much as I could, but he kept finding reasons for us to talk. By the time I left, I felt complicit.”

“That’s bullshit. You didn’t do anything wrong.”

Max took a big drink and nodded slowly. “And yet I’m the one who feels ashamed."

"Some people don't have the capacity. That doesn't mean you have to take it on."

Max smiled sadly. Cormac persisted."You should write her and put a stop to it."

"With what proof? The word of some kidnappers?" He put his face in his hand. "I'm going to need a little more before I accuse her favorite mage of anything."

"I take it she doesn't know about your history."

"Good heavens, no." He folded his arms insecurely across his chest. "We have enough difficulty, she and I, because I prefer the company of men. If she were to learn *specifics*, I think she may burst a synapse."

Cormac went quiet, looking down into his lap. "This is the real you, then? I mean, the original you? The prince?"

Max nodded dully. "Is this the three-drink story I owe you?"

"I think it's a rather important one." Max didn't argue. "Why didn't you say anything?"

"Believe it or not, I don't want everyone knowing who I am. Assassins. Political scheming. Revenge. Petty diplomatic moves. It's all part and parcel of the job. And it's more or less why I'm here now."

"May I ask what happened?"

He gave a strained laugh. "What I wouldn't give for three drinks."

Cormac leaned forward. "You know what's downstairs, right?" He chuckled and refilled Max's drink. "If you don't like this one, I can get another."

Max picked it up and drank stoutly. "What the hells, why not? In Saltrush, there are receiving hours, when the Queen hears from the people. Lately, I'd been taking on some of these. On a dark and stormy eve, at the end of receiving hours, an old woman came and asked to stay."

"I…think I have an idea where this is going."

"And I wish I had. I brought the request to my mother. We were due to host a summit of our allies, who could arrive at any time. She told me to refuse her, that all available room was spoken for by our guests. So, I returned and apologized and told the old woman I would walk her to an inn. She transformed into a fey woman and demanded if I had judged her based on her appearance. It…was at this point I started to realize I was in trouble. I assured her that was not the case, but she wouldn't hear it. She told me I would have to find a way to live with myself and disappeared from the hall. I thought that was that until the next morning."

Cormac looked at Max, his jaw set. "Of all the bullshit reasons to curse a person. It wasn't even your fault."

"I could have stood up to my mother, I suppose, or made my own decision."

"Oh, rubbish. She stabbed the damn messenger."

"Cormac…."

"What's the grand lesson here? What are you supposed to be learning?"

Max remembered Flora urging him to be upset, encouraging

him to be angry. Why wasn't he? Because he'd been trying to figure out the *grand lesson*, because he'd assumed there had to be one. What if…?

"And your parents turned you out, even though it was your mother's decision?" Cormac said. "None of this makes sense."

Max knocked back the rest of his drink, reached across the table, and—briefly—touched Cormac's arm. "I appreciate that you're angry on my behalf." He watched Cormac's breath catch for a moment at the contact, and he felt it in his own chest.

"Right," Cormac said. "Forgive me, but I don't know that I like your mum very much."

"You're only seeing the shrewd piece of her. There's the part of her that is a very good queen."

"And a mother?"

Max hesitated. "That's…always been secondary."

Cormac's face scrunched while he wrestled with something. "Max…why go home?"

"Believe me, I've thought about it." He looked out the window at the fading sunlight. "But it's the people I keep coming back to. I make it a point to go out into the town and listen to people's problems and hopes and ideas and bring them, no matter how difficult, to my mother. And slowly, slowly, a bit at a time, things are changing for the better. I don't want to take that link away, from the people to her."

"But things aren't changing for the better for you, are they?"

"That doesn't mean they never will."

"You really think things will improve?"

"I think they have to," he said. "It's got to balance out, right?"

Cormac laughed and shook his head witha roguish smirk. "I didn't know I had such an optimistic idealist on my hands. You're something else, Max, and not because you change shape."

"What?"

"I can't imagine a single other person in the world could be in your spot and not be furious."

Max looked at Cormac for a moment. "May I—may I kiss you?"

Cormac blushed, a dark purple coming to his cheeks. "I, er—yes, please."

Max abandoned his crate and knelt next to Cormac. Cormac's hand traced the side of his face, and Max pressed his lips to Cormac's, his heart fluttering against his rib cage. When they parted, Cormac leaned in again. His hand found Max's and he held it for a moment. "I'm sorry," he said at last. "I'm sorry you're having a shit time of it, and for my part of it. But I'm not sorry it's brought you here."

Max shook his head. "Neither am I."

Cormac stood and lifted Max to his feet, raising his chin with a gentle hand under it and coming back for one more kiss. "Thank you," Max said dazedly.

"For what?" Cormac laughed.

"You helped me get Flora back safely. You didn't have to do that."

"You trust me for some reason. I want to be worthy of it."

Yes, he couldn't quite pinpoint it, either. He probably

shouldn't, given the way this all started. And yet…Cormac's hands were gentle, careful. He held onto Max's hand in both of his and smiled softly, a little nervously.

"That is extremely endearing," Max said. "And I'm glad."

"Are you hungry?"

Max realized he hadn't eaten much of anything all day. "Very."

"Come with me to the kitchen."

Max obliged, but he'd forgotten that the downstairs was not, in fact, empty. The bar was starting to fill with revelers. Flora sat at the bar chatting easily with Brenna, who spotted Cormac and Max. "There they are," she said.

Flora looked to Max. "You okay?"

"Doing much better now," he answered with a demure smile.

Brenna looked between her brother and Max, and at last she said, "I'm stealing him. Come on, brother. You owe me some answers."

"If I'm not back in five minutes, she's murdered me," Cormac said before being dragged into the kitchen.

Max sat down next to Flora, still feeling fluttery. "Are *you* all right?"

"Me?" Flora squeaked, surprised. "Oh, yes. They were careful not to damage me. I wish I could say the same for some of my cultures, but I'll start again."

"Well, I'm relieved. And sorry that I was too…shocked to say it earlier."

"That's okay." She leaned her arm on the counter. "Aubric,

huh."

"Mm."

"What you saw in him, I'll never know."

"He was smart, charming, and he gave me the time of day. I ignored so many warning signs. Now they're coming home to roost."

"You couldn't have seen *this* coming."

"No. I never thought he'd *attack* me. Let alone attack you to get to me. I'm sorry."

"Don't you be sorry for things he's done. I'll get an apology out of him yet."

Max attempted a smile. "I'd like to see that."

"It'll happen," she promised.

Cormac returned with Brenna and some food on plates that were very much not the Gray Goat's. "Careful," he said out of the corner of his mouth. "People might get the idea that we're a food-serving establishment. We are much shittier than that."

"Not for lack of wanting," Brenna said with a dreamy sigh. "I'd love to get an oven, bake some bread...."

"Not at the Gray Goat," Cormac said, horrified.

"And why not? Just because it's shitty now doesn't mean it always has to be shitty."

"I guess you're right." To Max, Cormac said, "I've been roped into helping down here. You're welcome to take the bed."

"I don't want to put you out," Max protested.

"Oh, don't worry about that," Cormac said. "Half the time I

sleep with my head in the wood shavings."

"He's not kidding," Brenna said. "Table three needs a refresh."

"All right, all right," he grumbled, but he smiled as he put on his apron and got to work.

Brenna leaned her elbows on the bar and looked at Max. "Sorry to hear you're having a hard time. I hope you don't mind —Cormac and I don't keep secrets from each other."

"I figured," he said with a little smile. "Did he tell you about the scarf?"

"Yes. That's very useful." She started to dry some glasses. "I hear a lot of sad stories on the regular, but this one is certainly the wildest. You seem to keep a pretty good sense of humor about it."

Flora nudged Max. "Even took his first period in stride."

"Oh, no, you have to worry about *that?* That just seems unfair."

"A lot of it seems unfair."

"Don't worry, you're safe here. Despite my brother's work." She rolled her eyes and sighed. "He works hard for us, and it saved us at one point, but it's like putting an oven in. Just because things were shitty once doesn't mean they have to stay that way."

Max tilted his head. "Perhaps this is an obvious question, but have you told him this?"

"Oh, more times than I can count. He's stubborn as all hells." Her eyes twinkled. "Maybe you can break him of that."

"Me?"

"He seems awfully fond of you."

He felt his face heat up. "I…am rather fond of him."

She leaned on her back foot and smiled. "A first."

Flora looked back and forth between them. "Wait, wait, wait, what? When did this happen?"

Max blushed vividly. "We've talked a fair bit."

Brenna beamed. "I'm so pleased. Usually he gets in his own way."

Flora smiled tentatively at Max, who busied himself with his plate. "Max does too."

"Should I leave the pair of you to talk about us?" Max asked, an eyebrow raised.

"Oh, don't," Brenna said. "I like watching you turn red."

"Enjoy it while it lasts. I have no idea what color my skin will be tomorrow."

"Really? That's wild. How do you know what to wear to bed?" Max just smiled thinly, and she nodded slowly. "Right. Well, if you want a robe…"

"Thank you, but I'll be all right."

"That goes for you too, Flora."

Flora smiled. "I think I'll take you up on that. Thank you for taking us in. I know it's not the most convenient thing."

"Oh, we're happy to." She winked at Max. "Cormac's happiest, of course."

Max wondered, if he counted himself, if that was still true.

Chapter Five
The Guild Man

Of all the days to turn into number two, it had to be when he was staying with Cormac and Brenna. Number two was a very petite underkin woman with purple skin and white hair, and the change was always difficult, compressing into such a short-limbed person. He tried hard to stay quiet, but between the soreness of walking so far yesterday and the fight, it hurt badly.

Cormac roused from his sleep in the battered armchair in the corner. "Max?" he asked blearily. "Are you all right?"

He pulled the covers over himself. "Mmhmm," he said, strained, his voice between registers.

Cormac came over to the bed and set his hand to the blanket lump. "You're shaking. Can I get you anything?"

His voice slid firmly into the higher range. "Thank you, but no. I'm almost—finished." He clenched, his eyes squeezing shut around tears.

Cormac sat on the edge of the bed and patted Max's back through the blanket. At length, Max's head emerged, long hair mussed up. "Hi," Cormac said, a little wonderingly.

"Hi," he answered, self-conscious. "I promise, I can't do this on purpose."

"It's okay," he said with a little laugh. "Does the sun hurt you, too?" Max nodded. Cormac tucked Max's hair behind his ear. "That seems unfair, to get the downsides of all the different lineages."

"Wouldn't be a curse if I only got the good parts."

"I guess so."

Max pressed the covers to himself and pushed the heel of his hand into his forehead. It ached a little with the morning light. "Cormac?"

"Yes?"

"Can I ask a graceless question?"

"I suppose."

There was no use beating around the bush. "Are you uncomfortable with my male forms?"

"Oh. Oh, goodness." He laughed. "It's rather the other way around, if I'm being honest."

"Really? You could have fooled me."

"I wasn't trying to."

"I believe you."

He looked relieved. "I've spent a long time fooling people. Maybe I don't have heirs to concern myself with, but it's... frowned upon, where I'm from."

"I'm sorry," Max said. "I know what that's like. If it helps, yesterday's form was my original, and preferred."

"I figured," he said. "You seemed much more sure of yourself."

"It's always a relief."

"And there's no way of knowing when it's coming back around?"

"No," Max said. "Is…that a problem for you?"

Cormac found Max's hand, spreading the fingers against his and looking at them. He ran his hand up Max's arm. "Are you you?"

"I…sometimes fear I'm not."

"I can tell. You're still you."

"How do you know?"

Cormac smiled. "Because moment to moment, your answer never changes. You want to break your curse and go take care of your people. I figure six different people would have different opinions on that."

"You're probably right."

He leaned over Max and placed a kiss first to his cheek, then to his neck, then his shoulder. "Besides. It feels like you."

He shivered, lightning activating at his core, heating his belly. "Cormac…you should know I haven't…since…"

"Do you want me to stop?" he asked.

"No, gods, no."

"I'm going to walk to the door," he said. "If by the time I come back you've changed your mind, no hard feelings."

"And you? I am a woman, if you hadn't noticed."

"You're Max," Cormac answered.

He hadn't known how much he needed to hear that until that precise moment. Max managed not to cry and wiped at his eyes, clearing his throat. "Well. Yes. But there are definitely some parts of me that are different."

Cormac chuckled. "Max, I'm gay, I'm not allergic."

"No, of course not—" he sighed in slight exasperation, more than a little longing. "I just mean—I want to be fair to you."

"There's nothing *unfair* about you," he told him. "You're just you. That's what I like. Now. Here I am at the door. Shall we?"

Max bit his lip. Who was he to hesitate on Cormac's behalf? He nodded.

Cormac took his hat, hung it on the doorknob outside, and shut the door. Max tilted his head. "What was that?"

"Previously agreed-upon code. Essential when you have a sibling and don't want to be interrupted," Cormac said, making his way back to the bed. He stood with his hands on his hips. "Now, what do you think—?"

Max grasped him by the fabric of his shirt and pulled him close among the folds of the covers. Cormac kissed him, running his hand through Max's loose hair. Max lifted his head to better feel his fingertips against his scalp. The coil in his belly heated to an almost unbearable tenor. Something between his legs went wet. He had little idea what was happening, but he knew it was meant to do this. Cormac undid the front of his shirt, and Max slid his hands in. The smoothness of Cormac's skin was interrupted by a snarling burn mark that cut across his chest and down his abdomen. Cormac froze.

Max asked softly, "Does it hurt?"

He shook his head, and Max leaned in and kissed the burn. Cormac slipped his hands down Max's petite body, and he shivered. Cormac placed his lips underneath Max's chin and tipped him back until he was reclined. He watched Cormac dispense with his pants and then lower himself down. Max set his hands to the hollows of Cormac's hips and held on as Cormac positioned himself between his legs. "Is this okay?" Cormac asked.

Max nodded, and Cormac kissed his neck, his ear, and his shoulder for a while before sliding into Max. Max gasped, gripping at the sheets. It wasn't all pain, but neither was it all pleasure. Cormac seemed conscientious of this, moving slowly, gently. "If you need me to stop, let me know."

Max put his hand to Cormac's chest. He wasn't exactly sure how he could feel both like something was too tight and that they had been made to fit together at the same time. He felt like every time Cormac looked at him when they were joined, he could see straight through him to whatever was on the inside. And once again, it was a study in dichotomies, because he felt both so very seen and very exposed at the same time.

Cormac whispered in his ear, "You all right?"

"Just—a million thoughts and feelings."

"Want to stop?"

"No?"

Cormac kissed him deeply and stroked his hair, pushing into him at just the right angle for something to ignite. Max moaned, high voice plaintive. Cormac responded by doing it again. Max felt as though there were some kind of invisible chain strung between their sternums, and as Cormac got to the end of it, he pulled him back in and ran his hands down his back, his backside. Cormac's breath caught, and invigorated, he started pushing anew. Max held his hips aloft and felt that tinder strike again and again. He panted in time to Cormac's heavy breaths, which grew more and more urgent. He held his firm backside in his hands and squeezed, and Cormac withdrew and cried out. Max held his shaking body against him until he got the breath back in him.

Cormac trailed his hand down Max's front to the space between his legs. "May I?" he asked.

Max just nodded, and Cormac parted the fold, his gentle fingers seeking. Max still held Cormac to him, their eyes locked. The pleasure felt equal parts from Cormac's touch as well as the closeness of his body, until it gently lit on a part Max didn't know that he had, and his breath got knocked back into him. Instinctively, he clapped his hand over Cormac's, gripping it.

"Bad?" Cormac said.

Max just shook his head and urged Cormac's fingers back to that spot. When he found it again, he made sure Cormac didn't leave it. He squeezed his eyes shut and threw his head back, shivering from his unfamiliar places to the whole of his body. It was different from what he knew. It built to a crescendo, but there was no sharp drop; it was like his body carried the harmony as it continued to reverberate through him following the climax, and it could either gently settle or progress and rise again.

Cormac swept Max's hair from his face and held on, putting

his forehead against his. "Was that all right?"

"You were amazing," Max gasped.

Cormac edged closer and entwined his legs with Max's, his strong arms around him. "I don't know if I was all that skilled."

"I've never been with anyone who made sure that I...you know, after they did."

"Oh," he said quietly, troubled. "Max, that's not amazing, that's just polite."

Max sat and thought about it, bewildered. "I guess there's a specific sort of etiquette."

Cormac wove his fingers into Max's hair. "You okay?"

"Yes. Very much yes. You?"

"Also yes." He rested his chin on top of Max's head and held onto him.

"It was all right, even though I'm a woman?"

"Like I said. Felt like you."

Max pressed his head against Cormac. "I don't know that I could see past it."

"You make it easy."

He nestled into Cormac's strong arms and listened to his heart beat for a while. At length, Cormac looked down at himself, at the dark gray and purple mark across his torso. "Thank you," he said. "For not asking."

"It seemed to not be the time."

He laughed a little. "No, we were a little busy. I'll...tell you if you want to know."

"You'll tell me when you're ready."

"Well, that hardly seems fair. I've asked quite a lot of you."

"Some of those things really couldn't wait. A scar is, by definition, not going anywhere."

"I suppose you're right." He leaned his head back, then looked over at Max. "We'll say I owe you one."

"Okay." Max kissed Cormac, gently at first, then a little more insistently. Cormac beamed as they parted. "What?" asked Max with a nervous little laugh.

"This was nice. Really, really nice."

Max leaned his head into the hollow of Cormac's shoulder and closed his eyes, for the first time in a very long time perfectly content.

Brenna and Flora had hit it off and were chatting happily when Max and Cormac came down. Brenna exclaimed when she spotted Max, "Did you do that to match us?"

"No, I swear," Max said with a lopsided smile. "It does what it wants."

"Which number is this one?" Flora asked.

"Number two. The first one that showed up after the cursing."

"She's so…" Max lifted an eyebrow, and she finished, "Small. You're almost my size."

Cormac picked Max up and set him on a barstool. "Better for lifting."

Brenna said, "Speaking of your height, can you get down the cookbooks for me? I want to show Flora something."

"We could just put them on a lower shelf."

"We could, but I like making you get them," she said, poking at him until she'd driven him into the kitchen.

Flora's head swiveled to fix Max with a look. "There was a thing on the door. Brenna says that means you were doing it. Were you doing it?"

"I neither confirm nor deny anything," Max said blithely.

"You!" She swatted at his arm. "I'll get it out of you yet."

"It won't be hard," he said. "I crack easily."

"Did you—?" Brenna and Cormac returned, and she stopped leaning over on her stool.

Brenna plopped a large book that held scraps of paper attached in various ways to the pages to the bar. "This is the book of all the recipes I've cared to try in the last few years. The lady who comes to help at the bar writes them down, or I find them in library books, or on the last page of the newspaper. Obviously, not having an oven limits me somewhat, but I do my best."

Flora leaned in, intent. "Oh, that sounds good."

"Doesn't it? I can't remember how it turned out when I made it last."

"I've really come to love cooking," Flora murmured. "I wasn't really allowed to at home."

"No kidding? Oh, right, you're a noble lady."

"Not here," she said cheerfully. "Just an everyday, run of the mill cryptobiologist."

"Right," Cormac said with a little laugh.

Flora paused. "Oh, this sounds good. Why don't we make this

one?"

Brenna looked at the page. "Shoot, I'm out of eggs."

"We can go to the market. Pick up a couple of things."

Everyone looked at Cormac, who spread his hands. "Why are you all looking at me?"

"You're the one who knows things about how to stay safe in this city."

He pushed out a breath. "Right. Well, don't take the main thoroughfare. Even if the vendors don't get you, they'll sell your soul to the Guild. Max, have you got a hood?"

"Not for this body," he said, confused. "Why?"

"Not so many underkin around. That, and sunshine."

"I can disguise myself magically—"

"Not in the market, you can't. Pickpockets will just as soon scout out who's using magic and sell that information to the highest bidder. You can borrow Brenna's cloak."

This was feeling like a worse idea by the minute, but Flora was so excited. He let Cormac drape Brenna's green cloak over his shoulders and pull up the hood. "There," he said, turning Max's chin up affectionately. "Now it just looks like the shadows from the hood."

"And no one will think it's odd I'm walking around with my hood up?" Max asked.

"You won't be the only one," Brenna promised.

Cormac asked, "You sure you want to go? I can tuck down there myself."

"That's okay," Flora said brightly, tucking Max's arm into the crook of hers. "I think it'll be good to get out."

In other words, she wanted to pry information out of Max about Cormac. As was her right as his best friend, but she couldn't have been more transparent about it. Cormac said, "All right. If you're not back in a half hour, I come looking."

"We'd best get to it, then," Flora said. "Back in a bit!"

She pulled Max out into the bright day, and suddenly he was glad for the hood. His underkin eyes and skin were sensitive to the sun. He wasn't sure how Cormac and Brenna did this on a regular basis. Flora wasted no time. "So what's he like? Underneath all that gruff experience."

"Gentle," Max said. "And maybe just a bit soft."

"He's certainly the most interesting man you've slept with."

"How do you know I slept with him?"

"Please. I've known you your whole life. Plus you're walking a little funny."

Max looked down inadvertently. "I am—? Gods."

"Don't worry. I'm the only one who'll notice. How was it?"

Max finally gave in to her pulling him around by the arm as they walked through a long alley under some brightly striped awnings. "Sex as a woman is…vulnerable. Has it always been like that for you?"

"Oh, yeah," she confirmed. "There's definitely an element of trust that has to go into it. And, well. You know me. Really only did it a handful of times. Still, every time. Trust."

"I thought I understood that, but it seemed so different."

"Maybe because you're petite? Or is it something to do with

his bits? Were they unusual?"

"Yes, they were utterly abnormal. Good gods, Flora. For someone without interest in this sort of activity and this sort of person, you say the wildest things."

"I know. Nobody expects it. If it's not him, it's you. I bet it's different for all your bodies." She gave a tiny gasp. "You could try to find out!"

Max laughed quietly. "Leave it to you to make it a research project."

"It's probably the most fun anyone will ever have researching. Well. For you. I'd decline the opportunity. For lots of reasons." She paused. "It *was* fun, right? He was good to you?"

"Yes. Goodness, yes. As good as I've ever had and better."

"Good. Because otherwise, I'd get into a fight I couldn't finish."

"There's no need. He's very kind, and, well, our stories aren't so different. When it comes to being open about certain things."

"He's gay?" He nodded once. She squinted. "So why was he so flirty with number five? And why'd he have sex with number two?"

"He just says I'm Max."

"Aww. That's cute. And true! As far as I can tell, you're still my friend in there."

As far as he could tell, that was, in fact, true. Much as he feared splitting into six, he still felt the same day to day, with minor exceptions. "I think it truly doesn't matter to him."

"So what are you?" She asked.

"What do you…? I'm Max."

"No, no, I mean the pair of you. Are you courting, or dating, or just doing it for fun, or…"

"Oh. Um. I don't know."

"You slept together without talking about it?"

"Listen, there was a lot to discuss," he said. "Between Aubric, the curse, my title, we were a little tired of talking."

"It's just so unlike you to jump into things feet first. You're so measured."

"Well, maybe that hasn't worked out the best for me," he said, tilting his head to the side. "Maybe it's all right to just take it as it comes, just this once. And maybe *someone* strongly encouraged me to take a risk."

Flora nodded. "But you probably should still talk about it."

"You don't think that might be a little daunting for him?"

"For *him*, hmm," she teased.

"Yes," he emphasized. "I'm used to casual conversations about people's lives and livelihood over the dinner table. That might scare him a little."

"Mm." She hefted her borrowed basket higher on her arm and looked at the colorful stalls of produce and sundries. "It's not like you're asking him to marry you."

"No, but I am expected to marry. And, unless things change drastically, not a man."

"Why shouldn't they change? You've always been an advocate for the people. Maybe let them petition on your behalf for a change."

"You really think that could happen?"

"Why shouldn't you get to marry who you want?"

"Because the last people who did that were my great great grandparents, who are so notorious for eschewing tradition that there are literal ballads about them."

"The horror. I'm just saying, maybe don't take it all as read. You were ready to see where this goes; maybe it'll surprise you. Oh, aren't these pretty."

She reached for a red pepper and examined it in the dim light under the tent. She added it to her basket along with some spinach and tomatoes, then selected six eggs using some kind of grocer's sorcery Max didn't understand. He waited while she took them to the cashier, and he tried to busy his mind with the colors and smells of the market—anything to take his mind off an apparently overdue conversation.

He didn't see the man slip in right next to him. "Your Highness," he said. "A word."

Max turned, startled. He was a fey man with with light blue skin and shimmery gossamer wings of the same icy hue. His hair was a long and a dark blue that matched his impeccably fitted suit. Max wondered how the wings fit, thanks to number five, but didn't feel it particularly prudent to try to go around him to find out.

"Do I know you?" he asked suspiciously.

"My name is Lucien Hargreaves. I'm a representative of the Guild."

He wanted to turn over a table of produce and run. He'd literally been grappled in a dark room by a representative of the Guild, and it had felt friendlier than this. "You seem to think you know who I am. What do you want?"

He looked over Max earnestly. "I do know who you are, and your circumstances. Tell me, what brought you to Clockbridge?"

It was a common diplomatic technique to avoid asking questions to which one didn't already know the answer. It was in the periphery of his answers that Max would give away new information if he wasn't careful. "An old friend has been working and living here."

As if summoned, Flora finished her transaction and came to stand firmly beside Max. "Who is this?" she asked, though she looked to Hargreaves for her answer.

"Lady Nythera—" he began smoothly.

"Oh, good, he knows my name," she said. "And what does he want?"

"He says he's a Guild representative," Max said. "He hasn't exactly gotten to what he wants yet."

Hargreaves' poise was rocked by Flora's bluntness, or maybe by the confidence Max felt with his friend at his hip. Hargreaves even appeared to blush a little. "Not what *I* want—it's an offer. From the Guild. We can discuss it in the Gilded Hall, if you would—"

"I think we're both more comfortable out here," Max said, holding out his hand for Flora's basket. She handed it over, and he balanced it over an arm. "I assume that's all right?"

"Yes, of course," he stuttered.

"Good. Now, Mr. Hargreaves, I have to be honest with you, your Guild doesn't exactly have a sterling reputation. The aggression towards magic users makes this place very difficult to work in and around."

"The Guild is rather strict with magic users," he admitted.

"Oppressive, some might say."

"Max," Flora said. "Maybe we *should* talk somewhere else."

Hargreaves looked nervous. "If I'm being honest, Your Highness, I'm a diplomat. And a low level one at that. All I know is that I am to extend an offer of amnesty for any and all magical incursions on our city in the name of your...." He looked around as if to see if anyone was listening. There were enough people nearby that someone easily could have been.

"It's all right, go on and say it."

He kept his voice very low indeed. "Curse."

"If...?"

"If you will agree to let some of our scholars make a study of it."

There it was. Max suddenly felt as though the cobbles were dropping out from under him. Flora steadied him.

Hargreaves seemed to notice the discomfort, as he quickly added, "A small one."

"What will that net them?"

"A good number of our alchemists make their living making wards and protectives. Your situation is highly unusual. We aren't sure yet how much we can learn."

"Ah. I see. An anomaly all the way around."

Quickly, he offered, "And of course, any findings will be communicated to you in service of your attempts to have it broken."

"Why would you think I'm trying to break it?"

Hargreaves folded his hands. "You met with one of our men about a search for a cure. I understand that conversation was less than fruitful. We can help. Officially, this time."

Max's jaw clenched, and Flora set her hand on his shoulder. "Max is not an object of study."

"We will make every effort to be delicate," he promised. "We understand this is a sensitive thing."

"May I think it over?" Max asked, a growing pressure mounting behind his eyes.

"Of course. Where might I call on you?"

Not the Goat. The Goat was both safe and completely unsafe. As much as Max didn't want to give them anything, he wanted even less to have another unexpected visit. He looked to Flora, asking, and she nodded. He said, "I will be in Lady Nythera's home tomorrow evening. I will have an answer for you then."

Hargreaves made a little bow. "Thank you, Your Highness. Until then."

He disappeared too seamlessly into the crowd for someone that brightly tinted. Max sagged, and Flora asked, "Are you okay?"

"No," he said. "No, I am not—everything that was supposed to be secret, they know. Everything."

She put her hands on his shoulders. "Maybe that's not as bad as it seems?”

“How?”

“Well. They aren’t going to control or punish you.”

“Only if I agree to make myself into a laboratory rat.”

“Maybe—or maybe they’ll learn something that will help you!”

He pinched the bridge of his nose. “Flora, your undying optimism is adorable and not at all appreciated right now.”

“Sorry.”

“How would this be different from Aubric studying me?”

“It’s a different approach. He’s a wizard. They’re alchemists, enchanters. More heads are better than one. Plus, I’ll make sure they behave.”

He stared into the middle distance, trying to make sense of all of this, any of this. He felt eyes on him. “We should get out of here,” he muttered.

“Back to—?”

“Don’t say it. They’re likely to have us followed.”

“Well, what do we do?”

A very good question. In the midday crowd, salvation appeared in the form of a worried underkin-elf. Cormac caught Max’s eyes and hurried over. “Thirty minutes, remember? Thank gods, you’re okay.”

“Maybe,” Max eked out. “The Guild found me.”

“What?” Cormac looked around. “Not here. Follow me.”

He took them through the back end of the market, where pallets stood stacked and crates waited to be unloaded. He kept a nervous watch over his shoulder. "Don't look back," he instructed Max, "but we are absolutely being followed."

"What do we do?"

"Lose them." He took Max's hand. "Walk quickly and stay with me. Flora, walk a little behind Max."

She did, and Cormac doubled back and led them straight to the main thoroughfare, close to the center of the street. Max cringed, waiting to be descended upon by vendors, but to his shock, it was like they didn't see them at all. Instead, they all started calling out to the person behind them, who couldn't wave them away quickly enough. Cormac found another alley and rushed them through it, then another, then another. He looked back. "I think that's done it. One more trick." He looked up at the brick building and pulled on an iron ladder, which unfolded with a screech. "Up we go."

Max found himself at odds with heights on the best of days, and this was not the best of days. Still, he clambered up to the roof and waited for Cormac to bridge the gap between them with a set of planks that seemed to have been kept here for that purpose. He helped Max and Flora across, then finagled his window open. He swung inside and held out his arms to receive them. Max stood for a moment, trembling and trying to catch his breath. Cormac put his hands to his shoulders and looked down at him. "What happened?"

"They know—everything. Who I am, what happened to me. They know I've used magic inside the city. I have no idea how." He shook his head. "Did you tell them?"

"No. Gods, no, Max, I'd never…." He trailed off.

"You know who did."

"I'm going to take care of it," he promised.

"It's too late. They want to study me."

"That could help you, couldn't it?"

His eyes flashed. "Help me? Is being treated like an animal, stripped of my dignity, and purposefully injured helpful? Because it hasn't been so far."

Cormac looked at the ground and swung his arms.

Flora gasped. She reached for Max then pulled back. "Research shouldn't be like that," she said. "We can make sure that it isn't this time."

"If they'll allow it." He pressed his hand to his aching forehead. "My guess? They won't find the answer, and they'll use that to justify more and more. Because those alchemists have to make a living, don't they?" He felt his eyes go wet, and he turned away. "Excuse me. I think I need to lie down."

Flora took her basket from him and gave his arm a light squeeze. Cormac lingered a moment longer, then let Max be.

Chapter Six
City of Dreams

Max laid among the fresh sheets and kept his eyes covered for a while, trying not to think too hard. The pounding of his head had subsided into a general dull thud. He was thinking about rejoining the others, as being alone with his thoughts was none too pleasant, when he heard shouting from the hall.

He rose urgently and grabbed his knives, leaving Cormac's bedroom door open. In a moment, however, he realized the shouting was coming from Brenna's room, not the bar. Cormac's voice was raised. "How could you do something like that?"

"Someone has to look after you." Brenna's voice was defensive.

"It's not just the two of us anymore," he returned. "These are good people."

"You really think there's such a thing?"

"Listen to yourself. This place is crushing you."

Pleadingly, she said, "I'm closer than ever. They let me put in an offer—"

"Is that what this was worth? Somebody's *life*, and maybe you can buy the bar?" Angry footsteps toward the door, and Max fled back to the room. Before he shut the door, he heard Cormac say, "My sister wouldn't do that."

Max put the knives away and sat on the edge of the bed. A gentle knock sounded at the door. "Come in," he said.

Cormac came inside the room, his mouth set in an unhappy line. "Hey," he said. "I...hope you didn't hear that."

"I did," he admitted. "Or at least the end of it."

"I'm sorry. That was neither of our finest moment." He came to the bed and sat down next to Max. "She thought she was... keeping me safe. Because I opted not to report you, she thought there would be scrutiny, so she reported for me."

"I suppose I can respect that."

"Well, I can't," he said angrily. "You could have—"

The end of that thought dangled precipitously in midair. Max said, "It's just been the two of you for a long time, hasn't it?"

Cormac nodded, putting his face in his hand. "I don't think I've told you how we came to be here."

"That one was a three-drink story."

"We've had three drinks if you add them all up. Besides, I think I owe it to you now. Our mother is underkin. Our father's an elf. I don't know if you know much about the underkin, but the whole society is paranoid. Comes from other countries actually trying to attack them generations ago. So there's a reason, but it pervades everything now. Everything's about trying to preserve the society. Mum started attending this group of displaced underkin and…I don't know if they got to her, or it was her idea to start with, but somehow she took it into her head that she did wrong by having kids with an elf. So one day, she tried to…erase that mistake."

Horrified, Max held his silence. Cormac nodded slightly. "She set the house on fire. All three of us in it. Dad didn't make it. Brenna almost…I had to go back for her."

"Cormac. I'm so sorry."

"So we left our town and came here. We'd heard about it, you see. Supposed to be the kind of place where anybody can be anything if you just work hard enough. Instead, it's the kind of place that pits people against each other by design."

Max took his hand and held it. Cormac looked down at their hands enjoined. "Max, if you want to go…I can't pretend I played no part in the Guild finding you."

"I don't know where I would go," he confessed. "I can't go home."

"Your parents would really prefer it if you suffered out in the world?"

"It's…."

"Complicated. But answer it, please, as simply as you can."

Max let out his breath. "Even after this, no, I don't think they would prefer it. But I also think that me going home still-cursed would be seen as a failure."

"All right. Still, if you want to go, I understand."

Max shook his head. "If anything, *this* is the only place I feel safe."

Cormac blinked, startled. He blushed, already a little tinted red after arguing. "Really?"

"Right now, I feel like I can only trust Flora," Max said. "And you."

"Not me," Cormac said wretchedly. "I told my sister everything."

"I don't blame you," he said. "Or her, really."

"Well, *I* do, the both of us. If *you'd* seen how scared you looked, you'd feel the same."

It was obvious Cormac was still stewing with anger for his sister, and that alone probably didn't sit well with him. "Yes, I was scared," Max said. He took Cormac's hand, noting how much bigger it was than number two's. "But knowing more of what happened and why, it's a little easier."

"You're not just saying that?"

Max shook his head. "It really was the pair of you against everyone else for a long time. It must be hard to change."

Cormac's expression shifted a few times as he worked through his thoughts. "But change happens."

"It does."

"I don't know that she ever…expected me to meet someone. Someone *good*, I mean. I love her, but she can't be the only person in my life forever."

Max shifted his weight. "I'm a little sorry it's me."

"What? Why would you say that?"

"Everything with me is just…complicated."

Cormac set his hand to Max's knee. So small, number two's

knees. It was such a funny thing to notice in that moment, but it didn't feel wrong. "Maybe I like complicated," he said.

Max smiled a little. "In that case, could we talk about it?"

"Sure, all right." Cormac let out a shaky breath and a laugh. "Can't say I've ever really had one of these talks that went anywhere. Go ahead."

"There are expectations of me."

"Which are complete horseshit."

Max nodded his concession. "I've always been a rapscallion, pushing back left and right. Doing so against those expectations would not be new."

"That's a word. Somehow, I don't see you as much of a rogue."

"Depends on who you ask."

"All right, you scoundrel, tell me what we're looking at."

"There are the societal expectations that say what I should and should not do—"

"Those are the horseshit ones," Cormac said.

Max continued through a grin. "There are also the expectations of my station and my future responsibilities. All the politics and schemes and assassins, those all come with me, if you want to spend more time with me. But I will say—for me, this would be worth the fight. If it's something you want."

"Can't rightly remember the last time anyone asked me what I wanted," Cormac said softly.

"You don't have to answer right away."

"For now, we're spending time together, and I want to keep

doing that. Is that okay?”

Max leaned and bumped his head into Cormac’s shoulder. “More than okay.”

“But what about you? What do you want to you do now?”

A little bit of Max’s headache resurged. “I’m going to have to take the Guild’s offer.”

“You don’t have to, Max. You could leave. …*We* could leave.”

“You’d go with me?”

“Always wanted to travel.”

“I don’t want you to decide to do that while you’re arguing with Brenna. Your answer might be different tomorrow.”

Cormac exhaled. “Fair.”

Max smiled and leaned up against Cormac’s arm. Cormac rested his head atop Max’s. It seemed that, for now, they’d decided things. Better than that, he’d made it through that conversation without breaking down or combusting.

He looked up at Cormac tentatively. “The alchemist you mentioned. He’s connected to the Guild?”

“That’s honestly the reason I don’t know more about him, because I didn’t want to tip anybody off that I was looking. If you take their offer, I wouldn’t have to worry about that.”

“Please do.” He took a breath. “If something goes wrong, we leave. But I think I have to give it a try. It’s the closest I’ve gotten to finding someone to break it in all this time. It would be a shame to walk away from it because of what *might* happen.”

Cormac nodded. “You’re brave.”

“Oh, nonsense.”

"No, you are. I can't imagine subjecting myself to Guild inspection. I'd be in jail, or worse."

Max was still terrified it would go that way. But the only thing for it was to try.

Max ventured down into the bar around dinner time. An unfamiliar woman with a pleasantly plump face and graying red hair stood behind the bar. "Hello, love," she said. "Can I get you anything?"

"Um, thank you, but no. I'm just staying upstairs."

"Oh, a friend of the family, then. I'm Becky."

"Becky. A pleasure. I'm Max."

"That's an unusual name for a pretty girl like yourself."

He smiled slightly. "I'm an unusual girl."

It was strange. The second it left his lips, he'd expected to cringe, or at least laugh wryly at himself, but instead it rang oddly true.

Likely because he'd told Cormac to refer to him how he looked. It made sense to refer to him by the way he looked. It was for convenience.

Max stared at the bar. Wasn't it?

Cormac came down and put his hand to Max's shoulder. "Hey, Becky. Where's the boss?"

"In the kitchen, with Miss Flora. It's a lovely thing, for her to have someone to cook with." She noted Cormac's hand on Max's shoulder and conspicuously said nothing, though she smiled a little extra.

He nodded. "I'll go see to setting the table, then."

"Do you need any help?" Max asked, desperate for a distraction.

"No, please, just take a load off." He gently brushed a stray strand of Max's hair behind his ear and disappeared around the counter into the kitchen door.

Becky held her dishrag to her chest. "I don't think I've ever seen Mister Cormac take to someone so softly. You must be magic."

Max laughed a little. "Me? No. That's all been there in him all along."

She smiled and fell to drying off the mugs on the draining rack. In a moment, Brenna appeared in the doorway to the kitchen. "Max," she said cautiously.

He went over to her, where she held her hands behind her back and looked at the ground. "I have to apologize," she said, anguish in the creases around her eyes. "I told the Guild about you, and I shouldn't have done that. I just—I thought he was getting himself in trouble, and I thought maybe I could fix it."

Max shook his head. "I understand. You've always looked out for one another."

"No, no, you're not supposed to be this wonderful about it," she said, pained. "Be angry with me, be—furious."

"I think Cormac's done plenty of that for the both of us," he said with a little laugh.

Her knee bounced up and down underneath her burnt orange skirt. "And I hate that too. I don't remember the last time he was mad at me. I do deserve it, but…."

"I heard you put in an offer. Did the Guild consider it?"

"They said it was too low." She sounded so defeated, even if she looked so confident. "I'll come back again once I've managed to save up a little more."

Max dug around in the pocket of his skirt and came away with one of the velvet bags of coin. He pressed it into her hands. "Go back and ask for a counteroffer. If they're serious, this should let you accept it. If they're not…well, then you'll know."

Her eyes widened. "I can't—I can't accept this. I hurt you, and you—"

"One of us should have the Guild off their back," he said, closing her hand around it.

She looked down at the bag in her hand and then up at him, her eyes watering. "You can't know what this means. Gods, you really are a prince."

"Just—for me, next time the Guild comes round asking about someone…?"

She nodded. "I'll say nothing. Thank you, Max. Now come eat. Flora and I made a quiche."

The table in the kitchen was clearly a bar table repurposed, but it had a little tablecloth on it and Cormac had in fact set the table. Flora was already sitting, beaming. Brenna plopped Max into a seat and went to get the pan. They ate and chatted, and Flora filled Cormac in about Lucien Hargreaves. "*That* guy?" He groaned.

"Oh, so you know him?"

"He's the one they send when they want a light touch. Too light sometimes, and we wind up cleaning up after his talks later."

Max said nervously, "I'd like to keep it light. No cleaning necessary."

"They will," Cormac reassured him. "They want something from you."

Flora leaned forward. "Did you figure out how he knew all those things about you?"

Brenna looked away, guilt and fluster on her face. Cormac looked torn between being angry and protective. Max stepped into the anxiety between them. "Yes," he said, "and it's not a big deal."

Flora looked back and forth. Realization dawned on her face, and she shrank back. "That's a—relief, then. But didn't it seem like he knew…too much?"

"What do you mean?"

"Well, he knew about *me*. Nobody here knows much more than my name."

That *was* odd, but, with their resources, they could have figured it out in short time. Couldn't they?

"You're right. He did seem to know a little too much."

"And that makes him shady," Flora pronounced.

Max was in the dungeon. The chill seeped into his naked body as he knelt on the floor, clutching the one blanket he was given to himself. There had been no knowing what he would turn into, what might happen if he was pressed into desperation. So he was watched, eyes in the dark just beyond his range of vision. "If you're there," he said, number three's low voice rumbling out of him, "can you please just—talk to me?"

"Oh, Max," Aubric's brassy voice returned. "You made it quite clear that you never wanted to talk to me again."

The keys rattled in the lock, and the cell door swung open. Max staggered to his hooves, still unsure how they worked, but before he could leave, the door clanged shut again, this time with Aubric on the inside. He looked up at Max, his bottle-green eyes glinting in a way Max had once found endearing. He'd found himself a puzzle, and there was very little Aubric liked more than a puzzle.

From his sleeve, he pulled out a dagger.

"Max," Cormac's voice cut in. "Max, it's just a dream."

Max shot up, entangled in the blankets and drenched in sweat. He felt for his face, found number two's small pointed nose and full lips. He breathed out hard and buried his face in his hands. "I'm sorry," he breathed out. "Did I wake you?"

"I just got back," Cormac said. "Are you okay? It seemed like that was going on for a while."

Max stared into the folds of the blanket and tried to search for words. "The first week of the curse," he said as calmly as he could, "was hell."

"I imagine that it must have been difficult, not knowing what was going on."

"I would have taken that," he said, strained. "Sincerely. But they put Aubric in charge of figuring out what was wrong with me."

"Wait. The guy who hired the—your ex-boyfriend. That guy?"

He nodded, rubbing fiercely at his eyes. "And he doesn't study *anything* halfway."

Cormac's fists clenched. "What did he do?"

"Don't—don't tell Brenna. I don't want her to think that this is what the Guild is going to do." He nodded, his eyes searching Max. Max pushed out a breath. "He put me in the dungeon with no clothes and people watching me at all times. And then he… took pieces off me."

"He *what?*"

"It started small, a bit of hair here so he could see if it grew back, a small cut there to see if it changed forms with me. Some webbing, excised from between number four's fingers to test. And then it was a fistful of feathers, to see whether they would retain their shape when I was no longer number five." He looked at his forearm in the moonlight coming in through the window, found the long scar. "Then it was just anything. To see if I bled like a human. To see if the celestial would heal herself. The worst—he took off my tail to see if it would come back. It did."

Cormac stared hard. "I'm sorry—I know you have a history, but if I run across this sadistic fuck, it's lights out. Does your mother know?"

"He fed her lies about me being dangerous. It took me the whole week to convince her to let me out of the dungeon and to finally obtain clothes that fit. I would not be surprised if he has her charmed, to be honest. Conveniently, when I was about to try finding out, I was exiled."

Cormac sat on the edge of the bed and helped Max straighten out the covers. "You…don't know if your mother was in control when she sent you away?"

"No," he stewed. "Because it's something that so conceivably could have come out of her mouth. But then why would he have sent people for pieces of me here if he was behind sending me away? I don't know."

"And your father?"

"Much of the time, he stands in Mother's shadow. If he has his own opinions, I don't frequently hear them."

Cormac nodded. "Something doesn't feel right. Maybe it's just because I don't know what it was like on the inside, but things don't add up."

"No, you're right," he agreed. "I'll try writing Father. I should probably do that anyway."

"I just can't see a world where my child, however old, got cursed and I'd send him away from me."

"Even if there's a league of assassins waiting for me to make a misstep?"

"Wait, there's a *what?*"

"It's a very, very long story, but the short version is my grandfather pissed off the King of Helmdar, and the king contracted the assassins to 'end my family line', and, well, they've been operating under contract ever since."

"*Especially* if there's a league of assassins waiting for you to make a misstep like, I don't know, walking into a tavern alone and unprotected. Max...."

"It...doesn't make much sense, does it? I suppose I was too close to it, too afraid, to see that." He laughed mirthlessly. "I was too busy being afraid of one thing to remember to be afraid of a whole other host of things."

Cormac put his arm around Max. "How are you not just a ball of paranoia?"

"I am," he said wearily. "But sometimes I have to turn it off, or else I'd be so busy trying not to die that I wouldn't live."

"Been there," he sighed. "Don't think I got the living part quite right. But I'm here, and as long as there's life in me yet, I'm not going to let anything happen to you."

"Cormac...I don't want you risking yourself for me."

He grinned. "You've seen the way I fight. It's not me risking myself so much as hitting the risks until they stop moving."

Max couldn't help a small smile. "Really, though. Would you say all this if I wasn't a prince?"

"Course I would. Though let's be honest, the reason you're getting such cushy treatment from the Guild is probably because they don't want to get in trouble."

"That's probably true."

"But I will go with you, and I will make sure nobody ever so much as thinks about treating you like that again."

Max rested his head in the crook of Cormac's neck. "Thank you," he said. "Flora said something similar. I hadn't thought to ask about taking someone with me."

"Don't ask. Make it a foregone conclusion."

"Okay." He pulled the covers closer, nervous. Cormac tucked them firmly around him and stroked his hair. "I kind of don't want to go back to sleep," he admitted.

"I know. I'll stay with you until you do."

"You could stay after, too," Max said. "That chair didn't look too comfortable. As long as you don't mind getting woken up at dawn."

Cormac smiled. "I don't mind at all."

He slipped off his boots and set them down on the floor, then settled next to Max. He gathered Max into his arms and held fast. "If you could do anything," he said pensively, "like you woke up tomorrow and the curse was gone, no more assassins, no more evil ex-boyfriend, what would you do?"

"If I got that kind of new lease on life? I suppose I'd…hmm."

"What is it?"

"I guess I'd finally get over the fear and give one of my symphonies to the national orchestra."

"*One of?* You've written *multiple* symphonies."

"When I had few responsibilities, and my only other hobby was championing social justice, yes. It's harder to find the time these days."

"What do you play?"

"I started with the lute, but if it has strings, I can probably figure it out."

"That's incredible."

"I left everything back home for fear of robbers on the road. I miss music."

"Do you perform?"

"No, not really. Composing is my real love, but I just…." He grimaced. "Need to get past the fear of actually *hearing* it."

"What's so frightening about that?"

"Well, when you're writing, you can still change things around, mess with it. If something's not right, you can obliterate it and start again. Once you've got it on the page and you've given it to another person, it's no longer malleable. You're bound by their impression of it, and it takes on a whole different life. Which I imagine is satisfying in and of itself, but I've not gotten that far."

"Promise me," Cormac said seriously, "that once you're all sorted out and you've had a moment to breathe that you will pick your favorite and show it to someone."

"Okay," he said, closing his eyes and leaning against Cormac. After all of his fear-facing lately, what was one more?

Chapter Seven
The Fine Print

Max knew by the sheer amount of pain he woke up in it was going to be a number three day. He tried to detangle gently from Cormac and shove himself into the wall so he had somewhere to expand to. Cormac stirred. "Max?"

"Just the usual. Go back to sleep."

"Isn't there anything I can do to help?"

Was there? Nobody had really tried. While he was considering, he felt his spine lengthen by half, which was always the worst part. "Would you mind…terribly if I asked…for a cup of tea?"

"Is that all——? Of course not. I'll be back."

Cormac slipped from bed and made his way to the door, and Max turned over onto his stomach, trying to will the change to go faster. It generally did, at least by a few seconds, if he didn't fight it, didn't think about it. So he focused on the sound of the clock ticking, a hearty metallic pulse in the wooden chest of the case. He loved the comforting beat of it and the delicate chime. Even this sparse room felt like a home when filled with those sounds.

His headache, usually present, grew when the horns did. He buried his face in the pillow and waited for the last of the miasma of pain to at least die back. He took a breath and went for his clothes in the bag.

He was finishing putting the scarf on when Cormac returned with an elegant teacup and saucer. He stopped in the doorway and laughed a little incredulously. "Max. Is that you? You're wearing the scarf, so it must be, but…damn."

"Just about the opposite of yesterday, yeah," he said, rubbing at the back of his neck. He stepped toward the table and prayed he didn't stumble. He made it intact, but he felt Cormac's eyes on him. "Never seen a fiend before?"

"No, it's not that. I'm sorry," he said sheepishly, setting the teacup in front of Max. "You're just so different. And tall. Really tall."

"Yes, number three has been the hardest in general, coming and going and *being*." He took a sip of the tea. "Thank you, this is lovely."

"It's supposed to be good for aches and pains."

"Ah. Good. I could use the help."

"I can see how this one might be difficult to change into and out of. How tall are you?"

"Just shy of seven feet, including the horns."

"Well, damn."

"The curse doesn't do anything halfway."

"No, I was just thinking…I haven't seen number four yet, but all of your forms are very striking."

"Otherwise known as difficult to hide," he laughed.

"No, you shouldn't have to—I mean, I know why you want to and sometimes need to. But if people weren't bastards, or at least less, you could turn all kinds of heads."

Self-consciously, he fiddled with the tea bag's string. "Well… thank you. On behalf of the lady who cursed me."

"No, I think that comes from you," he said. "I'm no expert, but the way you smile, the spark behind your eyes…that's always the same. And it's really—it's beautiful."

He covered Max's hand with his, and Max chanced a smile. "Even like this?"

"Especially like this. I didn't want to embarrass you, but number three? Definitely one of the top six forms."

Max shook his head, still smiling. "You always know just what to say."

"I really don't. I'm making this up as I go, and truth be told, I'm *terrified* I'm going to ass it up."

"You're doing brilliantly. No need for terror."

"It's just— the past few days have been the happiest I've been in…. You're just really wonderful, and I'm scared of stepping in it."

Max tightened his hold on Cormac's hand. "I don't see a way you could."

"Don't make that a challenge," he laughed.

"Sincerely, I am not worried."

"Kind of you. Oh, before I forget." He rose and pulled out a little drawer in his workbench full of brass parts. "I want to put in a new lock at Flora's. It's a little easy to pick right now. Of course, it won't keep the Guild out."

"Because we're inviting them in."

"Like the vampires they are."

"That's very much appreciated. I hope everything is where we left it."

"We'll go have a look." He withdrew a dense little brass unit and tested a set of keys in it. "Yes, this will do." He slipped it into the pocket of his coat, which hung on the hook on the back of the door. He put his hands to his hips and blew out a breath. "Look at me, fetching cups of tea and installing locks."

Max tilted his head. "Is that a bad thing?"

He rubbed at his chin. "No, no, not at all. It's just funny. A week ago I wouldn't have had anybody to call friend enough to bother with things like this. There's Estien, I suppose, but he's the one who usually gets the tea. Then you folk come in from Saltrush and all of a sudden, I'm sociable."

"I think you might have been," Max said, "given the opportunity."

"Maybe. I told myself I'm just busy with people who need their clocks cleaned, one way or another."

"I can bring you Flora's clock, if that helps."

He smiled. "No. I like this much better."

They made their way across town to the residential district in the late afternoon, the sun hidden behind some forbidding-looking clouds. Flora chatted a mile a minute, desperately nervous about the state of her house. When they arrived, the door was still shut. Max, playing the part of the large-and-scary-looking man today, looked to Cormac and they each nodded, telling her to stay put while they searched the rooms. Aside from her bedroom still in disarray, everything looked to be safe and accounted for. Max helped Flora clean up her room while Cormac tangled with the door. She looked sadly at some broken glass in the corner. "I'm going to have to start those titrations again," she sighed.

"I'm sorry, Flora."

"Oh, don't be," she said, brightening. "You and Cormac got me back. Did I say thank you yet? Thank you a hundred times, by the way."

"Flora, if I can, I will always show up," he said seriously. "It's just a matter of when."

"Well. Cormac certainly didn't have to."

No, he didn't, he thought fondly. He was glad he did.

Flora and Max methodically worked through her belongings strewn across the floor and returned them at least to neat piles on the dresser and bed. She waved him off. "I think that's enough for now. Want a drink?"

As time progressed toward the evening and Lucien Hargreaves' return, he found his nerves acting up. "Yes, please."

She patted his shoulder. "Don't worry. It's just talking tonight. You're good at talking."

He was, but he wasn't confident in his ability to negotiate his way through a topic that made him this nervous. She left him in the living room, and he went to see how Cormac was getting on with the door. He looked up and wiped at his forehead with a forearm. "It's putting up a fight," he said with a little grin.

"Need an extra set of hands? They're…reasonably useless at everything except music, but I can hold things."

"Sure, that might help. If you can hold this bit here…"

Max held the lock unit up for Cormac to tighten into the door. He furrowed his brow, stared intently at the mechanism for a moment, then gave the screwdriver a hearty wrench. The lock clicked into place, and he sat back. "I think that's done it. Go ahead and let go." Max did, and nothing fell. "Hey," Cormac said with a little fist pump. "Nice work."

"I did almost nothing." He stooped and gave Cormac a kiss. "But you, on the other hand…"

Cormac smirked and made a gentle grab at Max's waist. "Come here and do that again."

A throat cleared behind them, and they turned to see Lucien Hargreaves standing at the door. "Cormac," he said with an awkward little nod. "And you must be…"

"Max," Max said simply.

Hargreaves looked up at him—and up. He was by no means short, but Max was very tall. Cormac said, "Yeah, I know, it's weird being the short one."

Flora came out from the kitchen. "Max, I've got—oh. You're here early."

Hargreaves bowed his head. "Lady Nythera. Thank you for volunteering your home for this conversation."

"Sure," she said, holding up a bottle. "We were just going to have some wine to prepare for it. Want some?"

He laughed—a brief, strangled thing, and then seemed to realize she was serious. "Er. Thank you, but no."

"Suit yourself. Have a seat," she said, setting three glasses down on the coffee table and pouring them. Max helped Cormac up, who shut the door and went to stand behind the couch where Hargreaves opted to sit. Max tentatively tookthe chair in front of the clock, and Flora sat on the floor in front of the coffee table rather than sit next to Hargreaves. "We were just putting my house back together. I was kidnapped."

"Oh—oh, I'm sorry to hear that."

She shrugged and sipped her wine. "Max and Cormac got me back."

"I—wasn't aware you were all on first name terms."

Cormac folded his arms. "Guild doesn't know everything."

It occurred to Max that he was not on *last name* terms with Cormac. He'd never offered one because he didn't have one, technically. Hargreaves shifted his weight. "Well. Good to see you all. Prince Maximillian, I have to ask—are you comfortable having this conversation in so public a setting?"

"It's the only way I feel comfortable with it," he said, sitting forward.

"I see." He was clearly discomfited by the idea, but he soldiered on anyhow. "Have you given consideration to our offer?"

"I have," Max said. "I'm inclined to accept—with some stipulations."

Hargreaves' demeanor shifted. His face brightened, like some great dread had been lifted from him. "Of course, of course. What might those be?"

"What kind of study is this?"

"We will have an alchemist, an enchanter, an arcanologist, and of course a physician examine you. They will make notes on your transitions from their respective points of view. This could go on for a number of sessions."

"Just examinations?"

"They may adjust for a variable here and there, see what effect it has."

"No," he said plainly. "No experimentation."

"Your Highness," Hargreaves said diplomatically, "you must understand that there has never been and there might never be an opportunity to study someone with a makeup like yours."

"Then the information shouldn't be of much use, should it?"

"On the contrary. This could provide us with much-needed context for curses as a whole, humanoid transmutation, and of course, your own specific curse. To limit the breadth of the study would limit the data."

"You heard him," Cormac said.

"If I may," Flora ventured. "I believe what Prince Maximillian is concerned about is infringement on his bodily integrity. Perhaps if you laid out what exactly you expect to happen, he might reconsider."

Hargreaves looked flustered. "To be completely honest with you, Your Highness, Lady Nythera—I am a diplomat, not a researcher. I couldn't begin to tell you what I expect. I can say that the researchers involved will state their intentions clearly and ask permission before doing *anything.*"

Max lifted his eyebrow. "And I have the ability to say no without invalidating the agreement?"

"Of course."

"Under those conditions—and a strict adherence to them—I will agree. In addition, I will bring Lady Nythera or Cormac or both to every examination. They are to be treated as advocates for my well-being and given the same respect I am given. They have the authority to remove me for any reason."

Hargreaves bowed his head. "It will be done."

"And lastly—you, the Guild, will not use anything you learn from me to curse or otherwise harm anyone. You will not sell this information to anyone, and should you publish your findings, I insist that every precaution be taken to protect my privacy and to prevent this information from being used against anyone. I am familiar with the multinational court system and will not hesitate to use it if need be."

"Yes, of course. Is there aught else I might note?"

"You will communicate the timing and nature of these examinations...."

"Through me," Flora said firmly. "In writing. With at least two days' notice."

Max nodded his approval. Hargreaves said, "For the future, I can do this. For the first examination, we were hopeful you might come to the Guild Hall a half an hour before dawn tomorrow."

Max shut his eyes. He was unsure how far he should press

this. So far Hargreaves had been accommodating, but he didn't want to find out where that ended. "Very well," he said begrudgingly. "And I presume you will have this all in writing by then?"

Hargreaves looked startled. "Is a formal contract absolutely necessary? For your privacy, leaving your name off things would —"

"It's necessary," Cormac said.

Max nodded. "We will begin once I've reviewed and signed."

Hargreaves looked around and must have decided not to press his own luck. "So it shall be. I thank you, Your Highness."

Max stood and walked Hargreaves to the door. "We will see you in the morning, then."

"You certainly will," he said.

Cormac dropped to the couch where Hargreaves had sat and held out his arm to receive Max. Flora pushed Max's wine glass toward him. "Well?" Max asked. "How do you think it went?"

Cormac said, "Good call on the contract. I don't trust him. He's squirrelly."

"More than that," Flora said, "He wasn't aware of the realities of an examination like this one. There's a real danger in just letting diplomats handle this."

"Which is why I hope you don't mind coming with me," Max said. "I rather panicked."

"No, not at all." She toyed with the rim of her glass. "I wonder if there's not a safer living arrangement for you. Not that I don't want you here, but since they know where 'here' is, they could come by at any time. And if you aren't here, I can tell them to beat it."

Cormac nodded. "This is good for official things, but you can bet it's going to be watched. You're always welcome at the Goat. There are always other people around, and it's hard to spy undetected."

Flora smiled. "You can both stay tonight, since it's bright and early for us tomorrow."

Max nodded slowly. "Thank you both. I know keeping me is a risk."

They both went to shake their heads, but it was a touch hard to deny. Max drank deeply of his wine. Flora said, "We like you safe. I'll watch for messages from them and let you know when to expect to report."

Cormac told Max, "I do have to go back to work the day after tomorrow, but if they want all of these things to be around dawn, that's no trouble."

"You'll just sleep even less," Max said, setting his mouth to the side.

Cheerfully, Cormac said, "Oh, how much sleep do you even really need?"

"Six to eight hours," Flora answered.

"Of course you know that."

"Flora knows just about everything," Max said.

"Oh, that's not true," she returned. "I just studied a lot. And not even as much as some."

"But what you don't know, you're always excited to find out."

"I am. I have to admit, the prospect of your study is exciting. Mr. Hargreaves wasn't just blowing smoke—this information could help you, and a lot of other people."

A small comfort.

Flora's guest room bed fit two people much more comfortably than Cormac's, but when one of those people was number three, it was still a bit of a challenge. Max and Cormac arranged themselves and settled down. Cormac turned slightly. "Max? You okay?"

"I'm nervous," he admitted. "I don't think they're going to do what Aubric did, but I worry that the effect will be the same."

"I won't let them do anything that takes away your—what did Flora call it?—your bodily integrity."

Max knew that Cormac believed that firmly, and he wanted to believe him, too, but there were just so many ways that they could strip him of that. He decided to stop worrying about them ahead of time and instead said, "Cormac, what's your last name?"

"What?"

"I realized that I don't know. I feel like I've known you much longer than I have, but sometimes I realize that there's still so much to learn."

"Ah." He settled back. "We don't have one."

"Really?"

"It…Cormac isn't my given name. Neither is Brenna hers. When we left, we left everything. But being kids, we didn't think about anything like surnames. So when they asked our names when we registered here, we just told them the ones we'd chosen and they left the latter half blank."

"I'm sorry. I didn't realize."

"No, you're all right. Bit of an unusual circumstance. And I'm just lucky, being the silly boy I was, I didn't name myself something foolish. It's funny, though. Our last name was Graymoor. Now we've got the Gray Goat, which we definitely didn't name. Brenna will sometimes joke that she'll use Graygoat."

Max smiled a little. "Maybe it was meant for her."

"What's yours?"

"I don't have one, either, though admittedly for very different reasons."

"Ah. Everybody just knows who you are."

"At least in Saltrush. In other places, I still have introductions to make."

"How do you do that?"

"Depends," he said. "If it's official, it's 'Prince Maximillian of the Kingdom of Saltrush'. If it's just me, it's just Max."

"That is a mouthful."

"The poor heralds," he said. "For them, it's 'His Royal Highness Crown Prince Maximillian of the Kingdom of Saltrush'."

"What makes a prince a *crown* prince, anyway?"

"Intent to inherit the throne. Had I siblings, they would just be prince or princess."

"You're an only child, then," Cormac said.

"In a manner of speaking. I've always had Flora. We were

raised together until she went off to university. If something were to happen to the whole family, she would become Queen."

"Somehow, I can't see that."

"Neither can I."

He stayed quiet for a moment, and Max glanced at him. "Something the matter?"

"I'm sorry, it's still bothering me."

"What is?"

"It just doesn't make any sense for your mother to send her only son, the heir to her kingdom, away."

The longer he thought about it, the less he could deny it. "I truly felt that it was in line with how frustrated she was with me, with everything. Now, though...."

"Do you want to go home?"

Max hesitated. "I do want this curse broken, as she does. Would without intervention. And that isn't happening at home."

"If she's being controlled, isn't she in danger?"

"She's safe, as long as she does as suggested. A dead figure-head is no good. But you're right. As soon as I can return, I should."

"I'd like to see it," Cormac said.

"I'd like you to come see it. And me."

"Would I be welcome?" he asked quietly. "A nobody from Clockbridge."

"There's no such thing as nobody. And I will always welcome you."

"But."

He sighed. "It's less about you and more about the fact that I won't fall in line and marry a woman. They would never take it out on you."

"And you?"

"I think…if they saw me happy for the first time in gods know how long…they might change their minds. I hope. And if not, well…I don't have to be the heir. There's time enough for them to make siblings."

Cormac laid back and looked at him. "You'd really give up the throne…"

"I can't live a lie," Max said. "Not even for my people, whom I do love. What good does it do them to have a miserable king who can't stand up for himself?"

Cormac threw his arms around Max's neck and kissed him hard. Max breathed out and smiled in bewilderment. "What was that for?"

"You're one of the bravest people I know, Your Royal Highness Crown Prince Maximillian of the Kingdom of Saltrush, if not the bravest, and I admire you very much."

"Thank you," he said, his voice breaking a bit.

Cormac kissed him again. "I should stop keeping you from sleep." He looked at him in a little bit of bafflement. "How should we…I'm used to being the big spoon."

Max laughed a little and moved him gently to face him. "The horns point backwards," he said. "I'd rather not gore you."

"Ah, no thank you." He wrapped an arm around Max and brought him in close. Max's tail wound around their legs. "Oh," he laughed in surprise.

Max smiled tiredly and rested his head on top of Cormac's. Like this, he felt he could forget tomorrow and whatever came after and just be.

Chapter Eight
The Gilded Hall

Max didn't sleep much, and was awake well before the alarm clock rang. It was strange, being aware of the time of dawn. Usually he woke with it. The room was dark and cold, and he felt extra strange, wearing the clothes he'd worn the day before. That would change later, but he couldn't very well go through town naked.

Cormac groaned slightly and whacked the alarm clock. Max appreciated the sentiment. He stooped to kiss Cormac and went about pulling himself together.

Flora was already up with breakfast ready for all three of them. Max sat and looked at her gratefully. "Thank you for keeping me fed," he said.

"I like doing it," she answered, "but your thanks are well appreciated."

"I'm glad you've found something you like so well in your time out in the world."

"The trick will be convincing my parents to let me keep at it."

"You're thinking of leaving?" Cormac asked.

"Not yet, but someday I'll have to go back," she said. "Been thinking about that a lot lately, actually. They're not getting any younger, and I've put off my responsibilities for a long time."

"You should enjoy yourself while you can," Max exhorted. "The responsibilities aren't going anywhere."

"Well." She smiled. "Not until you're down to one face again."

"What are your responsibilities?" Cormac asked curiously.

"My family is in charge of running the Royal City and assisting the Queen in matters of diplomacy. So kind of like a mayor, I suppose?"

"That seems like a lot."

"Hence me avoiding it," she said with a little laugh. "I'll get there someday. Not all at once, thank gods."

"Our inheritances don't pass to the heirs when their predecessors die," Max explained. "We take on something of an apprenticeship, where we do the work and our parents oversee us, make sure we're ready. And then they retire."

"That seems reasonable," Cormac said. "As reasonable as anything with one person in charge of so much."

"Oh, we get help," Flora said. "Max will have advisors, and I'll have clerks. It's not *all* on one person; one person is just the face of it."

"The Guild doesn't have a face," Cormac mused. "It's just a bunch of people arguing with each other, and then decisions get handed down."

"How do you know whom to hold accountable?"

He frowned slightly. "I…hmm."

"And anybody can be in the Guild?" Max asked.

"If they know a craft and pay their membership. And then they elect the Upper Echelon."

"What if you don't know a craft? Say, you're a doctor or a teacher."

"I…suppose you don't get in the Guild, then."

"That seems strangely prohibitive," Max said.

"Any more than a single family being in charge of everything?"

"Not everything. In Saltrush, the people who make up the lawmaking arm are laypeople of all walks, chosen by their villages and cities."

"That seems fair."

"I suppose I am struggling to understand the Guild," Max admitted. "Maybe seeing it will bring some things into focus."

The Guild Hall rested on top of a hill, a huge stone building with a single public-facing door. Max glanced over his shoulder in the morning dim. It was hard to make out much, but he thought he could spot the Gray Goat below. Cormac heaved the door open, and Max tested his hooves on the slick marble floor. The tall ceilings were held up by stone columns, and fire burned in hanging bowls. To no surprise, no one sat at the polished mahogany reception desk, but on the arm of a plush sofa waited Lucien Hargreaves in another impeccably fitted suit. He rose. "Good morning! Thank you for coming. Your Highness, my

Lady." He paused. "Cormac."

Cormac folded his arms. Max acknowledged his greeting with a single nod. "Is the contract prepared?"

Hargreaves reached into a bag on the sofa and retrieved a stack of paper, then handed it to Max. Max held it and read through, line by line. Hargreaves said, "I trust it is to your satisfaction?"

It contained nothing that he hadn't said and nothing he shouldn't have, and everything seemed in order. He removed a pen from his bag and signed at the bottom of the last page, then watched as Hargreaves did the same, bearing witness. "I'll keep this copy," Max said, handing it to Flora.

Once again, Hargreaves looked defeated, but he nodded cheerily and said, "If you'll follow me, I'll show you to the room we've been given."

Flora trotted to keep up. "It's repurposed, then? Not usually used for experimentation?"

"It's an alchemist's laboratory, with a few added things." He led them out of the vast lobby into a long hallway. This must have been what the Brass Hall was mimicking, as each door had golden nameplates, but more, the reliefs along the doors all had gold leaf worked into the designs. There were torches ensconced in the walls in yet more smooth bowls of fire. They did not go into any of these rooms; rather, Hargreaves took them to a door at the very end and a stone staircase up.

The stairwell smelled musty and carried a chill that didn't leave when they got to the next floor. These rooms were much more modest—no gold in sight—but did still have nameplates. The one that Hargreaves let them into read *Laboratory Six.* Appropriate, Max thought grimly.

The room was not huge, but spacious enough to accommodate several benches and people to work them. There were already people assembled inside, who all looked up when they arrived. Hargreaves said, "Hello, everyone, and thank you for coming this morning. Please allow me to introduce—"

Max cut in, "Max. Just Max will do."

Hargreaves seemed surprised, but nodded deeply. "Max, please meet Dr. Henries. He's a physician specializing in all six lineages." A tall human man with gray hair raised his hand to greet Max, who nodded. "Then there's Dr. Gest, an alchemist with backgrounds in humanoid-magic interaction and curses." A plump elven woman looked up from the rig she'd made at one of the benches and smiled. Max felt very little warmth there.

Hargreaves continued, "And of course Professor Delsyn, who comes to us from the Solarian University. The Professor is a magical expert—"

"Not a mage," the old celestial man said gruffly. "Just an arcanologist. To be clear."

"Yes, of course. For magic, you want Enchanter Solana." He indicated a willowy fiendish woman with a pair of spectacles and grayish skin. "She has worked on the transmutation of several key figures across our Western Continent, including several curses."

She looked at Max critically. "I am told that's what we're dealing with here. If you would be so kind as to step over here, I think we are running up against time."

She indicated a rolling gurney with the back end propped up, like an uncomfortable chaise lounge. Dr. Henries said, "Please remove your clothes."

Max decidedly did not wish to do this, but they all kept waiting for him to say something or do something, so he took a breath and began to undress. Flora turned and faced the wall. He packed his clothes away into his bag and handed it to Cormac, then eased up onto the table. "Um…might I have a blanket or some such? It's rather cold."

They all looked at each other helplessly for a moment, and Hargreaves searched around. Cormac looked ceilingward, took off his coat, and placed it over Max. He signaled to Flora that it was safe to turn around.

"We'll remember that for next time," Hargreaves said.

Dr. Gest pivoted on her stool and looked at Max thoroughly. "Please tell us about the origin of your curse."

Was this really necessary? He supposed to understand it in full it might be, but he'd never really told anybody but Cormac. In the uncomfortable silence, he decided to abridge it. "A fey woman came to my home. She asked for a place to stay, and when I denied her, she left me with this curse."

Dr. Henries chuckled. "Ohh, never get on the wrong side of a fey. No offense, Hargreaves."

"None taken," he said with a slight shudder.

"I'd guessed it was fey in nature by the sheer amount of magic it must take to do what it does," Solana mused. "This one is innate, not in any book, and fiendish curses tend to be more… well, upon death. If celestials can innately bestow curses, we have no record of it."

Max had literally just told her it was fey. He hunched, the gurney cold against his skin. He could feel dawn inching ever closer. Henries pulled his stool over and picked up Max's arm, his hands also cold. "If I may just take your pulse here…it is in fact the elevated heartbeat of a fiend. And you are…which lineage to begin with?"

He answered, "Elven."

"That makes sense geographically for the region," he said. "I think your body is partially remaking itself every day. I'm hoping to see if that's true."

"It certainly feels that way," Max said.

"Does your height change?"

"Dramatically."

"Well, that bodes well, I think."

"Does it?"

"At least for my theory."

Dawn, and the whirlpool at Max's core began. Henries sat up straighter and put his hand to Max's shoulder. "Is it time?"

Max nodded, grimacing. The room started to move as all of the experts jockeyed for the right position to observe. Cormac and Flora stood in the back corner, various shades of disquieted. Max laid back against the gurney and tried to keep himself still. The impulse to scream was strong this morning, but he swallowed it. For their sake, he swallowed it.

Not for his examiners. They hovered, made notes, made quiet comments to each other that the blood pulsing in his ears made hard to hear. He shut his eyes and concentrated on breathing, tried to ignore the retracting, shrinking, and crushing of his body into a different shape. He could tell it was number four quickly by the way his fingers stuck together.

"Max, are those gills functional?" Henries asked, peering over his own nose.

"I—don't know," he eked out. "Haven't tried."

At long last, his body relaxed, as much as it ever did. The experts conversed, talking quickly, as though something might get missed. Henries gently lifted the gills at the sides of his neck. "They respond as other river fey's do. I think you would be safe to test them."

Why not grab a bucket of water and just dunk him in?

"That to me says your initial thinking was correct," said Solana. "From what I observed, the body adapts, rather than disguises itself."

Professor Delsyn harrumphed. "The cost of such a spell is enormous. This caster is a spiteful one with power to spare."

"It seems to me that the fact that this is clearly every dawn instead of every twenty four hours means it's a bespoke spell. Much harder to break inorganically."

Max's heart sank. Henries jostled his shoulder a little. "That doesn't mean impossible."

"What—?" Cormac spoke up for the first time, his voice croaking a little. "What methods are possible?"

"Well. That would be my colleagues' area of expertise," he said, looking over his shoulder.

"Alchemy is an option," Gest said. "A strong enough draught will obliterate just about anything. But the drawback is that it will obliterate just about anything. You'd be sick for a long while if we're looking at what I think we're looking at."

"And there are restoration spells," Delsyn added. "They're just rare in this part of the world. You might need to travel to the Eastern Continent—perhaps even Veritis to seek such a thing."

Solana said frankly, "What I would do? Seek out the caster and ask her to break it." They all looked at her, and she said, "There's a risk, yes. But she knows what she cast. If she can be persuaded, that's the least painful—and surest—method of removal."

"We may learn more in coming sessions," Delsyn said. "If we can pinpoint what was done, we can whittle away the power needed to reverse it."

Max's stomach developed a stone. More of this. More waiting. He sat there numbly as the experts dissembled to each other for a while longer.

Hargreaves watched from Cormac and Flora's corner. "Thank you, Doctors, Professor, Enchanter," he said. "I think this was a productive first session. If you would follow me so that Max can recover himself."

"Oh, yes, of course," Delsyn said. "We should discuss further what coming sessions should look like."

They gathered their things and with only a warm goodbye

from Henries, Max, Flora, and Cormac were left alone. They rushed to each side of him.

"Are you okay?" Flora squeaked.

"I'm fine," he said with a weak laugh. "This is…how it always is."

"Not with seven people *watching* you."

"No, that was thoroughly uncomfortable."

Cormac swept Max's medium-length blue-green hair from his face and set his hand to the side of it for a moment. "It was…apparent. I'm sorry."

"Thank you for the coat."

"Yeah," he said, trying on a little smile. He looked at the door, a hint of murder in his eyes. "Least we could do."

Max let his head rest back against the gurney and blew out a breath. "Not the news I was hoping for."

"They may still find something else," Flora said hopefully.

Cormac didn't look so certain.

Chapter Nine
Mahogany and Roses

On their way out through the Gilded Hall, Max passed by the experts and Hargreaves, huddled and talking. By now there were other people in the expansive space, so it felt a little less daunting. Hargreaves stopped them. "Ah, you're ready. Good. I wanted to give you this." He placed a pouch that clanked into Max's hand. "For your participation. We'll see you at the same time next week?"

He looked so hopeful. Max felt anything but. "Sure," he said at last.

The experts turned to go, but Cormac caught Dr. Gest. "Excuse me, Doctor— I wanted to ask—have you heard of a Professor Jenkins? An alchemist here in town."

"I can't say that I have," she said, tilting her head. "But if he works here, he'd be in the Guild Registry. You're welcome to give my name at reception."

He bowed his head. "Thank you. Much appreciated."

They walked away and Hargreaves escorted them to the door, and they were in the bright streets of Clockbridge, a little shell-shocked. Max asked Cormac, "What was that?"

"The alchemist I've been chasing down. I needed approval from someone to check the registry. She gave it." He grinned. "Easier than I thought. If you want to chase that down, we'll come back when there are fewer eyes on us."

Max smiled gratefully, then paused. "Is his name even Jenkins?"

"Ha, I doubt it. But the registry should match what I do know."

"Clever you."

He glanced around them. "I don't think they'll follow us today. Flora, I'd still like to walk you home."

"Sure," she said. "Thanks."

Max walked along in a state of general dissociation for a while while Cormac and Flora chatted. They kept glancing his way, but it seemed they didn't want to interrupt. At her door, Flora gave Max a hug. She didn't say anything, but the sorrow emanated. He hugged back, her face smushed against his chest. "I'm okay," he promised.

"Okay," she said fretfully. "If you need anything…"

"I know where you'll be. Come by every now and again, yes?"

"Yes," she said, brightening. "We have more recipes to try."

He smiled and gave her shoulder a squeeze before letting go. Cormac took his hand, and they walked back toward the mercantile district in relative quiet. "Sorry," Max laughed at last. "Clammy hands."

"Oh, doesn't make any never mind," he said.

"It is strange not to be able to put your fingers through mine."

"I wasn't going to say it."

"Oh, do," he said. "It makes it more palatable."

Cormac tilted Max's head onto his shoulder—a bit shorter than he was yesterday. "You think you'll try any of those things?" he asked quietly. "Going to a whole different continent or making yourself sick or anything else they might have said that I missed?"

"I don't know," he said. "I...want it gone."

"Do you?" he asked softly. "Because the more I get to know you, the more you're just...you. In different packages, but you're still Max."

That was what hadn't sat right since the examination. Doubt. "I *need* it gone."

"Max."

"I have responsibilities."

"You don't think you could do them as you are now?"

"My mother thinks I can't, and that's..."

"The most important thing?" Cormac asked with a wince.

"Well, for getting to ascend, yes."

"And that's what you want?" Doubt. More doubt. Cormac said, "I'm sorry. I shouldn't push."

"No. It's probably time I looked it in the face. There aren't any easy answers, which, I have to admit, is what I came looking for."

Cormac moved his hand comfortingly up and down his back, then pulled him in closer. "We need to get you some coats."

"Number one has one. I can only fit so much in one bag."

"I'll see what I can do. It's going to be a little different for you around the Goat starting tomorrow, with me gone most of the day. You going to be okay?"

"Yeah," Max said, trying to sound upbeat. Cormac looked at him skeptically, and he said, "All right, I'm no good being alone. I've never been alone once in my life. There are people everywhere, even if I'm not interacting with them. Perhaps, if I don't weigh things down too much, I can help Brenna."

"There's an idea. I can show you the ropes."

A distraction might do him some good.

What he wasn't prepared for was how physically exhausting being on his feet was. He'd thought that since he'd walked here he had a good idea of what that would be like, but it was a constant barrage of things across the room and back *all* day.

At the end of the day, Cormac laughed a little, but winced sympathetically. "It's hard to get used to. It's really not necessary."

"If I'm going to stay here, I'm going to be of help," Max said stubbornly.

"All right," Cormac chuckled, hauling him into bed. "Then you need your rest."

When he woke to the stretching and pulling of the next day made much worse by the soreness he'd inflicted on himself, he found a cup of tea waiting. And every morning as the soreness grew less, there was always a cup of tea on the table.

He didn't help the whole of every single day—Brenna said making him do that was patently unfair, since she'd been at this for years and he a whole week—but he balanced his time between polishing the bar and borrowing paper to hole himself up in Cormac's room with, carefully drawing ledger lines and humming lines and bars to himself. It was harder without an instrument, but he still wrote furiously, alternating between flurries of composition and punishing shifts at the Goat.

Inevitably, Becky had to be told about Max. They couldn't reasonably expect to keep up any sort of deception about his six different presences there, and Brenna insisted Becky could be trusted. She was right. Becky just told Max to let her know if there was anything she could do to help. He was surprised to note it was a growing relief, the more people knew and didn't recoil. Several Gray Goat regulars also noticed the revolving door of help at the bar, but Brenna worked her magic and asked them to keep that to themselves. "They think you're working under the table," she told him.

"Aren't I?" He asked, amused.

"Well, yeah, but they don't know it's just one of you and not six we're all calling Max for tax purposes."

"I see. I have never been six people for tax purposes before."

"Me neither! First time for everything, though, yeah?"

He supposed so.

At nights, Cormac came home, tired and usually covered in sawdust, but always ready with a kiss and to hear about what happened that day. Brenna mysteriously found a way to cover his night shifts between her and Becky, so he and Max usually spent their evenings talking into the night, sitting on the bed in the moonlight and keeping the flowers in the box growing. Cormac was particularly proud of his miniature roses, which persisted despite the coming chill. Max found himself opening the window to look at them throughout the day, never mind the cold.

True to her word, Flora came by to cook more and chat with both Brenna and Max, and Cormac when he happened to be around. She even wrote some of her current research at the bar.

"Honestly, I'm surprised she can do that," Brenna remarked, watching Flora hunched over her paper. "Between the noise in here and the fact that the bar is never really clean—though it's the cleanest it's been in years, so thank you."

Max leaned on his elbows against the bar, shaking number six's red hair out of his eyes. "Flora's always been focused. Comes from being in a castle full of people, I think. Otherwise you'd never get anything done."

"What about you?" she teased. "I see you getting more and more paper from the supplies."

"I'm getting there," he said.

"What is it?"

"A song."

"A song? Will you play it here?"

He laughed. "Probably not, unless you have a lute lying around."

"Not yet," she said.

"What are you up to?" he asked, amused.

"Nothing. Speaking of which, what are you up to with my brother?"

"What do you mean?"

"What do you get up to? Does he take you places, or…?"

"Mostly, we just talk," he said.

"Oh, he's so boring," she groaned.

"No, I love it," he said.

"Love?" She leaned over into him. "Are you thinking that word?"

"Oh, stop."

"A girl's got to know."

"A girl may have to wait."

She leaned on her elbows, too. "Oh, I'm not very good at that."

"I know."

She elbowed Max. "Does he talk about me?"

"Only all the time."

Her smile went a little sad. "Good. Cause I miss him. Oh, don't get me wrong, I'm thrilled he gets to spend time with you. But…that means he isn't spending time here."

"Brenna…."

"Oh, don't feel bad. It's good. It's not just the two of us anymore. But then—it's not the two of us, and that's a little sad."

Max leaned his head into her shoulder briefly. "I know what you mean. I took it hard when Flora went off to school. She was off doing amazing things, but I still missed having her around all the time."

"Yeah?" She looked down at her folded hands, coarse with work and washing. "How'd you get over it?"

"Had to, with time. Time and distractions."

"Did you make any new friends?"

"Well, no," he admitted. "Not until I came here. But I should have. That was probably my fault. I became pretty reclusive around then."

"There was someone else," she estimated. "Before my brother."

"Yes."

"I know that voice. It's heartbreak."

"It's…growing more distant," he said. "Now there's just anger."

"I think that's good," she reflected. "More people could stand to be angry instead of broken. It keeps you living." She looked at Max. "Don't stop."

"I'm doing my best," he said.

Max sat at the table upstairs one afternoon, number one this time. He looked over his composition again and again, afraid to admit it to himself but pretty sure it was complete. He set it on the table and sat back, blowing out a breath.

Steps thundered up the stairs, and he sat straight up when the door burst open. "Mister Max," Becky breathed out. "Quickly, you need to get out of here."

"What is it?" he asked, alarmed.

"There's a woman downstairs asking about you, and she isn't taking no for an answer."

Dread built up in his stomach, and he nodded and went to the window to use Cormac's escape route. Becky shut the window and curtains behind him, and he clambered onto the roof. He had every intention of standing up and continuing to run, but realizing the height knocked fear into him like a punch to the gut. He sat in stasis, his vision swirling. Internally, he screamed at himself to get up, get moving.

At length, the window opened below, and Brenna peered up. "You can come back now," she said. "She's gone." She helped him in through the window and eyed him up critically. "You all right? You seem a mess."

He filled his lungs again and nodded. "I am a mess," he said. "That woman—was she narrow and severe, with gray hair yanked back so hard it looks like it hurts?"

"Yes," she exclaimed. "Who is she?"

He collapsed to sit on the bed. "Captain Rhona. She was sent out with me, ostensibly to keep me safe, but…."

"But what?"

"I doubt her intentions," he said. "She let some things get out of hand in the villages. I think she'd as soon feed me to the lions as save me from them."

"Well, I insisted you're not here," she said. "Even let her look around a little. Hopefully that puts her off."

Max knew better.

"How did she know you were here?" Cormac wondered, setting down his things. "We've been very careful."

"I don't know, but she has a nose like a hound. If she heard that the Goat has six new employees, she probably zeroed straight in on it." Max sighed. "She's a tenacious old bag, I'll give her that."

"Why didn't you mention her before?"

"I've tried to forget her, and I hoped she'd given up on me."

"What does she want with you if not to protect you?"

"Not to have lost the prince, I assume. That would not look good."

Cormac paused. "So she wants to…let something happen to you, but also keep you around."

"I know it sounds strange, but yes, I think she genuinely wants both."

"Max."

"What?"

"Don't you think it might be a touch…?"

"You think I'm paranoid. Also consider that I am immature and did not particularly *want* a minder while going through the roughest period of my life so far. Let alone her. I was not kind to her, and she certainly wasn't kind to me."

Cormac laughed a little. "Running away from the nanny?"

"Perhaps a little," he said testily.

"Maybe you should see what she wants. What's the worst that could—?"

"Me to get back in line and go where she tells me to go, even when it might kill me," Max said morosely. "That's how we ended up on our village tour, chasing down the most ridiculous rumors of witches and healers, and that's how I ended up running away from angry villagers, hunters convinced I'm a monster, devious charlatans, and one incredibly ornery captain."

"You think she wasn't genuine? Or that these rumors weren't?"

"Maybe both, or maybe neither. But I don't believe for a second that she was ignorant of the dangers."

Cormac considered a moment and nodded. "Probably not." Max's shoulders loosened a little. He let himself unwind for a minute. Cormac sat behind him on the bed and rubbed at them. "Does this help?" he wondered.

"You mean the general aching? Yes, for a time."

"Good. I…hate that for you."

"It's not so bad," he said with a lopsided smile. "More of an annoyance, really."

"Max, I've seen it. It doesn't look like an annoyance."

"It has been the hardest bit to get used to," he admitted. He weighed the thoughts carefully, a little surprised he was having them. Double checking didn't make it any less true. "I've gotten over the six different shapes, but the actual changing always seems worse than I remember it."

"What *does* help?"

"Keeping busy."

Cormac placed a kiss in the crook of Max's shoulder. "I can occupy you for a bit."

He shivered. "Mm. I might take you up on that."

Cormac lavished attention on the curve of Max's neck, kissed the underside of his chin. He slid his hand up his back and laid him down on the bed. Max reached up and unbuttoned Cormac's shirt and pants, laying him bare. Quickly, they dispensed with Max's clothes as well, leaving them both naked, quivering in anticipation. Max held Cormac's gaze for a long moment. He wanted to remember him this way, eyes shining in adoration, his sculpted face both wistful and content. Cormac smiled a little uncertainly. "What?"

"I just…you're beautiful," he said.

"No one's ever told me that," Cormac almost whispered.

He put his arms around Cormac's neck. "I should tell you more often."

"You, on the other hand…" he ran his hand down Max's alabaster hip, his own light purplish gray skin standing out starkly against it. "I don't know anyone more beautiful. In any shape. But this one is particularly pretty."

Max traced Cormac's elven ear, pushing himself up on his elbows to gently pull at it with his teeth. Cormac's breath caught, and he pressed his mouth against Max's neck, settling between his legs, kneeling on the bed. Max leaned his head back and watched Cormac kiss his way down his body until he came to the hollow of his hip. There, he spent a few moments lingering before taking Max by the hips and spreading his legs.

"Are you ready?"

"Yes," Max said. He relaxed his lower body, and Cormac slipped into him. His breath caught.

"You okay?" Cormac asked.

"Very," he responded, trembling, gathering Cormac to him

and cupping his backside in his hands. Cormac pushed deeper, and Max's head lolled backward of its own accord. White hot tendrils of pleasure went their way from their join to his core. The rhythm of Cormac's thrusts nearly built to a numbing sensation, until he pushed in and held Max to him for a few seconds. Max's vision exploded into stars behind the black sky of his eyelids. He moaned plaintively, begging Cormac wordlessly to do it again. Cormac answered with a wanting sigh and lapped at Max's chest for a moment before lifting his hips to a new elevation.

Max's back arched, and he let go of a soft cry of surprise. His hands found Cormac's arms, warm with exertion and taut as he balanced carefully with his palms on either side of Max's waist. As Cormac went in deeper, he pressed against Max's front and Max could scarcely breathe for the aching want that consumed him. Every inch of contact seemed to set his skin afire, but rather than burning him, it renewed him, made him feel alive in a way he'd forgotten, or perhaps had never been before. Fervently, he gripped at Cormac's upper arms and craned his neck up to meet his lips. Cormac wrapped his arm behind Max's shoulders and held him aloft for what felt like a moment suspended in amber, joined above and below. Their mouths grasped for each other in search of ever more contact, and Max ran his hand along Cormac's jaw, slipped his fingertips into his hair behind his ear. Cormac leaned into his hand and his abdomen until they both began to shake.

Gently he lowered Max back to the bed but held his gaze.

Max felt his whole body rollick with a gasp as another wave of pleasure washed him over. "Cormac," he moaned.

"Yes, dear," he whispered.

He tried to formulate words, but in his sight he found them elusive for once. Before he could try again, what had been a wave became a swell that crashed into him, and he threw his head back and let it come until his cry faded in his chest. Cormac rose and kissed him stoutly, then softly, gently, holding him close.

All at once, Max's words crystallized, completely clear except for the sheer terror.

They lay there in the fading light entwined in each other's arms. Max rested his head on Cormac's collarbone, wrestling with himself. The words were just about exploding out of him, and he kept biting them back.

Cormac finally glanced down. "Max? Everything okay?"

Tentatively, he asked, "Can I say something a little frightening?"

"You can say anything."

"I love you," he ventured. Cormac sat stock still for a moment, not even breathing. Max lifted his head. "I—I'm sorry, I…"

Cormac shook his head wordlessly. He was frozen. Max put his hand to Cormac's face for the briefest of moments, watching him try to formulate. "Don't say anything. You don't need to say anything."

"Max."

"I shouldn't have said that, I should—"

He caught his hand. "No," he said at last. "You can tell me anything."

But it was never free from consequences. Cormac still seemed stiff, uncertain. Max put his face in his hand. "I should give you some space," he said softly.

"You don't have to."

"Flora wants me over for dinner one of these nights anyway." He kissed Cormac's cheek and slid out of bed and started to clean up and dress.

Cormac watched him, subdued, his lips pressed together. Max hastily threw himself together and kissed him, turning to leave. Cormac caught his hand again, and Max said, "We'll talk later."

Cormac's fingers slipped from his, and he nodded. Once Max arrived at the door, he said, "Max, walk so, so safe. Take the back route and check your corners."

"I will," he answered, and with that, he was gone.

"What the hells was I thinking?" he lamented, pressing his forehead into his hand. "It's hardly been a month. I *knew* it would scare him."

Flora looked at him sympathetically across the table, poking at her eggplant with her fork. "Sometimes you just know, right? And sometimes things just come out."

"That's it," he said, shaking a finger. "That's the thing. Things are not supposed to *just come out* of me. I've been trained better. I know better."

"And has any of that training ever prepared you for being in love?" she asked frankly. "Did any of our upbringing leave you ready to have your heart whisked away? Because I remember a lot of how to talk without offending people, and not a lot about how to *connect* with them."

Max was left staring, his jaw agape. "I…well…no."

She crossed her legs and sat back. "I didn't think so. It's something I had to learn the hard way. Still learning. And now you are, too. I'm sorry."

"I just—what if I ruined everything? What if I just took the foundation of that connection and broke it all up because I couldn't wait?"

"Max," she said patiently. "You didn't do anything wrong. Neither did he. Sometimes these things just happen. But you have got to talk to him."

"What do I say? How do I? Maybe it's best left alone."

She reached across the table and put her hand on his arm. "No. You're running. You ran here and you're running now. If you love him, and I know you do, you'll stay. Even if it gets scary."

Max shut his eyes and breathed. At length, he nodded. "Flora…thank you. You don't know how much you've helped me. Not just now, but always."

She smiled. "It's my wisdom. I'm very wise."

He couldn't bring himself to make a joke back. "Yes. You are."

"It's going to be okay," she promised. "Even if it isn't. You've survived it before."

"I don't want to lose him," he said, pained.

"I don't think you will," she said, bowing her head to see into Max's eyes. "Not for nothing, but I think he's in it for you."

"If you had seen his face…."

There came a knock at the door, and Flora tensed. Then her eyebrows drew together. "These Guild people always come by during dinner. Hold on." She rose and went to answer the door. He heard hushed voices for a while, and then she came back. "Max," she said, "there's someone here you should see."

Dread built in his stomach. Rhona? A Guild member? Who wouldn't Flora have sent away? Hargreaves was harmless; maybe it was him. Still, he set his napkin on the table and stood.

Instead, it was Cormac, standing sheepishly in the living room holding a cake. "Thought I would bring dessert," he said.

Flora took the cake and said, "I'll cut it up. Why don't the pair of you talk?"

Max felt as though he were taking a flying leap off of something very high, but he nodded. Cormac asked, "Want a walk?"

Maybe it would be easier while moving. He nodded again and followed Cormac out the door. Cormac put his hands inside his coat pockets and faced into the chill wind. Max tucked his arms in close, having forgotten to put on his jacket before leaving the Goat. They walked the bridge in quiet for a time, watching the clouds move over the black velvet sky. Cormac stopped, and they saw a boat heading for the part of the bridge that lifted up. For the first time, Max watched the great cogs at work, and suddenly felt small.

After a moment, Cormac said, "I'm sorry, Max."

"There's nothing to be sorry for," he insisted. "For you, anyway."

"Or for you," Cormac told him. "Those words...I have a hard time with them. Even when Brenna says them. And she's the only one who does. But that doesn't make it your fault."

"I shouldn't, if it's hard for you."

"Max," he said, taking his hands. "If that's what you feel, I'm so glad. Really. If you're saying you shouldn't have said it because I have hangups about the past, I'd like to know if you're a mindreader. If you're saying you shouldn't have said it at all, well..."

"No," Max said, his voice clogging. "No, I meant it."

Cormac pulled him into his arms. "I'm sorry. I'm sorry I couldn't just take it for what it was. I'm sorry that I can't—"

"You can't say it back."

"Not because—" He shut his eyes. "Not because of you. Not because of anything about any of this. You are amazing, Max, and with you, I am the happiest I've ever been."

Max's heart beached itself again and again against his ribs. "May I ask?"

"It's her," he said with a bitter laugh. "It's always her. Any time there's a hang up, it's my bloody mother."

"Cormac."

"It's not fair, is it? Not to you, not to me. She had to leave behind some bullshit that's nested in my head."

Max firmed his hold on Cormac. "No, it's not fair. She's taken enough from you."

Cormac's eyes went wet, and he wrapped his coat around Max to keep him from the wind. "I wish I were different."

"I don't," Max said softly.

"I just mean—I wish I were better."

Max held him tightly under the protective wings of his coat. "You are exactly as you are meant to be," he said. "And I care very much for you that way."

Cormac's cheek rested against Max's head. "I care for you, too," he said softly. "So much that I…I don't want to have fucked this up."

"You haven't. Have I?"

"No, no. Not even close."

Max felt himself collapse against Cormac, who held fast and kissed the top of his head. They stood there for a good few minutes, watching the boats come and go. At last, Cormac reached inside the bag he'd brought with him and retrieved a wooden box. "I, um…I made you something."

Max took the box and admired the top for a moment. It was beautifully scrolled, and smelled of rich wood. "This is beautiful."

Cormac put his hands in his pockets. "Open it." He did, and gentle music started to play. In the velvet interior, three dried miniature roses laid delicately. "I know you miss music," he said softly.

Max felt his eyes dampen, and he put his hand to the back of Cormac's head and pressed his head to his forehead. "Thank you."

Cormac kissed him once, then again. Max grasped him with the arm not holding the box, unwilling to let go. At long last, Cormac noted his shivering and said, "Let's go back."

They returned to Flora's for some cake and a bit of wine and then made their way back to the Gray Goat now that the bridge had lowered again. Max took the sheets of Cormac's song and folded them, nestling them against the roses inside the box.

Chapter Ten
The Director

Max's appointments with the Guild had been going surprisingly well. Henries and Gest kept careful notes of each of his transformations that they observed, and it became easier to be watched, knowing they were absorbed.

At least, until the first time the word *genitalia* was spoken aloud. He hadn't been quite paying attention to the chatter, vaguely dissociating as the dawn grew closer. He gripped the white sheet they gave him to cover the bits of number one he didn't wish to share and looked over his shoulder. "I beg your pardon?"

Henries stroked his chin. "Oh, we were simply discussing the physical implications of transformation on your genitalia."

Max blinked a little in alarm. It was slow burgeoning, but when it arrived it grabbed hold of his throat. He looked over at Cormac and Flora. Flora's hand covered her mouth, and Max supposed that made a certain amount of sense, between her sense of ethics, general squeamishness around those sorts of body parts, and the fact that despite Max's congeniality with the people, the number who would dare say such a word in his presence was very small. Cormac, on the other hand, simply looked like he was contemplating how hard he could throw the doctor. Max attempted to wet his mouth a little. "Forgive me, but is that really necessary?"

The experts looked at each other in a bit of bafflement. Gest said, "Aside from the obvious physical differences, there are considerable unknown factors with regards to your hormones. It's evident that they alter to some degree, based simply on the external changes. But to what extent? Are you ever in an androgynous state, or is the shift completely binary?"

"And how exactly does it work?" Delsyn mused. "Everything about this curse seems very carefully crafted. Was the caster considering making alterations or did it simply happen?"

Max choked out, "And studying my—parts is the only way to figure that out?"

He shrugged a shoulder. "You could tell us what it feels like."

"I can't say I've paid much attention!"

"You would likely notice some things in some of the contingencies," Henries said mildly, looking over his notes.

Max wasn't sure he *wanted* to know, but his voice creaked out of him all the same. "Like what, exactly?"

"Oh, splitting, retraction…inversion."

"In—"

"I found it rather unlikely myself," he said cheerfully.

His head was swimming. "I…I'm sorry, I just can't quite see

what these things have to do with the study of my curse."

Solana nodded placatingly. "I understand. The implications for your perceived gender and sense of self are upsetting."

"Actually, not nearly as much as this line of thinking."

She paused. "Oh. You mean to tell me you don't experience discomfort with the absence of a penis?"

Max stared into the middle distance. Should he end the study? This felt entirely invasive. He supposed it was only natural to be curious, but what use could they possibly have for this information? "I—no, not really."

They all looked at one another significantly and started synchronized note-taking. Max slouched against the gurney. Was it that interesting? "What...does that tell you?"

"Oh, maybe nothing," Henries said placidly. "But ordinarily cursed individuals experience a distinct sense of distress about the disparity between their internal self and new physical form."

Max guessed that made a little sense. And maybe he'd felt that in the beginning, but it had never really felt wrong. New, different, unknown, but not wrong.

He pressed at his forehead. That didn't seem right, did it? He was wrong, five sixths of the days. Sometimes extremely.

Wasn't he?

He looked again at Flora, who'd let her hand fall back to her side. She didn't seem eager the way the researchers did, but her horror had faded into a gentle sort of curiosity. The way she had been when he'd told her about his complete disinterest in the one girl he'd dutifully tried a dalliance with. At that time, she'd understood personally, albeit the other way around in her case. Now she seemed more studious.Cormac looked down at her, a mix of bewilderment and concern on his face.

"No," Max admitted aloud, to them more than the researchers. "I haven't noticed that."

Dawn drew closer, and with it, the usual tension. But not dread, he realized. Not anymore. The little bell Solana had enchanted to warn them of the impending sunrise chimed, and they readied themselves.

Number one started to give way, and Max thought about it—more than he ever had. He had to brush past the pain, where his mind usually settled. It was difficult—the feeling like he was being rended and compressed felt so urgent, but eventually he forced himself into a place of calm.

Today he searched for distress in the midst of everything. It wasn't *comfortable* by any stretch of the imagination, but he tried hunting for grief, fear, anxiety, despair. Number six's hips widened outward, hair brushed the top of his breasts.

Breasts. That alone should have been very strange.

It wasn't. Not today.

He did become very aware of them exposed to the room and grabbed for the top of the sheet to cover himself more thoroughly. Morbidly curious, he glanced under the sheet at his abdomen. No *inversion*, thank gods.

When the pain faded into the usual muscle aches and the experts descended on him to take his vitals and ethereal readings and gods knew what else, he stared up at the ceiling.

How could the strangest thing that had ever happened to him feel so natural?

Max shook himself out of his reverie to lay down some very explicit boundaries. The researchers would have to content themselves with what they knew of his nether region. The disappointment was uncomfortable and palpable, but faced with the prospect of his complete withdrawal on refusal, they agreed.

The strange feeling of wonderment set back in as he dressed, received the customary bag of coin, which felt especially odd today, and walked out with Flora and Cormac. They spent a good portion of the walk equally quiet, swapping glances that Max distantly realized were worried. Midway through the walk, Cormac set his hands to Max's narrow shoulders. "You know, I don't think Estien needs me all that much today."

Max brushed his long hair behind an ear. "Cormac, it's all right."

Cormac's eyes flicked to Flora again. "No, it's okay. Let me just leave him a note."

They were in front of the clock shop, Max realized. When they'd arrived, he didn't know. It all seemed like wandering in a fog. Flora fished out a pen and bit of paper for Cormac, and tucked her arm through Max's when Cormac went to slip the note under the door. A little numbly, Max sort of laughed to himself. What excuse did one make to one's employer when one's partner was on the verge of some emotional breakdown?

Was he? They seemed to worry he was. Maybe he ought to

have been. Apart from the surreal quality of everything and the occasional disconcert of trying to figure out what he should be, he felt all right.

They made their way to the Gray Goat, closed and quiet for the morning. Cormac posted them at the table in the kitchen and set to fixing the usual cup of tea and another for Flora. She thanked him and looked over at Max. "Doing all right, Max?"

He took a sip of his tea and considered. "I...feel like I shouldn't be," he admitted. "Apart from the *deeply* disturbing way they weren't at all bothered by asking those questions...I should feel strange, shouldn't I?"

Flora folded her hands on the table. "I don't think there's a *should*," she said softly. "I think a lot of people would. But you don't."

"And that's odd, isn't it? It doesn't make sense. From a biological standpoint."

"What do you mean?"

Max was going to have to say it out loud, wasn't he? It felt rather like he stood at the top of a large precipice, and if he spoke it, there was no climbing back up. In a rush of words, he veered over. "What kind of creature feels conditionally right both male and female? How can such a thing exist?"

He couldn't make himself look at Cormac in that moment. He was afraid of what he'd find there. Flora laughed, not at all unkindly. "Max, biology is *much* weirder than you could ever imagine. And that's before you add magic to it. There are so many variations on sex and gender. Some creatures start out one way and become another. Some don't seem to exhibit any signs at all, or some have many combinations of inward and outward presentations. They only tell us about male and female because most of us are one or the other. But it doesn't make anyone unnatural. We're all natural. We exist in nature, and nature exists around us."

Max's fingers trembled a little around the cup and saucer. He realized they were rattling and set them down, putting his hands in his lap. "I...don't think there's much terribly natural about me."

Flora shook her head earnestly. "Magical intervention or no, how you feel is normal. So normal. I could find you six examples in my books by lunchtime. Even if you were the very first ever recorded. There's nothing you could say nature doesn't already know."

"That's the thing," he burst out. "*I* don't know. I don't know what this means for me, this curse, any of it. What does it mean that I've found these other...feelings I didn't know I had? Are they even truly mine?"

For the first time, Cormac spoke up from across the table. "I think they are," he said softly. "You're...you're not upset, the way you were."

Max chanced a look his way. "But have I just made the most of it, or am I...?"

"That, I don't know," he said gently. "I don't think either of us can know."

He turned to Flora. "Can magic change a person like this?"

She shook her head. "The unknown quantity that makes a person a person is immutable. We don't know what it is. Some folk would call it a soul."

"What would you call it?"

"I don't know," she told him honestly.

He sat there, a little stunned. "And you're…all right with that? Not knowing?"

She nodded, an encouraging little smile on her face. "Yeah," she said softly. "It's kind of beautiful, isn't it? Letting go. Discovering what stuff is all over again, letting go, coming back at it. You don't have to be right, you just have to observe. It's freeing."

Max watched the steam rise from the surface of the teacup. Flora always had a way of distilling the biggest questions into uncomfortable but unquestionably gentle truths. He'd always been much more tempestuous, a crashing sea of questions whenever something uncertain came along. It was more a plea for comfort than it was a real question. "But what does it all mean? Am I right but the curse wrong? Can I be this—whatever it is—without it? Should I? Or is this how I'm meant to be? Or is it all a magical delusion?"

Flora reached out and set her hand on top of Max's. "Let it show you," she told him. "It will take time. And that's okay. It's *good*. You don't have to decide anything that way. It's going to feel weird, but that's good. That's real living. It's not the perfect certainty we were expected to have, but this is what it's really like for everyone else."

Max closed his eyes. All at once, he felt…not still, but quiet.

The squalls were still at the periphery, but there was shelter now. He felt himself smile. "You and your wisdom again."

"I'm so wise," she said, eyes wide, grinning. "Owls have nothing on me."

"That's true."

She glanced over to Cormac, then leaned back in her chair. "There's this lady by the bridge. She makes the best pastries. I think we could use some."

Cormac spoke. "You going to be okay getting there?"

"Oh, sure. I just ignore the salesmen at this point."

That wasn't what he meant and she knew it, but nobody said anything. She stood and put her hand on Max's shoulder. He looked up, and she smiled. "Good for you, Max," she told him. "It's gonna be great, no matter what."

For some reason, he couldn't bring himself to doubt. Cormac told her, "Walk safe."

"I will," she called, heading for the back door.

The kitchen fell into quiet. It wasn't oppressive. Cormac was good at letting Max just be while still staying nearby. He stood and tidied up the kitchen, started a dishpan for the day, washed a few dishes from the night before. Max sat with his tea and tried to find his words. At last, he said tentatively, "Does it bother you?"

Cormac dried his hands and turned to face Max. "What do you mean?"

"If I'm committing to not knowing, it doesn't just affect me. I'm choosing uncertainty for you, too."

He laughed softly. "Think, of the pair of us, you're the more important one."

"Cormac. That's not true."

"I don't even mean the kingdom thing. I mean, you're the one who has to feel it."

"And so will you. I'm not—" He swallowed. "No matter what. I'm not only a man. Not anymore. If I ever was."

Cormac stayed quiet a moment. At length, he crossed the room and knelt next to Max's chair. He set a hand to Max's knee, placed the other alongside his face, trailed over his cheek, his human ear, the long hair bundled behind it. "Feels like you. It is, isn't it?"

Max searched. That was what sat at the eye of this storm, so present and now more distant. Flora was right—he didn't have to know everything. But he felt like he needed this. "It is me," he answered earnestly.

Cormac met his eyes, that same sweet desire in them that he showed every face. "I'm sure," he said.

Max threw his arms around his neck and held on. Cormac pressed a lingering kiss to his cheek, and peace settled over the kitchen of the Gray Goat.

On the fifth appointment, Max sat on the gurney and waited, holding his white sheet around his abdomen. Henries came in before the others—not uncommon. He set his large bag down and came over to chat with Max, his hands in the pockets of his white coat. "Good morning, Max. How is it today?"

"Well enough," Max said. "And you?"

"As well as can be. Listen. I wanted to catch you before we began. I've noticed these last few times that you've been straining hard."

Max glanced at Flora and Cormac in their corner. Cormac watched suspiciously, and Flora seemed a little nervous. "Is it that obvious?"

"No," he laughed. "In fact, you'd need to be a trained professional to notice."

"I see. You're not part of the Guild, are you, Dr. Henries?"

He seemed surprised. "Goodness, no. They've simply retained me for the purpose of this study."

"I can tell," he said. "You're too humane."

"Oh, they're not all that bad," he said, leaning back. "They've given us the autonomy we need to conduct this with integrity. More than I can say for other grantors. But don't think I haven't noticed that you've changed the subject. What's going on?"

Max grimaced. "Nothing...clinical."

"I see." He glanced at Flora and Cormac. "From here on, I want you to do what you need to do to get through the transition. Scream. Cry. Thrash about. I promise that no one here will mind."

He thought that might not be true, but he appreciated the sentiment. When Henries turned back to sort through his bag, Cormac stepped forward to take Max's hand. "Have you been holding back?" he asked quietly.

There was no point in dodging. "Yes," he said frankly.

"He's right," he said. "Don't. Not for our sake."

"Cormac, it's not pretty."

"You don't need to be pretty. Not for us. Don't hurt yourself more."

Max bit his lip, but nodded.

One by one, the other experts arrived, and soon after, dawn. The work began. Cormac stepped back into the corner, and Max forced a breath. Number three was coming, and it wasn't going to be pleasant either way, so he let go. He turned on the gurney and rested on his elbows, squeezing his hands together even as they enlarged. He set his head against the gurney and groaned. Henries set his hand to Max's shoulder. "Good," he encouraged. "Don't hold back."

Max gritted his teeth and let his shoulders hunch. The lengthening would happen soon, and that was the worst of it. Just as it began, the door opened. "Director," Henries said in surprise.

Footsteps across the room, and Max faltered. There was someone new in here. "I came to check on progress," a man's voice said. Max managed to turn his head and sighted a narrow elvish man with a small mustache and goatee and dark hair. He stooped to examine Max briefly, then said to the experts, "How goes it?"

"We're rather in the middle—" Solana said.

"Yes, yes, don't let me interrupt." He stepped across the room and picked up Henries' notebook, leafing through.

Max's breaths came hard and fast. He hadn't been holding back, which made it difficult to start now. He let go of a strangled cry as his spine cracked, bent, pulled long. Henries turned, distracted, as he went to make a note and found his notes usurped. Gest told him, "I have it."

"Thank you."

Max pushed through the pain and let what was going to happen happen as it wanted to, but never quite stopped being aware of that extra presence. Henries told him, "Good work. You're all done."

Max rolled onto his back again and breathed out hard. Henries took his pulse and his temperature, then went to try to beg his notebook back. The Director stepped behind Gest and looked at her notes, which she reluctantly relinquished. "I see not much has happened," he said.

"That's not entirely true—" Gest said.

Delsyn puffed himself up. "Controls are the most important part of any experiment. I would expect the Director of such a Guild to know that."

The Director looked up, dark eyes narrowed. "And I would expect a visiting researcher to watch his tone."

Solana intervened. "All the Professor means is that we're still collecting data for the controls."

"Yes, well, we will discuss that after the subject has left."

Max lifted an eyebrow. "The subject can hear you."

The Director ignored him. To the experts, he said, "Meet me in my office in ten minutes."

He left the room, and Henries shook his head. "Don't worry about him."

"A bit hard," Max remarked. "What is he going to push?"

"Nothing we don't recommend," Gest said firmly.

Max somehow doubted that.

Chapter Eleven
The Master

By the time he'd received his notice of summons for the next appointment, Max found himself incredibly nervous about going back. Cormac looked him over one evening when he returned from work. "Max," he said carefully. "Maybe you should think about that alchemist."

Cormac had found his information in the registry. Max had argued with himself for a long time about seeking him out. Now it was all coming together in a perfect storm of anxiety. Max put his face in his hands and tilted his head back. "I'm still not sure I want to *eradicate* everything in my body."

"Maybe he'll have something different to say," he said. "It never hurts to get a second opinion."

"Hmm."

Cormac gently eased him up from the crate he sat on. "Let's at least hear him out. I think it'll make you feel better, ticking it off the list."

Max sighed and nodded, taking up fistfuls of number two's skirt to avoid getting caught on the bannister on the way down.

It was dark by the time they got to the street, and Cormac took Max's arm protectively. Once again, the street vendors didn't bother them. Max leaned in. "What did you do to get them to leave you alone?"

"They just know I work for the Guild," he said with a shrug. "Talked to a few of them, years back."

"Talked to them, or *talked* to them?"

He chuckled slightly. "What is it you think I do?"

"Well, I know you intimidate people."

"On occasion. Mostly, I just talk. The fact that I look like I might make something of it is just insurance so they don't start anything."

"And do you hug all of the people who do start something?"

"Easy way to deescalate, especially mages. Can't say I've done it *too* often, but you were not the first."

"Oh, now I feel bad," Max joked.

"Don't worry. You're my favorite person who's ever started something."

"That is reassuring."

Cormac indicated a side street that wound on a ways, warmly lit shops spilling light onto the cobbles even after many of the shops of the main thoroughfare had closed. "This is called Alchemy Alley," he informed Max. "I wasn't shocked he'd be here, but it was good to have it confirmed."

They passed apothecaries and metallurgy shops, all brightly advertising miracles. Max felt like he could use one. Cormac found a set of stairs leading up into a dark passageway, and held out his hand to help Max up. Max hesitated. "You're certain he's the one."

"As sure as I can be on secondhand information," he said. "But my source was good." Max set his hand cautiously on the railing and looked up. Cormac touched his hand to Max's lower back. "I'll be with you."

Max nodded and started up the stairs. They wound up to a hallway that was dark except for a dimly lit shop remained open at the top. Cormac pointed to it, and Max opened the door.

The front room was mostly empty. There was a glass counter with herbs and crystals displayed in it, and a beaded curtain separated the front from something better lit in the back. The door hit a bell, and Max jumped. "Easy," Cormac told him.

From the back, a gruff voice called, "Be right with you." Some heavy steps sounded, and a large fiendish man appeared between the strands of the curtain, his skin a deep purple, his lower jaw and nose clearly broken at some point in his life. "Can I help you?" he said.

Max nearly turned on his heel and left based on nerves alone, but Cormac held him gently by the shoulders. "I hear you're the one to come to with curses."

The alchemist looked left and right, then stepped out from behind the counter to douse the sputtering candle that lit this room. He locked the door, and rounded on Cormac, his height on full display. "And who told you that?"

"I can't tell you," he said.

He set his crooked jaw and nodded brusquely. "Good answer.

I take it from the trembling you're the one with the problem, dear?" Max cleared his throat and nodded. The apothecary said, "You have nothing to fear from me. I assume if you're still alive in Clockbridge you know not to go spreading that about, and discretion is of utmost importance to me. I value my patients' privacy." He held the curtain open. "Come, come, into my study."

Max bowed his head and passed through the curtain, down a hallway into a brighter-lit room with a rug and a large, scarred wooden desk. A chair sat in front of and behind it, and the apothecary stumped away on large hooves to go find another. He came back with a wooden chair and set it beside the leather one he offered to Max. Cormac gamely sat on the wooden chair and held Max's hand in his.

"I," the apothecary said, "am Davitt Molas, an arcanist and apothecary, but that, I'm sure you know." He sank into his own chair, then sent the door closed with a wave of his hand.

Max sat up higher. "You're a mage."

"Of course I am," he laughed. "I'm a fiend. That won't be a problem for you, will it, Master Cormac?"

Cormac looked up, startled. "How did you know—?"

"Don't know of any other underkin-elves looking up my name in the Guild Halls."

Cormac shook his head admiringly. "No, sir. No problem."

Molas folded his hands in front of him, leaning his elbows onto his desk. "That's the thing about the Guild," he rumbled. "Always willing to break their own rules when it suits. And I know it suits, because you, too, are a mage, aren't you?" he asked Max.

Max stuttered for a moment, and he said, "No need to deny it. This is a safe room."

Max leaned forward. "How can you tell?"

"Those knives strapped to your leg are sorcerer's blades. Lightly enchanted, just barely. But unusable by most."

Max started. The knives were fully covered by the skirt. "All right, you're a wizard."

"And a pretty good one, too," he chuckled. "You've come to the right place. Why don't you tell me what's been happening?"

Max nervously pushed a bit of his hair behind his ear. The story came spilling out of him—much more detailed than the one he'd told the Guild experts. Molas sat and listened carefully, his bushy eyebrows bunching at times as he considered.

Max said, "The Guild has been observing me. The alchemist among them says that the curse could be removed by alchemy, but that it would make me ill."

Molas laughed once. "That's *a* way of looking at it. Of course the Guild alchemist wants to go scorched earth."

"Sir?"

"If I am hearing you right, the primary concern is pain. Is that right?"

Max thought. "I mean, the primary concern is that I keep turning into other people."

"But what you mentioned more often was how it hurts." He stood and went to a bookcase, squinting at spines until he pulled out a tiny pair of silver spectacles and placed them on his nose. "I can't break your curse. It's much too strong. It would be irresponsible of me to try—it would cause you pain, distress. But I can ease the pain, and I can give you means to control it."

"You—can do that?" Max asked.

"If you are indeed a mage," he said.

"I would be indebted to you," Max told him earnestly.

"Careful to whom you say that. But you've learned that by now."

"I figured if you were to try to harm me, you'd have told me that you could cure it completely."

"You'd be right. Don't trust anyone peddling cures. I sell mitigations."

"Is there no hope of breaking it?"

"I didn't say that, child. But there's no easy route, no tonic I can give you that will burn the curse out of you. This is where we start."

Cormac's hand tightened around Max's. Quietly, Max asked, "Will you still…even if I don't break it right away?"

"Max. Of course. It's you I like. And I especially like you hurting less."

He blushed vividly at having this conversation in front of Molas, who graciously busied himself with his book. "Thank you," he answered, hushed.

Cormac squeezed Max's hand with both of his and held on. Molas glanced over the edge of the book corner. "Now then. Shall we begin?"

The tonic brewed while Molas spoke, his voice a gentle rumble, like thunder in the distance. He uncovered a large crystal that had been wrapped in a velvet cloth and passed it to Max. "This can serve as your focus. Imbue it with your resonance and it will respond."

"How do I do that?"

"Spend time casting magic into it. Any spell will do. In the mornings at the rise of the sun, hold that close and concentrate. Focus on becoming whichever version of yourself you like. The crystal will hold that potentiality for you, and cycle it back into you with your renewed focus."

Max examined the pinkish stone in his fist in the candlelight. "So...I could theoretically turn myself into the first version of myself every day."

"You could. The timing, I expect, will be tricky. It's important to remember that you want to begin right as the transformation is starting, not before, or the effect of the crystal will be overridden."

"That seems difficult."

"It can be, but I bet you'll get the knack for it before too long. You're smart enough to learn magic in the first place; this will be much easier."

Max hoped that was true. He was almost certain the wizard was humoring him, but the possibility was too tantalizing to turn his back on. Molas rose and checked the tonic burbling in the pot over the burner in the back corner of the room. "Good, good," he murmured to himself, reaching up to a shelf for a green glass bottle and pouring the contents in. He set the bottle down on the desk. "Let it cool. This will make your body more malleable, more receptive to transmutation. By this process, the pain will decrease—not masking it, but taking away the cause for inflammation. You will take this once weekly—this bottle should last you three months or so."

"Thank you," Max said. "Truly. How much do I owe you?"

"Oh, five gold will do it," he said.

"And for the crystal?"

"No, no, five gold total."

"That doesn't seem enough." He took out one of the bags that the Guild had given him and put it on the desk. "Please, accept this."

Molas' long fingers twiddled the medallion on the bag's clasp. "This is Guild money."

"And hard-earned," Cormac said.

"Is that a problem?" Max asked.

"No," Molas said. "Guild money *tends* to be hard-earned. You're certain you want to give it to me, without even knowing if what I've made will work?"

"Please, take it," Max said. "You're the first person who's tried to make a difference instead of a name."

Molas turned his head. "Who are you?"

"No one of any import," he said.

"I highly doubt that," he said with a deep chuckle. "But that's only because I've never met anyone who wasn't important to *someone*." He indicated Cormac with a crooked finger.

Max smiled and took the tonic. It was still warm in the bottle, but cool enough to touch now. "Thank you, Master Molas."

He stood to show them out. "One sip tonight. Not too deep. It's going to taste terrible."

Cormac helped Max to his feet and out the door. He put his hat back on and tipped it to the alchemist, then fell to navigating the streets. Max clutched the bottle and the crystal close until they arrived safely back at the Gray Goat. Cormac scratched at his head. "Max, I know you want to hope, but maybe temper your expectations a little."

"You don't think he's legitimate?" Max asked.

"I think that there's a type of alchemist that gets by on promises. And he made some pretty big ones."

"But not the biggest," Max countered. "If he were trying to swindle me, he'd have sold me a cure, wouldn't he? And he'd have asked for more money."

Cormac nodded his concession. "Let's just see what tomorrow brings, hmm?"

Max held the bottle for a moment longer, then took a drink. It burned like alcohol with undertones of something muddy and runny. He coughed. "Oh. Oh, gods. He was right."

"Well, that's one point for the old man," Cormac said, patting Max's shoulder. "Let's see if he's right about everything else."

Morning, and Max opened his eyes. Since yesterday had been a number two day, whatever would come would be unpleasant. He waited, tensed. When the stretching began, he flinched and covered his head, but instead of the usual tearing feeling, there was a sort of warmth flowing through his limbs. Max unclenched and looked down at his hands. They were fading into number four's blue, but with none of the burning he usually felt. He laughed incredulously, his voice sliding into the lower register. It all seemed to be moving faster, as though the lack of resistance made it roll downhill.

He wasn't even sure when it was done, because there was no moment of release. Instead, the warmth faded away, and he was left feeling—good. He sat up, the covers slipping off him. Cormac, who was in the middle of bringing the daily cup of tea, started in surprise. "Max," he said. "You're done?"

"It didn't hurt," he said in wonderment.

"It didn't?"

"No. I mean, it felt like—when you stretch out for a moment. There's tension, but it doesn't outright hurt."

Cormac put down the tea on the table and went to sit next to Max, who still looked disbelievingly at his hands. "Really?"

"Molas did it." Cormac kissed Max's cheek, and Max pulled him into a hug. "Oh, I feel like I have to celebrate. This is—I can't remember the last time I felt this good. At least two months ago."

Cormac beamed. "I'm glad. Previous doubts happily rescinded. I—" a banging sound from down below interrupted his sentence. "What the devils is that?"

Footsteps on the stairs, and Brenna's voice came through the door. "That old bag is at the door. Your captain."

Max shrank. Cormac looked at him. "Listen. I can make her

go away. But you said yourself, she's tenacious. Maybe you should see what she wants."

Max gritted his teeth. "And let her know I'm here?"

"I think she already knows."

The banging persisted. Brenna asked, "Am I telling her off or what?"

Max put his face in his hands. "Let her in but make her wait," he called to Brenna. "I'll be right there." Then he muttered, "Gods, what am I doing?"

Cormac patted his shoulder. "I'll be with you."

"Good. Someone might need to step in." He shook his head and fell to dressing.

When he reached the bottom of the stairs, Rhona was seated at one of the tables, patently ignoring a cup of tea. Her head whipped around, and she stared daggers through him. "You."

"Captain," he said, trying not to sound sheepish and failing.

She stood and stalked over to him, leveling her pointed chin and glaring him down. "Where have you *been?* Imagine my distress when I awoke and found you gone in Redune."

"I did leave a note."

"Your Highness," she snipped. "A note is cold comfort for your poor mother, the Queen."

He faltered. "You've spoken to her."

"What choice did you leave me?"

"Did she seem—? Never mind. Captain, I formally apologize."

"I should hope so! You disappear into a major city, and I find you staying *here,* of all places."

"What's wrong with here?"

She looked appalled. "Your Highness. It is not for you to associate yourself with the tavern-going sort."

"And I think it is not for you to tell me with whom I cannot associate," he said sharply. "The proprietors of the Gray Goat are good people, without whom I would be terribly lost. We should be thanking them."

"You wouldn't have *been* lost had you—"

"Stayed in the villages where people tried to kill me?" he asked bluntly. "I did what I had to to keep myself safe. Something you seem oddly unconcerned with."

Rhona puffed herself up. "Of course I am concerned. It was under control. We were there for a purpose—one you seem to have abandoned."

Max laughed. "What purpose was that? Seeing just how many pitchforks could amass in one location?"

"You are meant to be finding a solution to your ailment."

"Call it what it is."

Distastefully, she pronounced, "Your *curse.*"

"I will have you know that I have found a way to control it."

Cormac started, but Max held firm. Rhona looked genuinely surprised for the briefest of moments, and at last said, "Is that so?"

"Yes. It is handled."

"In that case, you should have no qualms about accompanying me back to Saltrush, per your mother's instructions."

Max faltered. "I—"

Rhona looked around. "You will either come with me or begin searching at once for a complete solution. You will find me at the Haltered Pony. I will give you three days to discuss your answer." She stalked from the bar and let the door slam shut behind her.

Cormac folded his arms in the quiet aftermath. "What will you do?" he asked quietly.

"She's bluffing," Max said. "She can't order me home."

"But your mother can."

That much was true. "I'll tell her I'm looking for a cure. That's technically still true, working with the experts. I'll just let her stew in the meantime."

"You were doing some bluffing of your own, and she called you on it," Cormac said. "You don't know that the crystal will work."

"No, I don't," he said.

"Then why did you tell her—"

"I'm not ready to leave you, all right?" he said, a little heightened. Cormac pressed out a breath and came to hug Max. Max felt the tension leave his shoulders, and he sagged against Cormac. "I don't want to go."

"Okay," he said, making comforting circles on Max's back. "Okay."

Chapter Twelve
Nullify

Two days to go, and Max had an appointment. He paid sharp attention to everything, making note of what he'd tell Rhona about his progress. He looked over Henries' notes while the doctor bustled about number three. Six appointments now, and six transitions. This one would be different.

He looked over the descriptions of each of his forms. Though the language was clinical, they were each thoughtfully rendered. He recognized himself in each of them. That was new. He'd always thought of them as a costume forced on him daily, but reading these descriptions, it was far more like different aspects of himself. The thought was uncomfortable. How could he be any more himself in these foreign shapes? Of course he wanted it broken. Who wouldn't?

Henries noted, "You seem much more relaxed this morning, Max."

"Truth be told, I worked with an alchemist," he said. "The transitions are far less painful now."

Gest looked up. "You've taken something?"

"Yes. A tonic that makes the body more changeable." He paused. "Is that a problem?"

"It damages our controls."

Henries said firmly, "Patient comfort is more important. We can adjust."

Gest said, "I don't know that that's going to fly—"

The door opened, and the long, thin elven man stalked in, a wave of gloom following. "What's all this chatter? I can hear from the hallway."

"Director," Gest said, flustered.

"We were just discussing a change to the controls," Henries said, keeping his chin level.

"A change? By nature, controls must be constant," the Director said, frowning. "What *change* is this?"

"The subject has seen an outside alchemist," Gest filled in. "He seems to have taken an intervention that decreases the pain of the transitions."

"No," the Director said, shaking his head. "No, no, no. We can't have that. That will irrevocably damage the data on the nature of the transition itself."

Max interjected, "Why? What difference does it make if I'm in pain or I'm not?"

"It's not about that," Gest said quietly. "It's about what the intervention does to your body."

The Director looked at Solana. "Nullify it."

Henries interjected, "That will make everything worse—"

"Doctor, you are here at our pleasure," the Director said coldly. "I remind you of that."

Gest spoke up carefully. "He's correct, Director. Nullifying the agent will cause a reaction in the subject that can't be——"

"I did not ask for an opinion." He stared at Solana. "Do it."

Henries nearly lunged. "Don't——!"

Solana looked as petrified as Max was. After a moment, she raised her hands, and Max felt something run cold in his limbs. A few seconds later, the dawn came. The stretching felt more like shredding, and the pain rose to a fever pitch. He doubled over. His body trembled, breaking into spasm. He couldn't see straight, couldn't think. He let go of an unbridled scream, thrashing against the gurney until his sight faded entirely, and he fell slack.

There were furious footsteps. "What did you do?" Cormac demanded.

Someone came to Max's side and took up his wrist to take his pulse. When they pulled back his eyelid and observed his eye movements, he saw it was Henries. "He'll be all right," he murmured, but he frowned deeply at someone else. Solana, probably.

"No, I'm going to need a little more than that," Cormac said. "What did you *do?*"

"She turned off the active ingredients in the intervention," Gest said, "which leaves his body starved for the help it was receiving."

Solana said defensively, "It will even out!"

"After gods know how long of this," Henries argued. "You wanted stable controls—how is this any better?"

Cormac came closer and scooped Max up, holding him close as another spasm of pain twisted inside him. He couldn't even tell which one he was becoming, if he'd fully taken leave of number three. "We're done here," Cormac said.

"Cormac," Hargreaves said, "consider—"

"I'm not considering shit," he said. "You people did this to him. It's over. Flora—"

As Max was carried away, he saw Flora holding the door, looking horrified.

"That's far enough," the Director said.

Hargreaves pointed out timidly, "Director, it is in the contract. Either of his companions have the ability to end the study at any time."

"What fool allowed that in the contract?" He fixed Cormac with a look. "If you value your employment here, you will return the subject immediately."

Cormac stopped. "Guess that's over, too." He left the room and walked to the stairwell, then down the Hall and out the door. Then he broke into a run. "They're going to be coming for us."

"Where do we go?" Flora said between huffing breaths. "What do we do?"

Max put a weak, shaking hand to Cormac's chest. "Rhona," he said. His voice was strange—high and low at the same time.

"No, dear, it's Cormac."

"No, take me—to Rhona," he got out.

"She'll take you out of here," he realized. "Yes. Yes. Good. The…Harnessed Pony?"

"Haltered," Flora said. "It's on the other side of the bridge."

"Oh, we're going to have to run fast," he said, looking over his shoulder. Already people were gathering at choke points. "Through the Brass Hall. Come on."

Flora followed close on Cormac's heels, and they sprinted through the alleys until they could avoid the main thoroughfare no longer. They burst into the clock shop, where Fletcher looked up. "Cormac," he said. "What on earth are you doing with that naked—person?"

For the first time, Cormac seemed to realize Max was between shapes. Number five's wings were coming in, pushing off the sheet that he was wrapped in. It was like the changes were coming in agonizing bursts now, instead of a steady transition. Cormac readjusted his grip and pulled the sheet closer around Max.

Flora started talking, a stream of nervous chatter, and Cormac joined her.

Fletcher held up his hands. "All right, all right, I have no idea what's going on, but clearly something is quite wrong."

"The Guild," Cormac panted. "The Guild is chasing us."

Fletcher stood. "Why didn't you say so? Come on, come on." He locked the door and gestured to the back room, looking uneasily out the wide window. Cormac rushed to the dumbwaiter and got Flora situated before Fletcher unlocked the mechanism. "I'll stall them."

"Thank you," Cormac said.

"I take it you won't be in for a while," he said dryly.

"Probably not," Cormac said, setting Max down to run the mechanism. Unlike when he'd quit the Guild, he sounded genuinely sad now.

Banging came from the shop door. Fletcher looked back. "Hurry. Hurry, now." He folded two large wooden doors down on top of the dumbwaiter, and Cormac kept on, hand over hand, until they landed in room four.

It must not have been unusual in the Brass Hall for people to go dashing through trying to avoid something or another, as people pressed themselves out of Cormac's way and kept on as though nothing had happened. Flora opened the hatch for Cormac, then helped him get Max up and out, and they sprinted out through the rest of the mercantile district.

As they ran toward the residential district, the bridge whistle blew. It was about to raise.

Cormac said, "No, no, no, we cannot get stuck on this side."

"Book it!" Flora squeaked.

They made one final dash past the lowered barriers and over the widening gap between bridge halves. Once they landed on the other side, Cormac looked back, breathing hard. No one watched from the mercantile district. They'd lost them.

Cormac and Flora tried to walk as naturally as one could when holding a person wrapped in a white sheet. If they exposed Max's head, people would see a struggling, pained person changing very slowly. If they covered it, it looked very much like Cormac was carrying a body in a shroud. They decided the second one was better. So they walked along with Max's shivering body bundled up, quickly, but no longer running.

The Haltered Pony was a classy establishment, with tile floors instead of wood. Cormac paced them while Flora went to the desk and asked for Captain Rhona. Max shuddered, every so often unable to help a small cry. Cormac tried to quiet him.

At last, footsteps came from upstairs. "I have to say, I'm surprised, Your Highness. I expected you to—" Rhona stopped short. "What is this?"

Cormac hoisted Max higher and briefly opened the top of the sheet to show her. "Max suffered a setback this morning at the hands of the people who were supposed to be helping him. He needs to get out of here. Now."

Rhona looked at Cormac suspiciously. Flora interceded, "And we're coming with him. Aren't we?" she asked Cormac beseechingly.

He nodded. Rhona looked between them. "Lady Nythera— this is highly unusual."

"So is everything about Max's circumstances," she said, throwing up a hand. "Please, get him to safety. That is your job, isn't it?"

Rhona pulled herself up. At length, she said, "Carriage. Around the back."

"Thank you," Flora said hastily, going to hold the door for Cormac. To him, she echoed, "Thank you. For coming."

"I can't rightly stay here, can I?" he asked.

"But that's not why you're coming."

He stayed quiet, clutching Max to him as they waited. Max groaned quietly. Cormac held his head against his shoulder and set his chin to it. "What about you?" he said. "Your house, your research."

"I can start again," she said. "I can't do that if the Guild wipes me off the map."

He nodded.

"This isn't—this isn't normal," Flora said, hushed. "They want Max too badly. Why?"

"I wish I knew."

The sound of hooves plodding against dirt and wheels dragging along interrupted them, and Rhona drove a carriage into sight. "In," she said imperiously.

Flora again grabbed the door, and Cormac stepped up inside. Two brown leather cushions sat opposite each other in the plushest interior he'd ever seen. He laid Max down on one and pulled the blue velvet curtains closed. Flora closed the door and sat down, patting the front wall of the carriage. Rhona clicked the reins, and they were off.

Cormac held his breath until they crossed the stationary bridge out of town, then let it all out in a rush. Max understood. Once on the road, they would be safe. Had to be. He uncovered Max's face and checked on him. He looked much more like number five now, but still hadn't quite settled. Cormac put his hand to Max's face. "It's going to be okay," he said. "We're out."

"Back on the road again," he said distantly.

"You've got Flora and me now," he said, trying on a smile.

"We'll keep you safe."

"I'm sorry," Max said. "For mixing you up in this."

"Max. No." He found his hand—incredibly clammy—and held it within his. "You didn't do a damn thing wrong. It's that Director, and the Guild's got people too scared to stand up to him."

"You won't—be able to go back."

"Not yet. Things'll die down."

Max still looked troubled. "Brenna…."

"Will be fine without me for a while. I'll write her when we stop and let her know." Cormac wove his fingers into Max's hair. "Don't worry about me."

"That's hard—to do. Your face."

"You had me scared," he said a little more honestly than he was comfortable with. "They had me scared."

"I didn't think much scared you," Max said with a little laugh.

Cormac rested his forehead against Max's. "Yeah, well, that does it."

"I'm sorry."

"No, no, it isn't your fault. It's—I love you," he said, his voice thin.

Max opened his eyes all the way for the briefest of moments, then the last of his strength was gone, and he drifted off.

Part Two

–

Saltrush

Chapter Thirteen
Homecoming

The throne room seemed bigger to Max than it had before. The guards milled about awkwardly, knowing full well why he was here. The only one more petrified than Max was Cormac, who said he wasn't sure if he'd *been* in a room this big for any purpose. Flora was her usual chipper self, happy to catch up on what she'd missed. The guards chatted with her. Max supposed it was just her preternatural talent for making people feel at ease. He wished he had that.

The grand blue doors opened, and in swept Her Royal Majesty Queen Anora. Everyone in the room bowed, and she waved them off impatiently, coming to stand in front of Max. She held her hands out. "My boy," she proclaimed. "Home at last."

"Hello, Mother," Max managed, leaning forward to give her cheek a kiss.

She patted his and smiled. "I would hear of your journey. Come, sit by me."

"Mother, before I do—I'd like to introduce you to someone."

Her eyes caught on Cormac and Flora. "Yes, whom have you

brought with you?"

Max stepped back and took Cormac's arm. "This is my partner, Cormac. Cormac, if I may present my mother, Queen Anora of Saltrush."

Cormac clumsily made his much-practiced bow. "It's an honor, Your Majesty."

She nodded deeply, but said nothing further. Max said quickly, "And of course you remember Flora."

Flora smirked at Max. "Of course she remembers me!"

"I could hardly forget, my dear," Anora said. "It has been too long since your cheerful presence has graced this court. Welcome home."

"Thank you, Your Majesty."

"Maximillian," his mother said tautly. "Come here. We will speak in private."

Max lowered his voice. "Flora, could you please take Cormac to the guest chambers? I'll be along shortly."

She nodded and whisked Cormac away. Max went and sat on the edge of the dais. Cormac caught his eye as he was leaving, and Max attempted a smile. Anora clapped her hands, and most of the guard exited, leaving only her personal bodyguards behind.

"Mother," he said, "was that really necessary? You've given school friends of mine more consideration."

"I haven't the faintest what you're talking about, dear," she said. "More importantly, we need to discuss your journey. Rhona tells me you were unsuccessful."

Of course she would put it that way. Max bristled. "Actually, I was able to find a means of controlling the curse."

"She said that when she found you, you were struggling with…changing."

"Because an enchanter I visited to try to break the curse made it temporarily worse. I'm better now. And I am able to produce whichever form I wish." That was somewhat of a simplification, but his mother didn't need to know about all the trial and error on the way over.

"That is something."

"Mother."

"And it seems that the Helmdarian league is unaware," she fretted.

"Yes. Now that it's controlled, there won't be cause for worry. There may be a slip here and there if I don't get it exactly right, but—"

"This is what I mean," she said. "A slip here and there is all they need. If they knew how easy it could be to have a stranger pose as 'the prince', they could infiltrate our walls with ease."

Max leaned his head forward. "We are well-guarded within the walls, too."

"We were well-guarded when…." She trailed off, unable to finish.

Max grasped her hand. "It will be different now. It is different now. We have learned from that. And I am only vulnerable at dawn. I can still fight back if I don't look like they expect. Can we please talk about Cormac?"

"And what of him?"

"You are treating him like no one. He is not no one. He is very important to me, and more than that, he saved my life. I understand you are disappointed in my proclivities, but I at least expected a kind welcome for my chosen partner."

He watched his mother carefully. She seemed to be formulating a response, but she was far slower to it than he'd ever known her to be. At length, she said, "My son. I am not disappointed. I am simply…it is the way things are."

Max straightened in surprise. "Mother. This is the first I'm hearing of it."

"Your father…may have impressed on me that if I don't love the son I have, he may leave. As you did."

"Mother, you told me to go."

She spent a moment trying to find her words. Max found this odd, as being lost for them was counter to the job she did. "I didn't expect you to find a new life. Rhona says you were *working.* At a tavern, of all things."

"Yes, well, I found myself indebted to the proprietors. As I said, I was kept safe in a city that was really rather inhospitable thanks to Flora and Cormac."

"Then why did you go there?"

"To search for a way to break the curse. I sought Flora's help."

"And what made you return?"

"I was always going to come home. If home would have me."

"Dear heart, of course—"

"Please don't say 'of course' like it's a foregone conclusion," Max said stiffly. "I was cursed, and the first thing you told me to do, aside from submit to humiliating and painful examination, was leave. And I did it, and I came home when summoned. Remember that." He stood. "As far as Cormac goes, I love him. I will not accept him being treated poorly."

He moved for the door. As he reached for the polished brass handle, Anora said, "Maximillian." He turned. "Perhaps we might all have dinner this evening. With Father, Flora...and Cormac."

Max inclined his head. "As you wish." He exited the chamber, a mess of thoughts and feelings. He let his feet carry him as though without a brain to guide them at all back to his bedchamber.

It was quiet, untouched, apart from the bed being made. He sat on it and felt underneath it for the flask that lived there. He took a stout drink and promptly made a face. Apparently leaving it for the better part of three months unattended took a toll. He set the flask down with the intention to wash it out and found a pile of books on his nightstand.

A note on top read: *A few good ones. -Father*

He crooked up the corner of his mouth and examined the spines. History, philosophy, and the occasional novel. His father had been busy. He set his hand to the top of the pile for a moment and took a breath.

There was also something bundled at the foot of the bed. He picked up a midnight blue velvet cloak that crackled with static when he touched it. No, he realized, it was potentiality, magic not yet come into being. The note on this one read: *To keep you safe. Love always, Mother*

If his mother had come by an enchanted item, it would have passed through Aubric's hands—at best. At worst, it had come from Aubric directly. The thought curdled his stomach slightly, and he set the cloak back down, at least for the time being until he could investigate what it did.

He left his chambers again and headed for the guest wing, which was just around the corner. He found Cormac and Flora conversing in an open doorway.

"There he is," Flora chirped.

"How is it?" Cormac asked, rubbing at the back of his neck. "Everything okay?"

"Surprisingly," he answered. "She wants to have dinner with all of us tonight."

Flora looked at Max sideways. "And you didn't get into an argument?"

"Sort of." He glanced up the hall and spotted a pair of guards and pulled Flora and Cormac both into the guest room. "She was strangely understanding," he said.

"You think she was being controlled?" Cormac asked.

"I mean, I've never won an argument with her," Max said. "Then there was…she was pausing."

"Pausing."

"My mother doesn't pause. Unless it's for dramatic emphasis."

"Perhaps she's turning over a new leaf, and it's hard," Flora said.

"I want to think that, I do."

"But it's easier to believe that a wizard is puppeting her?"

"Yes."

Flora shook her head. "Max, sometimes I think you've let the danger clog up the works in your brain. Not everything is a threat."

"Enough things are," he said seriously. "I'm not going to overlook the possibility and endanger a kingdom."

She sighed. "All right, all right. I'm going to go see my parents and pick up something to wear tonight."

"Something to wear," Cormac said, confused. "What you have on is nice?"

"You don't—oh dear." She looked to Max. "You're going to have to teach him."

"Teach me what?"

"There are certain ridiculous rules for eating in the presence of the Queen," Max said. "Start with the outside utensils and work your way in. Never place the blade of the knife towards anyone, as that implies unsavory things. And wear nice clothes."

"I don't have nice clothes," Cormac said, dread in his voice. "I left all my stuff in Clockbridge and I don't have nice clothes."

"That's all right, I'll take you to get some things. It'll be okay."

"Good luck," Flora said, bemused.

A few flash lessons in etiquette later, Cormac and Max headed out of the castle into the upper town to find a fine clothes shop. Cormac gripped his own upper arm a little insecurely as they stepped down the last of the white marble stairs. He turned and looked back at the vast building of similar marble and topped with turquoise spires. "I didn't really get to see it before," he said. "That's your house?"

"It's the people of Saltrush's house," Max said. "In exchange for tending to the government and economy, we're allowed to live there."

"That's…certainly a way of looking at it. I mean, you grew up there?"

"Yes," Max said.

"That's…wow. The pressure must be—"

"Immense," Max said with a little smile. "Never allowed to forget for a minute that I'm the product of my parents' and my country's hopes and dreams. Never mind child development. Carrying all that around while trying to learn to share, to read, to interact with other children—and let's not get into adolescent behavior."

"You seem to have turned out pretty okay," Cormac said weakly.

"Thank you," Max said, and meant it deeply. "It's really a credit to my minders that I am able to carry on a *normal* conversation and not just ones I was prepared for."

"You have something to do with it. You want to be down-to-earth."

"Desperately. The last thing I want to be is the privileged

prince, with no idea how the world works. And yet sometimes I still am."

"We all have that, sometimes," Cormac said.

"You're trying to make me feel better," Max said. "You really don't have to console me. Look at what I was surrounded with."

"You spent a few months in a back room of a bar without a single complaint. That makes you all right in my book."

"That is a home," Max said earnestly. "It's yours. That's not nothing."

"Sure feels that way, compared to…." He looked around and shook his head.

Max stopped and took his face in his hand. "I don't want you to ever have to feel that way. This is lovely, and opulent, and I am lucky to have had it. But I treasure those days in the Gray Goat, because you were there."

Cormac smiled. "And you're here."

"We are here," he agreed.

Some whirling of fabrics later and Cormac was fitted with a new lawn shirt and beautiful black velvet jacket, some black trousers, and boots. Max picked him a few more things, and Cormac wore them out into the town. He looked down. "I expected to feel foolish, but this is pretty good."

"You wear them well," Max said.

"This shirt is soft. I didn't know fabric could be this soft." He patted his front, then looked up at Max. "Do I seem silly?"

"No. You seem like you're learning new things. Same as I did when I was learning how to work the Goat."

"This is much fancier."

"But no less of a learning curve."

"And you're sure your mother *wants* me at dinner."

"Yes," he said. "I know she can seem severe. But it's really paranoia. Flora thinks *I'm* unreasonable, Mother is much worse."

"All this over some old assassin's league from far away?"

"There are a few more dangers than that."

"But that one is up there?"

"Yes."

Cormac considered his words. "Can I ask why? You said it's an old grudge. How do you even know how hard they're trying?"

"They nearly succeeded."

Cormac looked up. "What do you mean?"

"You know that scar above my collarbone?"

"Yeah."

"I was a boy. Making one of my first public appearances, and an arrow came from a tower. I was taken off my feet and they swore I was dead before the healers got to me."

"Max, I'm—"

"Don't you be sorry," he said with a skewed smile. "It wasn't as though you had anything to do with it. Mother has never quite recovered from that, even as I have. She's convinced any amount of extra danger is too much."

"Which is why sending you out of the country makes very little sense."

Max nodded. And in their conversation, either she had been

trying to rewrite history or she didn't really think she'd banished him. "I want to watch her tonight," he said. "See if there are other signs. Flora might not think it's likely, but I'd like it ruled out."

Cormac nodded. "I haven't the faintest what to look for, but I am with you."

"That's the best I can ask for."

When Max showed Cormac the shops in the middle town, Cormac was much more comfortable doing his own shopping. He picked up everything he could need to feel comfortable, something to replace everything he'd had to leave behind. Except for Brenna. He didn't talk about her, but Max could tell she was on his mind.

At each shop, Cormac was shocked when Max didn't have to pay for anything. "They send the bill to the castle," Max explained. "Normally, I wouldn't do it this way, but I feel like Mother will appreciate every thing I do the 'proper' way. That, and…."

"And?"

He felt that she owed Cormac a little, after the reception he'd had to endure. But he didn't want Cormac feeling any responsibility for that. "I left all my Guild gold in my bag. I'll find a way to spend it all in town next time."

After a few more shop visits, they headed back, Cormac lugging their purchases. "I should show you how to find my room," Max said. "Should you need anything. This way."

Instead of using the grand front stairs, Max took Cormac in a side entrance hidden by some shrubbery and flanked by guards who gave an informal bow of their heads to Max. They walked along the colonnades, high arches in white marble that looked out on one of the grounds' many gardens, and then inside. "Your room is here," Max said, "and mine is just around this corner."

Cormac looked. "There's someone there."

Max picked his head up. "Oh, Father."

"Max," the King boomed, throwing out his arms. He was, like Max, tall and lanky, and his dark hair was streaked with gray. He, unlike the Queen, didn't wear his crown, claiming it weighed his head down too much when reading. Max gave his father a brief hug, and he held him out at arm's length. "That's more like what I remember."

"It's still temporary, Father," Max said. "The curse hasn't gone anywhere."

"Still, I hear you're controlling it. That's good! That's good. And who's this?"

"Cormac, this is my father, King Eren. Father, I'd like you to meet my partner, Cormac."

Cormac bowed, and the King clapped him on the shoulder and straightened him, holding out his hand to shake. "There's no need for that. I'm not my wife. It's a pleasure, Cormac, a plea-sure. I wanted to come meet you before dinner."

"Likewise, Your Highness." He refrained from bowing again, but seemed caught in the lamplight.

"You met my son in Clockbridge, was it? It's been some years since I've been there. How is the place?"

Cormac glanced at Max. "Truth be told, it's…being run by a rather domineering guild. We had to leave in a hurry."

"That's too bad. I recall it being a lovely city back in the time of the republic."

"Really? What was that like?"

"Oh, well, it was a bustling city, fair and open with its allies. They have closed off trade to all but a few partners now since the oligarchy. Things change, I suppose."

"Yes," Cormac said, sounding troubled.

"Are you both all right? When you say you had to leave in a hurry, it sounds like things were bad."

Max said tactfully, "There was an incident with the people who were supposed to be helping me with my curse. It quickly turned from help into harm, but thankfully short-lived."

Alarmed, Eren asked, "Harm?"

"It's really technical, but essentially they drew out the transition so they could study it further. It was temporary, but Cormac and Flora withdrew me from their study."

"They didn't like that," Cormac added.

Eren nodded slowly. "I'm glad you chose to come home. Your mother is too."

"Father—has Mother been acting strangely, do you think?"

"Strangely? No, she's just missed you. As have I."

"Before I left?"

"Well, she was worried for you."

"Never…never mind."

Eren set his hand to Max's shoulder. "There's nothing to worry about, son. Things are how they usually are here."

That could be good, or it could be bad, and Max wasn't sure which.

Max helped Cormac prepare for dinner, then escorted him to Max's mother's favorite rose garden, where the air was magically warmed and the coming winter was trivial. Flora arrived in a scoop-necked dress with a stole and quickly found she didn't need it. The Queen rose and kissed her cheek. "Flora, my dear, you look lovely."

"Thank you, Your Majesty. You look well."

Anora smoothed down her pale gold gown, contrasting with the premature silver hair she shared with Max. "It's every bit my tailor's work, darling. I've been dreadful, without Maximillian around."

Cheerfully, Flora said, "Well, he's back now!"

"That he is. Reason enough for celebration. Tell me," and she looked to Cormac too, "was keeping him too onerous?"

"Not at all," Cormac answered, a game smile in place.

The King inquired, "How did the pair of you meet?"

Max sent a panicked look in Cormac's direction. The truth of that story might be a bit much for them to handle. Cormac stayed measured. "Well, my sister runs a tavern. He posted an advertisement there looking for advice. I gave him some."

Max went lax. A version of their story that didn't make either of them look terrible. "A fateful meeting, then," Eren chuckled.

Cormac took Max's hand under the table. "I'd say so."

"What do you do, Cormac?"

"I, um, I was pretty busy. I built cases for a clockmaker, and I worked at my sister's bar at nights. Occasionally I ran messages for the Guild."

That was a relatively benign way of putting that. Anora raised an eyebrow. "That's quite a lot. But you *were?* You don't plan on returning to those things?"

Of course she'd seize on that. Cormac swallowed, blotting his mouth with his napkin. He placed it back in his lap. "When Max had trouble with the Guild, I had to leave. We all did. They have a tendency to make what they don't like disappear. So, for the time being, what I do is look after Max."

"Good heavens. Maximillian—"

"Mother, it's fine," Max said dully. "Leaving Clockbridge took care of it. And it was no more dangerous than any of the little towns that Rhona had us stop in."

She frowned. "What do you mean?"

"Well, people are superstitious. They think that people with curses can spread those curses. We weren't treated kindly."

"*How* unkindly? Were these little towns part of Saltrush?"

"No, no, past that. Well, I was attacked, swindled, and run out of more than one town."

Upset, the Queen sat back. "Why is this the first I'm hearing of this?"

"There's very little to be done for it after the fact."

"Yes, but before—"

Yes, Max thought vehemently, there should have been some

thought about it before.

His mother seemed lost in thought, as though wandering through her memory of the incident. The King leaned forward. "Are you all right, Anora?"

She shook herself. "Just fine. Regardless, I am pleased you are home and safe, Maximillian, and I thank you both for ensuring it. How are you finding our city, Cormac?"

"It's lovely," he said. "Max described Saltrush many times, but words don't do it justice. I hope I have some time to see more of it."

"I'm sure Maximillian will make some time to show you," she said, looking pointedly at Max.

Max nodded deferentially. As long as untangling Aubric's schemes didn't take too much of their time. "I was thinking about showing him the waterfront tomorrow."

"A splendid idea," Eren said. "Practical and beautiful. As many Saltrushian things are."

"I've been meaning to ask," Cormac said. "Does Saltrush export salt?"

Delighted, Eren said, "Yes! For its entire long history, salt has been a primary export. The ocean deposits it routinely in the caverns to the north, and then we send people to mine it. The -rush part comes from—"

A servant snuck in and whispered in the Queen's ear. She didn't look troubled or frustrated or even annoyed, but she rose and said, "Please, excuse me. Something has come up."

"Anora," Eren said, frowning. "Max just got home. Surely it

can wait?"

She did not pause or even acknowledge him, just followed after the servant.

The King sighed. "I'm sorry, my boy. She's throwing herself into work as ever these days."

"Does this happen often?" Max asked, trying to sound casual about it.

"No," Eren replied, eyes widening. "It's far rarer that she actually *makes* it to dinner in the first place."

Flora tilted her head. "That's strange. She's usually so well-mannered."

Max looked up at the sky, glittering with stars as a blanket of clouds moved in from the west. "She is the Queen. She sets the manners."

Flora made a face at him. "You know what I mean, Max."

He did. His mother would ordinarily never abandon dinner guests, even her own husband and son. But after he'd already confronted her about being dismissive of his partner? She was obsessive about work, that much was true, but at most she would have issued a few orders at the table and gone back to it.

He wondered who had called her away.

Chapter Fourteen
Implications

Max took his time walking back with Cormac from the rose garden, dallying along the colonnades. Cormac wondered at the height of them, at the lithe elven architecture, at the mosaics on the floor.

"They tell a story," Max said. "Here, here, you start here."

He led him to the leftmost panel of mosaics and showed him the goldfish in the bottom left corner. They followed it along as it escaped a bowl, found itself in the mouth of a seabird, flew over the vast tumbling ocean rendered in grays and greens, and dropped safely in a small pond with other colorful fish.

Cormac grinned. "I'd never have spotted that."

"I spent a lot of time playing here." Cormac slipped his hand into Max's, and they walked back across the tiles toward Max's room. Shyly, Max asked, "Do you want to come in?"

"I think that might scandalize some people, no?"

"Oh, hang it," he said crossly. "There are people who are scandalized if I choose the wrong shade of blue."

"Really?"

"Yes, actually. I—"

They rounded the corner, and Max froze. A tall, red-haired man in a purple coat was at his door with his fingertips pressed to it.

"Aubric," he got out.

Cormac's gaze narrowed and his grip on Max's hand tightened as the elven man turned around to face Max. He had a strong chin and an inexplicably handsome nose, but his green eyes were just a little too close together. "Max," he said, his voice congenial. "Welcome home."

"You lost the right to my name," Max said brusquely.

Subdued, he said, "You're right, Your Highness. My apologies."

"What are you doing here?"

He rubbed at his hairline. "I, ah…wonder if we might have a word in private."

"Anything you need to say to me, you can say in front of my partner. And I presume there will be a completely benign explanation for why you were just touching my door."

His eyes flitted to Cormac for a moment, who folded his arms. Even in his well-made jacket, they bulged. "I was just getting ready to knock, that's all."

"Right."

"Your Highness, I have something to say about recent events. You may wish to remain private. If you would just ask your partner to wait inside."

Cormac said through his teeth, "His Highness already told you no."

"A minute is all I ask for," Aubric said, still addressing Max instead of Cormac.

Really, Max wanted Cormac with him, but he didn't think Aubric would slip up in front of him. "It's all right," he told Cormac. "If it takes more than a minute, please come back."

He handed him the key to the room, and Cormac didn't argue. He gave Aubric one last threatening look before giving Max a kiss to the cheek, opening the door, and shutting it behind him.

"What?" Max asked bluntly.

"I understand you've controlled your curse," Aubric said, crossing his arms over his chest and rocking back and forth on his feet. He'd always been bad at concealing his eagerness. "Well done."

"I didn't do it for your praise."

"Of course not. I do wonder if you'd tell me how you did it."

"Another privilege you frittered away, Aubric."

"I am asking nicely, Your Highness. I can get at it another way."

"You mean my mother."

Aubric said nothing, fiddling with a longer piece of his hair. At length, he said, "I am still the authority on magic in this kingdom. Whatever you've done may be unsafe."

"Unsafe for whom?"

"Anyone."

"It affects only me. I suspect you know that."

"And your weal does not affect only you. I expect you to know that."

Max wanted to grit his teeth, swear, trip him—any number of terribly unflattering things. "Your concern is touching and overbearing."

"If you'd just tell me, it would be over sooner."

Somehow Max doubted that, but still he wanted to be rid of Aubric right now. "I saw an alchemist, all right? He gave me a tonic to make my body more receptive to change."

Aubric studied the ground, his hands to his belt. "I see. So you've gone for a mitigation rather than a solution."

"Yes. And if that is sufficient for my mother, it will be for you as well."

"You've still yet to tell me how you're *controlling* the change."

"It's rather personal."

He gave a long-suffering sigh. "I know you were hurt by what you thought you saw, Your Highness, but that's no reason to impair our working relationship. As I said—"

"I don't *think* I saw anything, Aubric. You were very clearly in bed with a student. And we have no working relationship. You want to study me, and I am in a better position to tell you no this time: No."

He started to stalk in the direction of his room, then thought better of it. He directed the guard standing between the doorways, "No one save the guard should be loitering in these halls tonight."

"Yes, Your Highness," the guard said, standing up straighter.

The guard looked to Aubric as though to ask if he intended to make something of it. Aubric sighed deeply and put his hands in the pockets of his coat. "Very well, Your Highness. Good night."

Max watched as he left the hallway, then went to his door and passed a hand over it. Faint traces of a spell lingered. Max's eyebrows lowered, and he went inside.

Cormac was at the door waiting. "I hate him," he said.

Max chuckled wearily. "Is it the smugness, the half-assed attempt at a beard, or his tendency to woo much younger men?"

"All of it," he answered, flustered, "but mostly what he did to you. And then he has the audacity to demand things?"

"Aubric's audacity has gotten him pretty far. He knows just when to push, and he can hardly help himself from asking questions."

"He didn't *ask* a damn thing," Cormac said. "He just expects you to tell him. What did you see in him, anyway?"

"He's very, very smart. When he wants to be, he can be kind. And the audacity can be a little rakish." He paused and watched Cormac for a moment. "You know I don't feel anything besides contempt for him now."

Cormac nodded. "Are you okay?"

"I'm nervous," he said. "He left some magic on the door. It's faded and inert now, but I wonder what it could have been."

"Was he trying to spy?"

"That would make too much sense for him." Max listened for magic inside the room and heard only the low hum of the cloak, still folded on the foot of his bed. He narrowed his gaze at it. "Then there's this." He picked up the cloak and examined it.

"What is it?"

"Something my mother left for me. But if she got her hands on something enchanted, it means he had something to do with it." He looked it over appraisingly. "I think, if I'm guessing right, this is a cloak that extends potentiality."

"And, uh, what does that mean?"

"Say there's an arrow coming at me. There's a moment where the arrow could hit me, or it could miss. Lengthening that moment, just by a little, gives me a chance to get out of the way. But in me, this could also draw out the transition."

"Why is everyone so obsessed with that?"

"I'm not sure," Max said, tired. "But it would be a shame for this to go to waste." He draped it over Cormac's shoulders and clasped it. "It looks fetching on you."

Cormac looked down. "Are you sure?"

"I want you to have it."

"And you're *sure* it's safe?"

"For you, as sure as I can be, yes."

"Thank you." He put his hand to Max's face and kissed him, lightly at first, then more insistently. Max pulled Cormac toward bed.

In the pre-dawn haze, Max rested with his head on Cormac's collarbone and his torso in Cormac's arms. Cormac stirred a little. "Is it time?"

"Almost."

He rolled over and picked up the stone from the nightstand, handing it to Max. Max held onto it, felt the weight of it in his hand. It had been three days of number one consistently. He'd doubted Molas, but he was pleased to be wrong.

Cormac traced Max's cheek with a finger. "What are you thinking about?"

"Just that this will be day four of number one in a row."

Cormac observed Max a moment. "Do you miss any of the other forms?"

Max was about to snort, tell him no, but something made that answer not quite truthful. He puzzled over it. What on earth could make changing bodies appealing?

He almost missed the trigger for his spell, caught himself at the last possible moment, and felt the urge to stretch die away. Cormac sat up a little. "Max?"

"Sorry," he said. "Lost in thought. I…guess I do. Huh."

"I mean, they are all you," Cormac said with a shrug. "Just different bits of you. I think it's pretty normal to miss them."

"Oh, there is nothing normal about any of this."

"A different word, then. With the tonic working again and you being able to choose what you look like when you need to, I'd almost say…."

"It isn't a curse anymore?" Max said slowly.

"Is that offensive?"

Part of him wanted to say yes, but that wouldn't feel true. In fact, it felt like realization was setting in. "No. No, it's—"

A knock at the door cut him off. He hurriedly put on his robe and went to the door, opening it only a few inches. A messenger stood there, his head bowed. "Your Highness," he said. "The

Queen requests your presence in the Rose Garden at seven-thirty this morning. She has instructed you to bring your consort."

Max nodded. "We will be there shortly. Thank you." He shut the door and turned to Cormac. "Well. That's…"

"She's not one to give notice, is she."

"No."

"I also feel a little strangely about being 'your consort'. I do have a name."

"She *acknowledged* that you are my consort," Max said wonderingly. "That's actually a pretty big deal. In the past you'd have been 'my friend'."

Cormac nodded in concession. "I've had a 'friend' or two myself," he grumbled.

Max started to pull himself together and stayed lost in thought. Whether or not his mother was under Aubric's thumb, it wasn't lost on him that she was trying, when she could. That in itself was a little unusual, but even still. Not in a bad way. As they walked into the Rose Garden, he took a breath and resolved to try, too.

She was already sitting when they arrived. She stood to greet them, and Cormac bowed. "Please, that's not necessary," she said. "Here, we are just talking over breakfast. Come, come, sit."

Max eased himself to the metal chair with its plump cushion and edged in closer to the table.

Cormac eyed the place settings tentatively. With fewer forks to manage, breakfast must have seemed a little less daunting. He put his napkin in his lap. "Thank you for inviting us," he said.

"Thank you for coming. I'm sorry I had to leave dinner in such a rush last night."

"Yes, I thought that was unusual," Max said. "What was it that pulled you away?"

"It was urgent," she said vaguely.

"Right, I got that." A servant came and set down a large waffle in front of each of them. The Queen smiled her thanks, and Max nodded, distracted. "Do you remember what it was?"

"Maximillian, of course I remember," she said. "Do you think I'm so old?"

"It's less about being old and more about—"

"The matter is hardly important," she said lightly. "Consider it dropped."

For now. He poked at his waffle and tried to keep from openly setting his jaw. If it had been some confidential matter of state, she'd have said so. The fact that she was so distant about it gave him pause.

She smiled again. "Tell me more of you."

Cormac swallowed. "Me, Your Majesty?"

"Yes. I am curious about the man who's stolen my son's heart. It's not every day he speaks so ardently of anything."

"I'm afraid I'm not all that interesting," he said with a laugh.

"Oh, that's not true," Max put in. "Cormac is a talented woodworker. Self-taught. He made me the most beautiful music box."

"Is that so?" the Queen asked. "You'll have to show me."

Embarrassed, Cormac said, "It's...made of off-cuts."

"Nonsense," Max said. "It's gorgeous."

"Still," he said with a nervous laugh, "it's nothing compared to what Max can do. He's written symphonies."

"Has he?" Anora asked curiously.

Cormac looked to Max. "You hadn't told…?"

"Much of anyone, really," Max said, his face heating up.

"Whyever not?" his mother wanted to know.

"Inevitably, someone will want to *hear* one, and the prospect of that is frightening."

"Nonsense. You ought to show it to Master Farrow."

"Oh, no. It'll have a good chance of getting played if I do that."

"Isn't that rather the point? I'll call for him tomorrow."

"Eventually," he said, his voice thin. "It's not—I'm not ready."

His mother looked at him for a long moment, as though something opaque between the pair of them suddenly became clear. "All right," she said, busying herself with her plate. "But when you are, I want to hear it."

"I was afraid of that," he mumbled.

"What was that, darling?"

"Nothing worth repeating."

"Then it ought not have been said," she chirped. The opaqueness was back. She turned to Cormac. "And what of your family? Whom might I look up?"

"Mother, no," Max said, mortified.

"I have to ask," she said seriously.

"Why?"

"Because if my son is going to spend time around someone, I think it's only safe to know with whom we are dealing."

"It is a difficult topic," Max said plainly, pointedly.

He fully expected his mother to drop it. There was one thing she detested, and it was rudeness. She folded her hands primly. "There are many difficult topics when one is spending time with royalty."

Cormac shuffled in his seat. "Ah…we're nobody."

"There's no such thing as nobody," Anora said. It lacked the comforting nature of Max's words.

"I—I mean you won't have to worry about them," Cormac stuttered. "My sister n'I are all that's left."

Anora's demeanor shifted. "Ah. I'm sorry." Max looked at her, frustrated, as if to say *I told you so*. She didn't look back at him. "Still—a family name would be appreciated."

"*Mother*," Max said, appalled. "Let it lie."

"Really, there's no one of any repute," Cormac said. "We were woodworkers, all. Except my mother, but she gave up her family ties when she left the underground to live in Brighton."

"So there is an extended family," Anora mused.

"Well—yes. I mean—no. I mean that they couldn't care less if I died, much less if I'm seeing the prince of a surface country."

"You'll find that things change quickly when money and power are involved. A name, if you please."

"Let me save you some time," he said tensely. "My mother is Fenrith Prism Graymoor. She killed my family and retreated underground, where she is still, for all I know. If knowing that about my family helps you decide whether I'm suitable company for Max, great."

"I decide who is suitable company for me," Max said, glowering at his mother, who looked stricken. He stood up and held out his hands to Cormac. "I think that's quite enough. Thank you for breakfast."

They left quickly.

Back in the halls, Max said, "Cormac, I'm sorry—"

"I can't be here right now," Cormac said, his shoulders clenched.

Max nodded, taking his hands again and pulling him along to the side gate, where they slipped into town without fanfare. Cormac took his hands back and stuffed them into his pockets against the cold. Max led on down a winding cobbled street to the waterfront, where the gray ocean lapped against the piers. Across the way, the mountains of the Carapace Islands jutted out of the waves as though someone had transposed a mountain range into the middle of the sea.

Cormac stopped and stared into it, the unknowable depths sobering him. Max ran his hands down Cormac's arms. "Cormac...."

"Really makes a person feel small," he said with a quiet laugh.

Max followed his gaze out to the ocean, trying to decide whether he meant the vista or the conversation, then decided it didn't matter. He leaned his head against Cormac's shoulder. "I'm so sorry."

"Why did you think she would be any different?"

"Because she is…she was…doing better. She was trying." He shook his head, looking up at the gray clouds rolling above. "I am sorry. I should never have subjected you to her."

"I wanted to go. I wanted to help you…have a good time with your mother. Something I haven't had in…ever." Angrily, he said, "But it's the same shit she started talking about. Whose family is better. Whose family will screw whose over."

"I don't believe in that," Max promised.

"You don't, but you—" He deflated slowly. "No. You tried sticking up for me. But you shouldn't have to *stick up for me.*"

"No. You're right. And I will have words with her about that."

"Do you still—do you still think she's possessed or some shit?"

It was the last thing Max wanted to do, but he went over the conversation in his head again. The vagueness, the rudeness, that one moment of clarity, the way even she looked shocked at the end of it. "I don't know," he said despairingly. "Is it horrible that I hope so?"

Cormac shook his head. "I do, too. For you. Because mine *wasn't,* and it was fucking horrible."

"I have to figure out how to tell for sure," he said. "The problem is all the wizards report to Aubric."

"What about Molas?"

"He might not know. Mind control is its own niche. But I think it's worth a try. In the meantime, you don't have to come to any more meals with her. I'll deal with her on my own."

"You're sure?"

"The power dynamic…she was the one who taught me never to wield it like that. If she is under a spell, I don't think she will like herself very much when she comes around."

Cormac hesitated for a moment, looking around them at the people who stared at Max. Max tilted his head questioningly, and Cormac at last must have decided he didn't care. He put his arms around Max and held on. Max cradled the back of his head in his hand and stroked his hair. Cormac rested his forehead against Max's shoulder for a moment, then peered up over it. "They're all looking at us."

"Let them."

"Did they know you're…?"

"Not officially."

"I think they know now."

"Good," Max said. "I won't be someone I'm not. Not even for them."

Cormac kissed him, holding his head against his. "I love you," he said softly.

Max smiled. "I love you too."

Cormac let go and took a good look at their surroundings. "There are mountains in the sea," he said in wonderment. "Close enough I feel like I could hit them with a rock. That's…wow."

"What does your sea look like?"

"A big empty. Sometimes there are boats."

"Maybe we'll go out there one of these days."

"I'd like that."

They walked along, glancing in the shop windows. Max

waved at some people who greeted him and held fast to Cormac's hand. There were whispers here and there. Cormac asked, "You're sure you want to be seen with me?"

"Darling. There is no one I'd rather be seen with."

A little flustered, he said, "I'm sure at least there's a nice eligible prince you could break it to the kingdom with."

"I don't want one. I want you."

Cormac smiled a little and let Max hold his hand all the way back to the castle.

Chapter Fifteen
Truth and Consequences

Max remembered double-checking that the door was locked. He wasn't sure why that night; there was just something about it that put him on edge. He put it out of his mind and returned to bed, where Cormac waited for him.

Quickly he was distracted from his nervousness by a string of kisses down his spine and shortly thereafter, much more.

They lay in each other's arms, panting their exertion and breathing out their adoration to one another. Max looked over at Cormac, who laid with his eyes shut and a little smile on his lips. "I didn't get to ask," he said. "Do *you* miss my other forms?"

"I do," he said honestly, opening his eyes and looking at Max. "I'm glad you have this option now, but there was something nice about getting to see all those different sides of you."

A little insecurely, he asked, "Do you...dislike having this one all the time?"

"No, goodness, no. You're you."

Max buried his face in the crook of Cormac's shoulder. "I

think I'm going to let it happen tomorrow," he said softly.

"Yeah?"

"I'm just…a little tired of being the same. Is that strange?"

"No. Well, perhaps a little, but only because no one else has this option. Can you imagine if we all did that?"

He laughed quietly. "No, I really can't."

"Maybe we'd all be a little better for it."

"It has let me see things differently," Max reflected. "Myself, specifically."

"I don't think that's a bad thing. Now that it's not hurting you and you're somewhere safe."

Max nodded. "You don't mind two, five, and six?"

"Let's just say I'm attracted to exactly three women and they're all you."

Max gave Cormac a squeeze. He was about to speak when he heard the door slide shut. "Who's there?"

"What is it?" Cormac said.

"The door." Max leaned forward and stared into the dark, his eyes adjusting slowly. He couldn't see anything near the door or in the corner. "Cormac—"

A pair of hands seized him from the shadow next to the bed. Cormac sat up abruptly and wrenched them off of Max. Whomever they belonged to pulled hard, and Cormac went sprawling atop Max before recovering himself enough to lunge over the side of the bed into the dark. Max produced a bit of light in his hand and sent it up into the air.

It was a burly person dressed entirely in black, their face obscured by a solid black mask. At the very least, they seemed to be the only one. They struggled against Cormac, rolling to try to veer away from the wall. Max tilted his head, a little curious. In their last fight, Cormac had utilized the walls to great effect. He hadn't heard any thumping before they hit the floor. Were they familiar with his work?

He shook himself. It didn't matter. Right now they were too evenly matched, and he didn't like the way the assailant kept bringing their arm to bear against Cormac's throat when they managed to get the upper hand. He threw the covers aside and reached under the bed for one of his knives.

The tricky thing about magic was that it tended to be an all-or-nothing proposition. If he tried to affect the attacker, he had a decent chance of hitting Cormac, too. Max squinted for a moment to consider his options. They weren't many. It had been some time since he'd attempted a displacement, but it would have to do. He held the blade point-up and focused on the ether clustered around the blade, then pushed his will into the space between the assailant and the armoire.

Max never liked the feeling of dissipating, like his senses were fading. When he rematerialized in the place he chose, he gasped for air and took a moment to reestablish himself before approaching the scuffle, aiming very carefully, and bringing the butt of the dagger into the assailant's head.

They sagged but didn't fall, but the extra seconds were enough for Cormac to get the wind in him and land a punch square in the temple. They dropped like a stone. Cormac breathed out hard and drew his arm across his forehead. "Fucking hell, I thought the palace was a pretty safe bet, but he just sauntered in, didn't he?"

Max went slack and caught his breath. "Who is it?"

Cormac wrested the black mesh mask off of the assailant's face. A human man, bloodied and unconscious. Cormac let his head hang forward. "I knew him," he said. "He's Guild."

"Ah. Wonderful. They've followed us." Max froze. "Flora."

"Shit," Cormac said, scrambling for his clothes.

Max too pulled on whatever was closest at hand and dashed out the door. He shouted to a shocked-looking guard to take the man to the dungeon, and they hurried across the grounds. The first bits of snow scattered over them as they went, and Max wished haste had permitted him time to get a coat.

Flora stayed in her parents' house, which sat adjacent to the palace grounds on a hill overlooking the upper town. He knew the way by heart—he'd gone here so often as a child, Flora's parents had come to accept him as another part of the household. The house sat dark and still in the early morning dim. Instead of heading to the door as Cormac did, Max circled the house and looked up to a second-story window that was, in fact, ajar. "Fuck," he said, mounting a trellis at the side of the window.

Cormac waited, bracing the creaky wood frame as Max went, unsure that the thing would bear both of their weights. Max lunged for the casement and pulled himself up and in.

The room was dark, and just like theirs, Flora's assailant wore black and a black mask. She held them off in her nightgown with a sword, taking wild swings to keep them back. "Max," she cried.

Max summoned all the magic he could muster and fixed the attacker in space so they could only move fractions of inches at a time. This wouldn't hold forever, but he didn't need forever. He just needed long enough for—

Cormac tumbled into the room and barreled into the attacker, grabbing their arms and twisting the long knife out of their hand. Flora gave a hefty thump to the head with the pommel of her sword, and the assailant sagged forward to their knees, albeit very slowly. Cormac knelt on their calf and pinned their hands behind their back, and Max relieved them of their mask. An elven woman this time. She twisted and looked at Cormac in disgust. "How does it feel?" she asked. "To be on this side of things."

He grunted, "Not great, and hello to you too, Elis."

"They'll catch you, you know. There's nowhere on the continent that's safe."

"I'm sure the Queen of Saltrush will love hearing that her sovereignty has been violated."

"No, she won't," Flora said grimly.

"Was it him who sent you?" Max asked. "The Director."

Elis laughed. "You'd like that, wouldn't you?"

A noise from the hallway, and Flora's father appeared in the hallway in his nightshirt bearing a candle. "What is going on—Prince Maximillian?"

Flora said, "They saved me. From her."

He took in the scene again and drew in a sharp breath. "I'll call the guards."

Max knew that once the woman was taken away, the chances of asking her any more questions was slim, so he looked at her sharply. "How many of you are there?"

"Hundreds," she said, grinning.

"Not in the Guild. Here. Now."

Cormac said, "I can hold you tighter."

"You don't scare me, Cormac. You've gone soft."

"Gone? No. I've always been soft." He pulled her arms and put more weight on her legs, forcing her to arch her back. "You've just pissed me off."

"Three, okay? Just the three."

"Three," Max repeated.

"One for each of you."

Lord Nythera returned with several guards in tow, and they relieved Cormac of his load. As they walked off, she looked back over her shoulder with a grin. Flora balled up her fists. "Oooh, I don't *like* her."

"I did once," Cormac sighed. "It's a godsdamned shame."

"More importantly," Max said, "there's a third loose—"

"She was bullshitting. There are just two."

"How can you tell?"

"Because they were only planning on taking you alive. It's far easier to get in and out of a place like the palace with two people than fumbling around with a third."

Max sagged. "I'm sorry. Both of you."

"This isn't your fault."

"If I hadn't gotten you mixed up with this…"

"You'd still be in pain and alone." He grasped Max's hand and kissed it. "I don't regret it."

"Me neither," said Flora firmly. "I don't want you to go back to running."

"Okay," he said with a fond smile. "I won't."

Cormac looked around uneasily. "I don't want to speak for anyone, but maybe Flora should come stay at the palace, too. There are guards much closer."

Ruefully, she said, "Yeah, and I don't want my parents to be in danger."

Lord Nythera came stalking back up the stairs, and he fixed Flora with a look. "What the devils was that?"

She winced. "It's a really long story, Papa. But Clockbridge is run by this Guild, and they're not very nice."

"Why on earth are they attacking *you?*"

"We kind of took their scientific advancement."

"*What?* Why would you *do* something like that?"

"It was me," Max said. "I was their scientific advancement."

Lord Nythera's bushy eyebrows knit together. "You, Your Highness? I don't think I understand."

"They were experimenting on me. And at first, I agreed to it, because I needed help, but—"

Flora's fury lit her round face behind her crooked glasses. "But it turned evil! They hurt him, all so they could keep their data sets pure. So we took him out, just as we agreed we could. And then they started chasing us."

Lord Nythera nodded slowly. "I'm certain there is more to this story than I can comprehend before dawn—"

"Dawn," Max said in dread. "I need to get out of here."

"Is everything all right?"

"Yes," he said, heading for the window. "And no. Um—"

"It's no good," Flora said, rounding up her father and Cormac and pushing them toward the door. "You're going to have to do it here."

"My stone is back in my room."

"There's no time."

He knew she was right. He could feel it coming, tension building at his core.

He could hear Lord Nythera demanding what was going on while Flora shoved him out the door. "We'll explain downstairs," she said, and she shut the door, leaving Max alone.

He sank to her bed, still mussed up from her rude awakening, and put his face in his hands. Well, he'd been thinking about not changing into number one out of duty today. This just made sure of it. He felt for his bare neck. He didn't have his scarf. He hoped the guards recognized him.

As the dawn came, he stretched and kept growing. *Of course* it was number three. Hastily, he unbuttoned his shirt and pants and slid off his boots. Number three actually wasn't all that much wider than number one, but the sheer length of him and the fact that he needed somewhere for his tail to go made number one's clothes uncomfortable. He could deal with it for staggering back home, but any amount of extra duress right now felt unbearable.

At length, it was done. He awkwardly ran his tail through his waistband and rolled up his pant legs to accommodate the oblique L-shape of his lower legs. As he was finishing cuffing his sleeves, a knock sounded at the door. "Max? You okay?" Cormac asked.

"Just a little mortified," he answered, opening the door and wriggling slightly to try to get his clothes to stop pulling in uncomfortable places. "And unprepared."

Cormac reached up and kissed him. "It'll be all right. Flora's handling her parents."

"It's *both* of them now?" That was bad. Lady Nythera was a good friend of his mother's, and an incorrigible gossip.

"Her mother overheard."

"Brilliant. Just what I needed." He doubled back to pick up his boots and held them insecurely to his stomach.

"Hey." Cormac held Max's forearms and looked him in the eye. "What did we say? It's not a curse. It's just a part of you. You're just sharing it. No need to be embarrassed."

"I'm not," he said, pushing out a breath. "It's just the whole…circumstance. I guess I wasn't as ready to embrace it all as I thought."

"And that's okay too." Cormac held his arm as they made their way toward the stairs. "You'll get there if you want to. For now, let's just slip out and walk back."

"We shouldn't leave Flora alone."

"The guards will escort her."

Max's slouch started to reverse itself. "All right," he said, to himself as much as to Cormac.

It was all working until Lady Nythera came into the foyer. "Max?" she said softly.

He froze for a moment, thought about running, then turned slowly. She looked up at him earnestly, her gentle features so similar to her daughter's. "So it's true, then. You are changing."

"Once a day," he said with a nervous laugh.

"That must be so difficult."

"Actually…it's not so bad," he admitted. "The hardest part is other people's reactions."

"So that's why this Guild wants you?"

"They were using me to study transmutation, yes. Apparently I am a rare specimen."

"You're no such thing," she said, drawing herself up to her deeply unimpressive full height. "You are Prince Maximillian of the Kingdom of Saltrush, and you will not be *used*."

He smiled a little. "Thank you, Lady Nythera. Please—keep this between our families for now."

"Of course, of course—"

"I mean that no one outside of our families can find out. They must not know."

"I understand," she said seriously.

"Thank you. I should get back before my mother hears of the attack."

"Wait," a voice called, and Flora hustled into the foyer, a small pile of clothes and things bundled under her arm. "I'm coming." He smiled and put a hand to her shoulder. She patted his arm. "Sorry, Mum. I'll come back when things slow down."

"Be safe, my love."

They went out into the swirl of snow, Max taking careful mincing steps to avoid falling on his tail in it. Max looked up at the white vortex above. "I am sorry to have interrupted your time with them."

"It's all right," she said with a little smile. "It's mostly interrogations on when I intend to get married. But hey, at least my research didn't get damaged this time! I don't have to start over *entirely* from scratch."

He winced. "But you do need to start over."

"It helps to be in a consistent place."

"Well, you know Mother will be thrilled to have you for as long as you like."

"Careful. I might just stay there and become that strange spinster with weird toads who haunts the guest wing."

"I don't think anyone would mind that."

"Least of all me." She clucked. "Your poor tail."

"What's wrong with it?"

She balanced her bundle under one arm and tried to adjust the waistband of his pants. "You're squooshing it."

"I'm what?"

"Squooshing. Hush, it's a word."

"I'll change when I get back. Hopefully I get the chance."

As he feared, there was Rhona, waiting for him outside his room. She took one look at him and said haughtily, "Your mother would like a word. Privately."

"May I please take a moment to get dressed appropriately?" he said, trying not to sound peevish.

She threw up her hand as if to say it was his funeral. He turned to Cormac. "Would you accompany Flora to a new guest room, please? I'll meet you back in my room."

He nodded, spared Rhona a glance, and gave Max a kiss on the cheek before heading away with Flora. Max retreated into his room, where he hurriedly dug out number three's clothes. He had yet to unpack the other forms' clothing. Perhaps this was the sign he needed to do so.

He felt much, much better in clothes that fit. He girded himself and stepped back outside, where Rhona waited. She led him along in stony silence for a space. "I understand you gave the intruder quite the welcome."

He looked at her incredulously. "Is that praise, Captain?"

"Hardly. It is not a prince's place to scrap." She paused. "But if you insist on doing so, you may as well win. Well done."

"Thank you," he said with a small laugh.

"I will be increasing the guard along the corridor. It will not happen again."

He believed that. Not only were the guards now aware of the possibility of infiltration, they would be watching for it. He was fairly certain the Guild blew their one and only chance to gain access on the inside. If he and Cormac and Flora were careful about their trips into town, he was confident they were safe.

Convincing his mother of that would be difficult. Convincing her of anything would be difficult. He steeled himself as they walked up the hidden staircase to the Royal Wing, where his parents kept their rooms. He could have been here, too, but he insisted on keeping his distance. He reached out and knocked hesitantly.

"Enter," his mother said. Max left Rhona standing outside and went into his mother's sitting room.

She was wearing a light blue dressing gown over a simple chemise. Max could count the number of times he'd seen his mother in disarray on one hand. Even this was not unkemptness, just…unreadiness. She looked up at him and started as though he'd hidden around a corner and jumped out at her. Anora put her hand to her chest and breathed out.

"That frightening, hmm?" Max asked dryly.

"No. No, of course not. I was simply…not expecting it." She took up her teacup, took a stiff drink, then set it down. "I have heard of the attack. I am told you put it down yourself."

"Not entirely. Cormac was invaluable."

"Maximillian! Do we or do we not have guards?"

"We do, but I wasn't going to let the fellow kill my partner while I ran for them."

"And that is the other thing! What were you doing, *spending the night*—"

"Mother, I'm not going to argue about this. I am an adult, I am in love, and if I wish to spend the evening with my equally adult partner, I will do so. Without shame."

"Would that you had more shame! Kissing and holding each other at the waterfront!"

Max folded his hands behind his back and looked at the floor. "The horror."

"Without so much as a formal announcement. The people have had no time to react to the reality you have foisted on them."

"What reality?"

"That you will be eschewing tradition. That you will not put aside your own wants and feelings for them."

"I have done quite a lot of the latter, Mother," he said, his voice deathly calm. "In this area, they will need to learn to deal with it. I will not *lie* to our people about who I am. About whom I love."

"Oh, please, Maximillian. As though that hasn't been done for decades. Your great great grandparents both had mistresses."

"And it wasn't a secret, was it?" He started to pace the carpet.

"An unkind friend made it the talk of the town, but they remained respected. Why? Because they did what was right for the kingdom and married each other out of duty."

"Duty."

"Yes, duty. Not love. It was the way of it for them, for my parents, for—"

He stopped. "You and Father."

She flushed. "I didn't—I didn't say that." He felt strangely like he'd been flattened. He knew they maintained separate bedchambers and private lives, but he'd thought that somewhere in there, they must have loved one another at some point. Anora swiped a bit of hair loosening from her silver chignon behind her ear, her voice softening. "Your father and I have been very fortunate in that we came to grow into compatible people, despite being very young and inexperienced when we were made to marry."

"Made," he repeated numbly.

"Yes, made," she answered gently. "That is the way of it, Maximillian. It always has been."

Max found himself walking to the sofa and sitting right next to her. She looked flummoxed, as though he had done something thoroughly foreign to her. He gripped her hands and looked her in the eyes. "Just because something has been shitty doesn't mean it always has to be shitty."

"I beg your pardon!"

He closed his eyes. "Sorry, sorry. But it's something that I learned while I was away, and it's true. Just because something has always been one way doesn't mean it has to *stay* that way. Just because others have endured it—doesn't mean we can't change it."

"Maximillian—"

"I am *happy*, Mother," he said. "For the first time in my life, I am happy. Can you imagine?" She held her quiet. He laughed. "I am cursed, and I am so happy. I am myself. And I think that frightens you."

Anora looked at him, her eyes wide and vulnerable. "It's all I ever wanted for my child," she all but whispered.

"Then let it be. Let me be."

"If I could…."

"You can. I promise you. Nothing will fall apart. Nothing will end."

"There are still responsibilities. The people will wonder."

"About my heirs, is that it?"

"You speak of them so flippantly," she said. "To them, that is the future. The future of Saltrush. *You* are the future. And right now, everything is uncertain."

"I have never been more certain in my life."

"Yes, but who will you sit on the throne when your time to retire comes?"

"Mother, you know there is more than one way to have children. Just because I won't be siring anyone the traditional way doesn't mean that I don't plan on having children."

She paused. "You…"

"I don't know when. I don't know if it'll be with Cormac. I don't know how just yet. But I have time. I have so much time in front of me."

"The fact of the matter is that tradition is reassurance," she said. "The people require that."

"Is there no way to give it to them without giving them my soul?"

"Perhaps…perhaps if we were to host a welcoming ball for Cormac."

Max raised his eyebrows. "You'd do that?"

"Maximillian, I do not hate your partner."

"That's news to me, given the way you raked him over the coals yesterday morning."

"I did not—"

"You pressured him into talking about something that hurts him very deeply so that you could—what?—look up his family and make sure they're not secretly out to grab the throne?"

"Maximillian, you may not like it, but it is a valid concern."

"And what if they are? Cormac is not them. We are not beholden to our families' mistakes."

"If that's meant to be a jab—"

"It wasn't. But you know, perhaps it *is* time we talk about that."

"Careful of your tone, young man."

"I mean it," he said, looking at her shrewdly. "Not once have we discussed the fact that I did not want to turn that enchantress away."

Anora pursed her lips, her eyes welling up. This alarmed Max. The Queen did not cry. She blustered, ordered, made matter-of-fact statements that she sometimes came to regret. "You are right," she said, her voice thin. "It was my doing."

Max looked down. "That's not...entirely..."

"You came to me for direction and I made an order. That alone.... If any should have been cursed, it is me."

"No one should have been cursed," he said.

She reached out to put a hand to his face and drew back. "I look at you now and I can't bear knowing that it was me who did this to you."

He took her hand and put it back against his cheek. "You didn't lay the curse. And I'm not...I'm actually becoming rather fond of it."

"What?"

"I know, that sounds strange, doesn't it? A month ago I'd not have believed myself. But now that it's controlled and painless… it's like seeing the world, seeing myself through different lenses."

She furrowed her eyebrows and gestured to the length of him. "You *like* being like this?"

"Am I that hideous?"

"No, no."

"You don't sound convinced."

"I just…I look at you and I don't see my son. I hear him a little when you speak. But I don't see him."

He took her hand and placed it to his chest. "I'm right here," he said. "Where are you?"

Her tears spilled over, and she threw her arms around him. Awkwardly, he compressed himself into her hug and patted her shoulder. Even when he was young, she wasn't much for displays of affection. "I'm sorry, my boy," she all but whispered.

"Mother, I feel like you and I are going in circles. We've had this talk, but there will need to be another one."

"I know," she said, wiping at her eyes. "I don't know what's *wrong* with me—"

The door burst open and Max stood without provocation. Then he saw who it was and he put himself deliberately between Aubric and his mother. "We are in the middle of a private conversation," he said, his voice low.

Aubric ignored him. "Your Majesty, it's time for your medicine."

"Medicine? Mother, what—?"

The Queen fiddled with her hands. "I am unwell. Aubric has been kind enough to make and administer treatments."

"Unwell? With what?"

Aubric folded his arms. "An idiopathic condition of the nerves. The physician has been unhelpful."

"The only unhelpful thing in this room is you," Max spat.

The Queen took Max's hand. "Maximillian. I'm sorry you had to find out this way. But Aubric has been most considerate."

"Aubric is a liar. A snake."

"Maximillian!"

"His experiments only benefit himself and his own twisted desires. When you had him working on my curse…." He trembled.

"Go on," Aubric said, bemused. "I'm enjoying hearing all about my evil schemes."

He looked entreatingly at his mother, trying to shut out Aubric. "He cut into me. Took pieces off of me to see if they'd grow back. Kept me without clothes for days on end, caged like an animal. Please, Mother, whatever he's giving you, it's not help."

She looked to Aubric. "Is this true?"

"Of course it isn't," he laughed. "Max had a high fever the first week of his curse. He clearly dreamed some things."

"You bastard," Max muttered.

Anora stood, cupping Max's face in her hands. "My poor boy. You've been through so much."

"Mother, he's doing what he does. Manipulating. Making you doubt. Please, you have to listen to me."

"I know you must have believed those things—"

He slumped. "You don't believe me."

"I do, darling, I do, but I also know you were very unwell." Aubric held out a crystal vial, and the Queen took it in her hands. "Thank you, Aubric, Maximillian. That will be all."

Aubric bowed and left the room. Max stood a moment longer, numb, as she downed the contents of the vial and coughed slightly. She patted her chest. "I need rest. I will see you soon, dear."

Max exited into an empty hallway. Aubric was gone.

Chapter Sixteen
Disillusioned

Max entered his room in a whirl of emotion. Cormac rose from the end of the bed where he'd been talking with Flora and caught him by the arms. "Easy. What's going on?"

"He's giving her something," he spat. "Aubric. And I *know* he was listening, because we were finally getting somewhere, and he showed up to dose her again."

Flora jumped up. "What do we do?"

"I don't know. I tried talking her out of taking it, tried telling her what he did to me, but he told her I was feverish. Was I feverish?"

"No," Cormac said flatly. "When you told me what happened, you showed me a scar. Don't let him get in your head."

Max nodded, putting his hand to his forehead. "Ugh. I was so close. So close to getting her to acknowledge that something was wrong. And then he swooped in."

Flora narrowed her eyes. "The first thing we have to do is keep him from spying on us."

"How do we do that?"

"Barriers and wards. Simple alchemy. Leave those to me. Then, we get our own wizard."

Cormac nodded slowly but enthusiastically. "Molas. He'll probably favor the ability to get out of town right now anyhow. Offer him money, a place to stay. He'll probably bite."

Max took a breath. "Okay," he said. He felt better having a plan of action. "Just...what is he making her do in the meantime?"

"I don't know. We should probably talk to your father."

Weakly, Max said, "My father."

"Is everything okay with him?"

"I think so. She just dropped the fact that they aren't in love."

Flora nodded sympathetically. "I remember figuring that out. It kind of crushes a little childhood fantasy."

Cormac said, "For once, I can relate."

Max sighed. "It's not the most important thing right now, but it makes me a little sad."

Flora patted his shoulder. "Let's get that letter written so we can take it into town."

"I can't," Max said with a wince. "If I leave like this my mother will not be happy."

"Cormac and I will take it, then."

"Yeah, I've got to watch for a letter from Brenna anyhow," Cormac said. "Speaking of people who likely aren't happy."

"You don't think she'll forgive you?"

"I think we might get there eventually," he said with a wince.

Max wrote a quick letter to Molas promising reward and more information if he came, stamped it with the royal seal, which would keep anyone on this side, at least, from opening it, and handed it to Cormac. Cormac kissed his cheek. "Back soon."

Max threw himself onto his bed and folded his hands behind his head, staring up at the ceiling. It was foolish, he thought, to sulk about his parents not being in love. It was probably more foolish that he hadn't realized it until now. All those years of being threatened with an arranged marriage and he hadn't realized that's what his parents had? Foolish.

A little more contemplation later and a knock sounded at the door.

"Who's there?"

"Father," Eren replied.

Max sat up and smoothed down his hair so he didn't look a complete mess. "Come in."

The door opened, and the King slipped inside. "Oh—oh, goodness."

"Father, please," Max said. "I'm not that hard to look at."

"No, of course not. Just not what I was expecting."

Max sighed. "Is this the part where you work me over after a fight with my mother? I really thought I'd outgrown all that."

"No, no, you're too smart for that. Your mother was worried, though."

"About me?" he asked incredulously.

"Apparently you became quite emotional when Aubric arrived."

He supposed that was how she saw it. "Did you know he's treating her for some nonsense disease?"

Eren looked up, surprised. "No. No, I didn't."

"He's giving her a draught. And suddenly, she's losing her place in sentences, forgetting that we've resolved issues, and being outright rude. When has Mother ever been rude?"

"Max, are you sure?"

"I am very sure. Mother is a lot of things, but she's never been rude to a guest. Not once. But she won't believe me, because Aubric is Aubric and he has her believing that I dreamt the horrible things he did when he had free reign to experiment on me. Hells, he almost had me believing it."

"What horrible things?"

"He cut off pieces of me, Father," Max said, choking on the words. "My hair, the webbing between my fingers, my tail."

He leaned over to look around Max. "But your tail is…."

"It grew back. I didn't forget."

Eren folded his arms and considered gravely. "Your mother trusts Aubric deeply."

"I know. I don't know how to get through to her, apart from showing her the scar across my backside."

"No, don't do that."

Max took a breath. "Do you believe me?"

"Yes. And I've never much cared for Aubric. We'll have to watch him carefully. If he is out to harm her, he'll slip."

"I'm worried that he won't. He's very smart."

"He will," he said confidently. "No one can keep up a facade forever. If we can find out what specifically he's up to, we'll be able to head him off at the pass. Perhaps he won't expect it, coming from me."

Max couldn't help a small smile. "Maybe that's true."

"We'll have it sorted."

"Father...." He paused, sighed. "Do you and Mother love each other?"

"Good heavens," Eren said, coughing. "Where did that come from?"

"She told me. She told me your marriage was arranged."

"Yes, that is true." He reached out for the bedpost for support. "And it is certainly true that we did not love each other when we married. Truthfully, we didn't know each other well at all. But, over time, we've developed a deep and abiding respect for one another. A partnership. I don't know if I would call it romantic, but it is a kind of love." Max nodded slowly. Eren lifted an eyebrow. "That does not mean I wish it on you."

"You don't think I should suck it up and marry a woman?" he asked with a bemused smile.

"No. I'm far too invested in your happiness for that. Tell me. Cormac. Does he make you happy?"

"So happy," he said completely honestly. "Happier than I've ever been. Happier than I ever thought I could be."

"I'll accept nothing less. As should you."

He pushed off the bedpost and headed for the door, which opened. Cormac, flustered at coming face-to-face with the King, stammered, "Your, um, Majesty."

Eren put his hand on Cormac's shoulder. "I was just leaving. Take care, boys."

Max smiled as he left. "He's not one for long talks," he said. "But the things he does say make up for it."

Cormac took off his jacket and hung it carefully, then came to sit next to Max on the bed. "Good talk?"

"Mostly."

"Mostly?"

"Both he and my mother seem to be afraid of number three."

He frowned. "Well, that's unfair. I happen to like number three very much."

Max picked up his head, smiling a little. "Do you?"

"Mm. Yes." He leaned over and kissed Max's cheek, his jaw, his neck. Max shivered, and his tail lashed out and pulled Cormac in closer. "Oh, hello, there," he said, toying with the end of it.

"You seem to be the only one."

"I'm sure that's not true. Brenna liked that you could grab all the things off the high shelves."

"Did she write you?"

"Boy, did she ever," he said with a grim little laugh. "Such colorful language in black and white."

"Surely she's not *that* angry?"

"No. She even put that she'll forgive us because we're alive. But I'll never hear the end of leaving without saying goodbye."

"It's not as if there was time."

"I know, and deep down, she does too."

"Maybe next time I'm number one I can go find her a present."

He stroked the spade of Max's tail. "Bribery usually helps." Max sat for a moment, debating himself. Cormac glanced up. "You're trying to decide whether to say something."

"Is it that obvious?"

"You get this cute little pucker in your lower lip. What's on?"

"Something my mother raised today."

"Uh oh."

"No, it's good. I think it's good. You can tell me what you think. She asked about throwing you a welcoming party."

"What's that?"

"Well, what it sounds like, mostly. It's usually thrown for younger people for whom marriage is not yet on the table, but it's not unheard of at our ages. It's an announcement to the people that we are seeing one another, and a chance to introduce you to some of them."

Cormac stayed silent, running the edge of his thumb over his lip.

"Are you all right?" Max said.

"Um. Yes. Sorry. Just thinking."

Max sat up a little straighter, looking down at him. "What about?"

"This seems like kind of a big thing."

"It doesn't have to be, but I think you might like it if it were a larger affair. The townsfolk can come instead of just the noble houses."

"That does sound nice, but I kind of meant big for us."

"I suppose it could be considered that way. It is something of an official declaration."

He shifted his weight uncomfortably. "Is it…okay if I think about it?"

"Yes, of course," Max said, trying to keep the preemptive disappointment from his voice. He wouldn't push it, but he had hoped for, if not enthusiasm, at least some understanding.

Cormac laid back on the bed, reaching for Max's hand. Max gave it, but stayed sitting up. "We didn't get much sleep last night," Cormac reflected. "Want a nap?"

"That wouldn't go amiss," Max said. He eased down to the bed, and Cormac took him into his arms.

They laid there quietly for a moment, and Cormac asked, "Are you upset?"

"No."

"Are you sure?"

"Perhaps a little chagrined."

"I don't know that one."

"A little embarrassed, a little hurt."

Cormac firmed his hold on Max. "Oh, Max—it's nothing about you."

He closed his eyes. "Forgive me, dearest, but it doesn't seem that way."

"I just need time to put all my thoughts together. They're not as fast as yours."

"It's all right. It's time for a rest anyhow."

Cormac set his head on Max's chest and let go of a tense breath. "I love you, Max."

"I love you too."

Max grimaced. Was there some sort of rule that numbers two and three had to follow one another in some capacity? The tonic helped, but changing from a seven foot tall person to a barely five foot one was bound to be uncomfortable, and it was. Cormac drowsily lifted his head at the sound of movement and shook himself awake quickly to put a hand to Max's back, patting gently in a consolation attempt. When Max was able to breathe out again, Cormac turned to his side and rested his head on a propped up hand. "Doing okay?"

Max swallowed and nodded, unsure of his form yet. He wrung out his shoulder with a hand and sat up slowly, getting reacquainted with his senses at a lower elevation. He put his hand to his head out of habit and found he did have a headache today after all. The low grade tension of pointedly avoiding talking about a welcoming along with worrying about his mother fomented in his skull. "I don't think I'm getting back to sleep today," he said. "Don't let me keep you."

"You're sure?" Cormac asked, searching Max for something.

There was an unspoken tension hanging in the air that had only been growing since yesterday afternoon, and Max didn't exactly know how to broach it. The problem had been his forwardness, as it usually was, so he hesitated to puncture the silence. At the same time, he couldn't quite bring himself to apologize for wanting Cormac to hold an official place in his life. His title hadn't been a surprise for some time now; surely Cormac had suspected *something* was coming.

He managed a smile and leaned over to kiss Cormac's cheek. "Go on. Rest."

Cormac nodded slowly, but didn't lower himself back to the bed until Max had finished dressing and came back to kiss him one more time. "You'll be cold," Cormac said, straightening Max's blue scarf.

"Never did manage those coats," he acknowledged with a sigh. "That's all right. I have an idea."

"All right," Cormac said, settling back against the pillows. "Just be safe."

Max laughed a little gently. "What do you think is going to happen in full view of the guards?"

Cormac closed his eyes and smiled lopsidedly. "I know you," he said. "You're not going to walk in full view of the guards."

Max had to admit he was right. "It'll be all right," he promised.

His first stop was a few doors down to beg something warm from Flora, who was delighted to find that her clothes were just slightly too big for number two. "I've never been bigger than anybody!" she crowed.

Max tugged her blue wool coat around himself, shoving the sleeves up a little higher so they didn't engulf his hands. "Thank you. This is much better than tripping on number one's coat."

Flora tilted her head. "What're you up to?"

"Nothing nefarious. Just going to clear my head."

"Do you want me to come with?"

He considered. Once he'd told Cormac he wasn't good at being alone, and at the time, it had been true, but he'd come to appreciate the experience of solitude in the hours he hadn't spent working the Goat. "Thank you, but I'll be all right," he said. "Think I'll head to the park. Could you do me one more favor?"

"Sure," she said, looking at him curiously. "Not like you to ask for so much."

He laughed a little ruefully. "Maybe I'm learning. Can you keep Cormac company when he wakes up? Make sure he's not eating breakfast alone."

Flora nodded slowly. "Everything okay, Max?"

If there was anyone he could tell about the push-pull of the feelings vying for his attention, it'd be her. Still, as he looked into her open face, he found that he just couldn't muster the energy. "Just some things on my mind."

Some things weighed heavier and heavier on his mind as he slipped from the palace grounds to the streets of the upper town. The guards noted his scarf and awkwardly bowed their heads to him as he left their protection. He supposed number two's diminutive posture was hardly stately, hardly like the prince they'd known.

That must be why he was a bit fond of her. She held everything that didn't feel princely about him and kept it safe. As he walked past a few uncomprehending early risers in the cobbled streets, they looked a little curiously at him. Like Clockbridge, Saltrush was home to very few underkin, but here the glances felt benign.

Max made it to the park at the center of the upper town with no more recognition than a few friendly "good mornings" exchanged.

He'd been here many times, under the eyes of governesses or guards. He and Flora had played under the boughs of the great tree at the center, barren now but for drifts of snow. He cleared a bit of snow off of a bench and sat, watching the snowbirds ruffle themselves and chase each other around.

A few times, he attempted to make sense of the tangle of thoughts chasing one another around his head, but every time he grasped at one end of a question it felt like six more followed. After a time he simply closed his eyes and focused on the feel of the weak sun on his sensitive skin.

"Mind if I join you?"

He opened his eyes. Eren, free of the trappings of royalty in a very nice but nondescript coat, stood in front of him. "Father."

"I almost forgot how to find the place," the King chuckled, looking around the park. "It's been some time since you frequented it."

It had been some time since his father left the comforts of his favorite haunts. Like the Queen, he had familiar paths through the halls, and that had been enough for him for years. Max got his words in order. "Does Mother know that—?"

His father's lips twitched. "We've escaped?"

Flustered, Max gestured to the empty park around them. "Usually there are more guards."

"She does tend to insist on those," he said, bobbing his head. "May I sit?" It was a perfunctory question. He was the King. Still, he waited for Max's answer, which he finally managed with a nod. Eren eased to the bench and considered the surroundings for a bit. "Still. There is a reason for them."

Max knew. He'd felt the pressure, the prohibition of his leaving this morning. His mother wouldn't be pleased he'd gone into town looking the way he did without so much as a friend to watch his back. "I just needed space."

His father leaned forward ever so slightly, a smile beginning. "I know. You've not changed so much I can't see it."

Max let go of a weak laugh. "I haven't changed at all." Eren simply lifted his eyebrows and let Max sit with that for a minute, the way he used to when he told tall tales. Quickly, he said, "I mean, I *have*, but that's all outside."

Eren wrapped his hands around a knee and looked down. "Is it?"

"Of course. You don't think magic can fully rewrite someone, do you?"

"No, but experience may."

Max turned his head to face his father. "What frightens you?"

"Oh, Max, I'm not frightened. Just seeking to understand."

That was his way. Ever a student. Max appreciated that approach more than people who decided they knew everything. He supposed what sat next to the King was not what he'd presented to his parents when he'd first arrived. It wasn't what he'd expected, either. "I'm still me," he told him earnestly, "just learning." Some of the strangeness pressing at his head eased, and he blinked. Was that it? Had he decided he knew everything, and was reality reminding him that he didn't?

Eren observed him for a length, then asked, "What have you learned?"

Max wet his lips, drying in the cold. "That there is much more to me than I knew. Than I was allowed to know." Quickly, he said, "I'm not blaming you. Or even Mother. It's simply what was expected of me. I was meant to perform a certain way, and once I started pushing back at it, it sort of all fell apart."

"Which way were you meant to perform?"

"A prince. With everything that implies. I was never...never going to be a stoic man, seated next to a wife, making calculated decisions from atop the country. And the more I *tried* to be, the more it chafed. Then I was rather forced to be something else, and I realized it fits much better, whatever it is, even if there isn't a word for it, even if there's no neat box it goes in."

Eren thought a moment, tucking his chin to his chest and folding his arms. "But that isn't entirely true, either, is it? You took to your mother's teachings even as you found places they rubbed wrong. You took to the people. You took to the ideals. You may not be what we imagined a prince ought, but you are every bit what one truly should be."

Max looked at him, startled. "You—think that's possible? Being whatever I am?"

The King put his hand on Max's shoulder. "Not only do I think it possible, I believe it necessary. For your heart, and the heart of the kingdom. You can be many things. Only one of those is prince, with only what it need entail."

Max sat for a moment, turning it all over in his head. "Even if I don't really know what I am?"

"Do any of us?" Eren asked shrewdly. "Perhaps I have the comfort of surety in my masculinity, but am I the same man I was at your age? Do I know whom I will become?"

Max laughed, a little damp-eyed. "Leave it to you to turn it philosophical."

"Ahh. You don't need help with that, do you?" His smile softened, and he jostled Max's shoulder again. "You don't need help at all. You'll get there in your time. You always have."

Max's headache ebbed a little, and he turned abruptly to his father and put his arms around him. Surprised, Eren paused, then enfolded Max in a hug and let him hold on as long as he needed. For the first time, Max felt like perhaps he might actually get there.

In his time.

Chapter Seventeen
Logical Flaws

Max and his father returned to the palace a few pastries richer for it. Eren's anonymity held until it was time to return home. He hid a grimace and gamely waved to a slowly gathering crowd, hustling Max along so that he was mostly blocked from view. It had been a long time since that was necessary, and when they arrived safely on the other side of the guards' checkpoint, they looked at each other and laughed. "I'm sorry, Max. I don't mean to imply your current height makes you a child again."

"No, I'm simply impressed that worked," he said, swiping a bit of his long white hair out of his face. "Though, if Mother gets word—"

"It was all my idea." He brushed a bit of snow from the sleeve of his coat, then glanced up, his mouth quirking up. "I do believe you *have* caught someone's eye after all."

Max felt his pulse quicken, but relief set in as he realized his father was referring to the burly grayish figure and the slight wisp of an elf hustling across the courtyard towards them. Then his heartbeat picked up again as he remembered he and Cormac still had yet to straighten things out.

"Quick," Max said, "how do you handle when prince stuff gets in the way of relationships?"

Eren chuckled and jostled Max's shoulder affectionately. "*That* you will have to learn on your own, my dear. Good luck."

He started away, and Max lagged after him feebly, but took a breath and reminded himself that he'd just sorted through something much more nebulous than what he had to with Cormac. Flora stopped and looked up at Cormac, beaming and patting his forearm before waving to Max and heading toward her room. Cormac, too, took a large breath, betrayed by the cold air. He turned toward Max and jogged to meet him in the colonnades.

"Hi," he said, stopping short of Max.

Max smiled in spite of everything. Cormac looked nervous, but he recognized the spark in his eyes underlying it. It was the same way he'd looked at him across the Gray Goat, from next to him in bed, before he grinned and grasped him around the waist, no matter where it was that day. Something anxious in Max eased. "Hello."

He gestured in Eren's direction. "Sorry. We told him where you went. Hope that's okay."

Max brushed that irritating stray strand away again. He'd really only learned to pull his long-haired forms' hair back, and sometimes it came loose. "It was...good. Odd, but good. Besides, I sent you Flora, so I can hardly complain."

Cormac nodded, swinging his arms. "She, uh—gives a mean

pep talk. And by that I mean sort of threatening? But nice."

He laughed. "That's her specialty. I hope you know I didn't ask her to."

"No. It was good, too. Got some thoughts out. They get stuck sometimes."

Max nodded and wandered to the stone railing, holding onto it and stepping up onto the base the way he had as a child. Number two's height wasn't all awkward jokes and Flora's triumph. Cormac came to stand next to him, leaning his arms on the railing and looking quietly at the birds in the courtyard. At last, he said, "Max, I'm sorry. I didn't want to embarrass or hurt you. I just wasn't sure I was ready to consider...." He made a sweeping gesture encompassing the palace and the town. "*All of this* as part of our relationship."

"It's already there, Cormac," Max said with a skewed smile. "Whether we like it or not."

Nervously, he said, "It sounds like a big thing."

"You said that before. What's a big thing?" More of his hair fell loose, and he swatted irritably at it. "Damn."

Cormac left the rail and took up Max's hair, pulling the tie loose and dividing it into strands. Max had watched Flora braiding her own hair, but it had always seemed like magic to him. Cormac's hands were gentle as he worked. He answered, "You know, like life events. Like...marriage."

"No, it's not that," Max said. "It's just a chance for the people to get to know you as the prince's consort. If something happens between you and I, that's it. No commitments thereafter." He stayed quiet for a moment. "But I don't want us to end."

Cormac tied off the bottom of the braid and tucked it up into itself. "Neither do I. Even with all of this involved. It's just a step I didn't know if I was ready for. *Being known.* But I think, if you're with me, I can do it."

Max smiled and turned to face him, taking up his hand and kissing it. "Of course I'll be with you. As long as you want me."

Cormac flushed a little. "Thing is, I was thinking, like, forever."

Max tried to keep it off his face, but the thought took him off balance. Was it bad? No, not all reeling was bad. In fact, the more he thought, the warmer his cold skin felt. Still, he felt compelled to remind him, "Now *that* is a big thing."

"I know. I know. And it should scare me, shouldn't it? But it doesn't."

Max looked at him. "You know that would involve many more official…things. You would be King someday."

He looked a little queasy. "That is scary. But I figure they're not just going to bung a crown on my head and toss me in, right? They'll tell me what to do."

"Oh, so much telling you what to do."

"And I won't be *the* King. That's still you."

"Yes."

"If you're with me, I could try. I'd look damned foolish. But for you? I'd try."

Max finally crossed the last few inches between them. His face only came up to Cormac's chest, and Cormac laughed a little fondly and lifted him to the railing. He put his arms around Cormac's neck. "You're sure."

"This is all future stuff, isn't it?"

"Well, yes. Any engagement we have will be long by necessity. But I mean—this is what you want?"

He laughed nervously. "As long as everyone can live with me."

"It won't be easy," Max warned. "You've seen how they treat anything different."

Cormac ran his thumb along the edge of Max's cheek. "Maybe we try to change that."

Queen Anora began party planning at once. She summoned Cormac, and Max attended, and they were able to have perfectly benign conversations. Perhaps Aubric had no interest in social events.

On the day Davitt Molas arrived, Max put on number one in the morning. For whatever reason, he felt like he should be more official when greeting him, and he also felt that he should show him his handiwork working.

Ordinarily, Max would introduce his guests to the Queen, but the last thing he wanted to do was let Aubric know that he'd summoned an expert wizard. He did have Cormac, Flora, and his father gather in one of the studies off of the archive as he went himself to wait for Molas in the front of the castle.

Molas cut an imposing figure in the snow, dark-robed and not at all whimsical. He muttered to himself as he kept adjusting his glasses after slipping in the snow. Max hurried to offer an arm.

"Oh, thank you," Molas said, taking out Max's letter. "I wonder if you can help me. I'm looking for Prince Maximillian."

"And you've found him."

"Oh, wonderful," he rumbled. "I must confess, Your Highness, I was most puzzled by your letter. I am not well known, and I like to keep it that way."

"I understand." Max helped him along to the steps, where Molas shook the snow from his hooves and his staff. "I'll be plain. I was the underkin woman you helped some weeks ago with the tonic and the crystal."

He pushed up his spectacles and peered through them. "Oh! So you are. Both are treating you well?"

"Very, for the most part."

"For the most part?"

"Shortly after I saw you, the Guild learned that I'd taken something and turned off the tonic, essentially."

Molas frowned deeply. "Soulless bastards. Let me guess. It 'contaminated their control'."

"You are right."

"And when you resumed taking it, everything returned to as it should be?"

"Yes." Max ushered him in a side door, keeping his head on a swivel for any of Aubric's laboratory assistants or mage guards. Molas looked around appreciatively, but not in awe. Max didn't doubt that this wasn't his first castle. "Now I've asked you here for help with an even more sensitive matter."

"Even more? I am unsure I like the sound of that."

"I do not blame you, sir, not one bit. If you'll follow me through here."

They stood in the Archive. Molas stopped to look at the shelves of books built into the stone walls. "I will, on one condition."

"I will escort you back to look at these when we're done."

He chuckled. "Never could resist."

"You'll like to meet my father. In here."

He entered the study as though entering a hall of worship, quiet, respectful. Flora jumped off the table as he walked in, and King Eren looked up from a book. Cormac stepped forward to shake his hand. "This face I remember," Molas said. "You, um… may not wish to come home for a while."

"Figured as much," sighed Cormac.

Max led him to Flora. "This is Lady Flora Nythera, a good friend and a researcher in her own right. And this is my father, King Eren."

Molas made a creaky bow to both. "Whose study is this? It is a well-curated room."

"No one's," Eren said. "And everyone's. It's attached to the archives so anyone may use it. But thank you kindly! I spent many a day putting together this collection."

"Ah! Well done, sire. And a generous idea, to share the knowledge."

"I—" He took a look at Max's bemused expression and amended, "will talk about this later. I think Max had something he wanted to talk with us about."

"Yes," Max said. "Everyone, this is Master Davitt Molas, an alchemist and wizard from Clockbridge."

"And surgeon," Molas said with a chuckle. "When you get this old, you collect a few specialties."

"Impressive," Eren said, eyebrows raised.

Max explained, "Master Molas helped me rein in my curse. Now I'm hoping I can call on you for a threat. My mother, the Queen, has a favored wizard. It seems he is giving her some sort of draught that I believe is opening her up to his control."

"A grave accusation," Molas said. "I presume you have more evidence than that?"

"It is very difficult to get. He seems to be monitoring her as she speaks. She is acting out of character and seems to be surprised by it herself. She's forgetting conclusions she's come to in the past. The wizard was not able to name the condition he claims to be treating."

Molas stroked his chin. "You know your mother—and you know your wife," he said, indicating Max's father, "far better than an interloper come to meddle. If you say that she is behaving strangely, I believe you. The bad news is that there is very little magically I can do to disrupt this."

Max sagged, and Eren ran his hand along his jaw. "There's nothing to be done?"

"I didn't say that," he said gently. "Doubtless, you both have been speaking to her, and you know that she is defensive of her truth. It is critical that you talk her into seeing what is real. Do not try to tear down her reality; instead point out the inconsistencies and let her follow them to where they lead. Whatever you do, do not accuse the wizard directly. He may have some sort of fail-safe in place."

"And through this she can become free?"

"The only way she will become truly free is if she stops taking the draught. But this is a good way to get her to a place where taking it no longer seems a good idea. How much of her reality seems to be distorted?"

"It seems…variable," Max said. "Some days I doubted myself when speaking to her, and other days it seems as though the whole of her has been replaced."

"That's what I feared. It seems this wizard is a talented one."

"He is."

"He is likely only manipulating what he needs to get his desired outcome. What *is* the desired outcome?"

"He wants to experiment on Max," Cormac said, his arms folded.

"We don't know that that's all of it," Max said. "There was something about sending me away that seemed important."

"It's a big chunk of it. He kidnapped Flora to try to get his hands on you."

"He did what?" Eren said in disbelief.

"I'm okay," she replied cheerily.

Max persisted, "But I don't think that's the end goal. Imagine having de facto control of the queen of a mid-sized nation and only using it to get at her son?"

"The more ridiculous the request seems, the more likely the

target is to question it," Molas said, drumming his fingers on his staff. "That's why he is moving slowly, rewriting reality a bit at a time, for gods know how long. In response, *you* must move slowly, counter his points. Or rather, help her do it."

"How are we supposed to do that if he's spying?"

Molas sighed heavily. "What I wouldn't give for a few hanthis toads. They create a humming sound too high-pitched to be heard that disrupts scrying vibrations."

Flora's head snapped up. "How many do you need?"

He shook his head sadly. "They're quite rare in these parts and unlikely to be in season—"

"The hanthis toad secretes a hormone that reads an awful lot like magic. I've been studying them for years now," she said triumphantly. "How many do you need?"

Max grinned.

And that was how Max found himself sneaking a live toad into his mother's chambers in a little glass enclosure the size of a teacup. He had to come back every so often and sneakily feed it, but it was good. It was an excuse to have conversations with her and push back at what was ringing around in her head. Sometimes he brought Cormac and they talked about the coming welcoming party, and sometimes he came alone and tried disabusing her of heavier notions.

"I don't know if it's working," he told his father in a despairing sort of whisper. His father kept watch at the door while he unloaded Flora's dried insects into the toad's cage, a *tad* more difficult with number four's river fey fingers.

"Don't say that, lad."

"She's not interrogating her thoughts at all. Even if she notices I'm right, she doesn't follow it to the next step. In fact, sometimes she just doubles down. I think she thinks I'm arguing just to argue."

"Don't give up on her," he urged. "She can think, she can change. She's been doing it, even while someone else is in her head."

"I'm going to tell her today."

"That's kind of a big one to drop in her lap."

"Well? Does she want me to be the kind of son who tells her everything or not?"

Eren conceded with a small shrug. "Just…meet her where she is, all right?"

"Where is that? Not sure if she hates her son or not?"

"Max. She doesn't hate you."

"She sure doesn't seem to appreciate my interest in men."

"She understands it's part of you, and she loves you. She hasn't always shown it in the way you need to see it. But she's trying."

"And how much of that is him? When we break her of it, will we go back to barely tolerating each other's presence, or—?"

Footsteps down the hall, and his father made a break for the side door. Max hastily stuffed the toad back under the sofa and sat down. His father gave him an encouraging smile and darted down the hallway. The door opened behind Max, and in walked his mother. "Maximillian," she said. "You startled me."

"Sorry, sorry," he said, nudging the toad further under the sofa with his foot. "I thought we might talk."

She came into the room the rest of the way, Aubric at her elbow. Max felt panic rise in his throat, but he stayed still on the sofa. "Aubric, we will speak another time," she said.

He bowed, his eyes narrowed on Max as if to ask what he was doing. Max just folded his hands over his knee and waited. At long last, Aubric left, the door swinging shut magically behind him. The Queen strode to the sofa across from Max. "Is everything all right, dear?"

"Yes," he said, though his heart was hammering in his chest. He needed this to go well. For himself, for Cormac, for whatever relationship he would have with his mother in the years to come. She sat down and waved a hand to invite him to speak. If only finding the words were so easy. He cleared his throat and decided just to go for it. "Mother…I've decided to ask Cormac to marry me."

He didn't know what he expected. Alarm? Dismay? Disappointment? Instead, she sat forward with her hands folded primly. "Are you prepared for what that means?"

"What—? What do you mean?"

"You will be inviting speculation on a nationwide scale. Until now, we've contained it to the streets of the town. Everyone will have something to say, whether they agree or disagree."

"Agree?" he said weakly. "How can someone agree or not with love?"

"Oh, people will agree or disagree with just about everything. Are you prepared for that scrutiny?"

Max pressed out a breath. "The people have long been able to marry who they'd like. It's time the nobility followed suit."

"That is what we will argue, yes. But is your heart prepared to withstand the arguments?"

"'We'?" he asked, eyebrow raised.

"You don't think I would leave you to the wolves, my dear?"

"Honestly?"

Anora pressed her palms together. "If your heart is set, it's set."

"Do *you* disagree?" he asked, tilting his head down.

She turned to the table behind the sofa. "I knew this was coming," she said, picking up a small box. She extended it to him across the gap between the couches. He opened the box. A silver wreath of leaves, like his crown, but made so tiny. "Typically worn by a prince-to-be during an engagement. Your father wore it, and your grandfather, and so on. If you would put it on his finger, then a prince you will make of him."

Max's eyes stung. Gods, he hoped this was her and not Aubric. "Thank you, Mother."

"And are you—?" She flinched. "Are you sure he will have you?"

"Whatdo you mean?"

"It was one thing when you were controlling your curse." She gestured to him, in number four's body today. "Now you've let it run amok. Does he approve?"

"Yes," Max said earnestly. "He loves me. Not my face. Not what I wear, let alone my throne."

For the first time, Anora smiled genuinely, a rare and often-sought thing. "Good."

Max peered across at her. "Do you remember—? We talked about this. I'm happy changing faces most of the time."

She paused, thought. "I suppose we did. I didn't understand."

"Do you now?"

"You're trapped in the palace until you become yourself again."

"I am myself now, Mother."

She corrected herself, "Until you become more recognizable to the public."

"Yes. I'd like to change that someday, but until you feel more comfortable…"

"It's not me, darling, it's the Assassin's League."

She was so certain of that. "Why does this affect their mission? If anything, I'd think it would make it harder."

"I—" She paused. "That is why I had to send you away."

"Was there a specific threat?"

"There are always threats."

"But were any communicated then?" he persisted.

"Aubric told me…." She paused, thought hard, as though trying to access something beyond a barrier. "Aubric. He was the one who suggested I send you out." Her eyebrows lowered. "Why would he do that? Why would *I*…?"

Max tried to contain his excitement. Now they were getting

somewhere. "Mother, for me, please don't tell him that you remembered that, all right? Let's keep it between the pair of us."

She put her hand to her forehead. "My poor dear. You must have thought…how could I have sent you away?"

"It's—it's all right, Mother. It was a good thing, in the end."

"I'm so sorry, Maximillian. I don't know what I was thinking."

Someone had been thinking for her, and that was the problem. And they were getting closer to breaking the lies down.

It was about then that the rumors started. Max was generally disinterested in the gossip of the upper town, but Flora came to him, upset. "Max! I'm so sorry."

"Everyone's apologizing these days," he said, bemused. "What is it, dear?"

"People are talking about you sequestering yourself. They're saying all sorts of things, that you've been injured, that you're sick, something. Some people are even saying it's a curse. They've noticed that you only come out some of the time."

He sighed. "I suppose it was inevitable. I'll have to take a couple of number one days in a row to try to stop those tongues wagging. But why are you sorry?"

"Because the only one who could *accurately* say anything is my mother. She swears it wasn't her, but how would you get cursed from 'hiding himself' unless you knew?"

He considered. "Flora, people talk. And wildly. I wouldn't be surprised if somebody guessed it right by accident."

"I guess. Hmm."

"Do you have reason to think it was your mother?"

"No! Aside from the fact that she never could keep a secret to save her life."

"Let's give her the benefit of the doubt." He clasped her shoulder. "Besides, it'll be good for me to get out."

Max, Cormac, and Flora took to the town, where Max was approached by a number of people asking if he was well. He gently laughed off the questions and introduced Cormac, who was at first shy and overcautious, but as the interactions rolled on, he loosened up. Max stepped back and watched fondly as he and a local publican talked shop.

Flora said, "He's doing really well!"

"I know," Max said. "Turns out the fellow whose job was 'talking' to people actually likes talking to people."

"Go figure."

Max leaned an arm on Flora's shoulder. "I'm thinking of asking him to marry me," he said, careful to keep his voice low.

She made a high pitched noise that he cut off immediately for fear of alerting Cormac. She calmed herself down and clasped his hand. "Max, that's—I'm so happy for you!"

"You think it's a good idea?" he asked shyly.

"I think you both love each other a lot."

"We do." He looked back in Cormac's direction and felt the fondness wash him over again as it did any time Max looked his way and spotted him in his element. "But with the Guild being involved and my inheritance and all the complications…will that be enough?"

"I'm afraid only time will tell," she told him. "But that's true of anyone."

"I just…I see him, and I *know*. I *could* wait. We *could* dawdle along the socially acceptable timing train tracks."

"Socially acceptable for whom?" Flora asked skeptically. "Because you were fully expected to marry girls you'd known for a week."

"That is true. I suppose by my parents' metric I've really taken my time. I just don't want to frighten him."

"Haven't you talked about it?"

"Briefly."

"And what does he want?"

"Me."

"Aww."

"And he knows I come with marriage and children and a crown." He watched Cormac shake the man's hand and greet another woman nearby. "He's willing to learn. He's doing it now."

"That's wonderful, Max."

"But what if we become my parents? If we marry because we feel we have to?"

"You're not," she said. "Right? You're marrying him because you want to spend your life with him."

"Yes," he said, smiling. "Because the idea of a future without him is no future at all."

"And as far as people to become, you could do worse than

your parents. Mine fight like cats and dogs when they think I'm not listening."

"Mother just has the last word on everything, so there's little point."

"I think they like each other, at least."

He nodded. "Still, I don't think I could take that blandness, day in and day out."

"You won't have to. What does your mother think of it?"

"She gave me a ring." She started, and he said, "I've already checked it for magic, don't worry."

"Okay, good, because the last thing we need is Aubric screwing up your engagement."

"Just a very old very benign enchantment that allows the ring to adjust size based on the wearer."

"Clever."

"A good thing to put on an heirloom."

"When do you think you'll do it?" she asked.

He hesitated. "The part of me that is terrified wants to say never and then go hide in my bedroom. The part that's more rational is thinking of taking him to dinner sometime soon."

"Oh, oh, I know a place," she said. "My parents used to go there all the time. It's very discreet, very pretty. Over on the waterfront. I can make you a reservation!"

"That would be great."

"And then you can announce on the day of the party!"

"Announce what?" Cormac asked.

"Um—my research project is paused," she said quickly. "I'm

staying here for a while. Ta-da!"

"I'm sorry," he said in a confused sort of sympathy. "That's upsetting, after all you worked for and all those times you had to start over."

"You know, it's okay. Max has me thinking. Maybe it's time for me to be looking at my responsibilities."

"Are they mutually exclusive?" Max asked.

"Well, no, but I do need to figure out how to do them both."

"Good," Max said. "The world needs your strangely specific toad research."

She beamed. "When they get back from their missions. I'm so pleased they're helping."

Cormac folded his arms. "Still, that's kind of a downer, Flora. I don't know if you want to announce that at the party."

"Oh, Max's mother will be thrilled," she said hastily. "She likes having me around. Something about being a steadying influence for her son?"

Max made a bit of a face. "Honestly, she *would* be all too thrilled. But Cormac's right. Maybe we tell her another time."

"Okay, okay, you're right." She gave Max a little smile. "Just let me know when you want me to make arrangements."

"Yeah," he said, nerves jumping at his core. "I will."

It was a week and a half later that he finally worked up the nerve. His family didn't dine out due to the utter mess that it could become, with the Queen in demand to answer questions or explain her decisions or kiss babies, not to mention the guard protocols. But Max wasn't his mother, and Flora promised that The Spotted Tern offered privacy as well as good food, so Max tucked the ring in his pocket and screwed his courage up.

Cormac chatted lightly on the way there, pointing out people he'd met or shops he'd been meaning to visit. Max kept surreptitiously reaching for his pocket. So many times on the way over he wanted to just take the ring out right then, just stop him walking and tell him what this was all about. He'd never been good at surprises. But he'd look over at Cormac and find himself struck silent with admiration all over again and could only walk on, determined to wait for the perfect moment.

Cormac stopped him outside of the restaurant. "Hey. You all right? You've been quiet."

"Yes. Just, you ever want to tell someone something, but when you look at them, you forget what words are?"

"No," he laughed.

"No, you're right, you're confident."

"*I'm* confident," he said with a chuckle. "Hello, Your Highness."

"Yes, yes, there's that. I was trained into it, though. You just have it."

Cormac took his hand. "I learned it, too. My teachers were just a hells of a lot meaner. Something you want to say to me?"

"I just…I love you," he said, a rush of laughter coming out.

Cormac grinned and set his forehead to Max's. "I love you too. What's so funny about that?"

"Nothing at all. I think I'm laughing at myself."

"Not the easiest thing in the world to do."

"You make it a lot more fun."

Cormac kissed him and cradled the back of his head in his hand for a moment. "Shall we go in?"

Max found the moment slipping away from him fast, but there would be more. Inside, there would be more. So he agreed.

Their table was a lovely little booth curtained off from the rest of the restaurant at large, next to two great windows that faced out on the water. Cormac commented many times on the changing colors of the mountain faces as the sun went down. Max watched his delight with delight of his own. Cormac caught him and smiled. "What?"

"You've made these old sights new again."

"How could you ever tire of this?"

"Until now, I didn't know," he said. "I just—I got dragged into the day to day shuffle, and it got lost. Now I get to see it again with you, and it's all the better for it."

Cormac took his hand across the table. He looked about to speak when he sat up straight, eyes focused on the small gap in the curtain. Max leaned over to look and froze at what he saw. In walked Aubric, escorting a guest. At first he couldn't see it clearly, just that it was a long elven man. When he turned, Max felt his insides turn to ice.

The Guild Director.

Cormac leaned his head down and spoke quietly. "We have to get you out of here."

"How? They're standing right there—" They began walking into the restaurant proper, and Max's throat clenched. He waited for the curtain to be yanked aside, but instead, a server led them past to a table nearby. Max heard them start to order their wine.

Cormac let out a breath. "Now," he said.

Max left a bag of coin on the table for their partially-eaten dinners, and Cormac hurried him out of the booth. They rushed for the door, only to be stopped by a server. "Is everything all right, sire?"

"E-everything was lovely," he said. "We just, er—we need to go. But thank you. Truly. Lovely."

Cormac patted him on the shoulders and gently moved him out of the way, and followed Max into the night.

They didn't speak for the entire tense walk back, Cormac periodically peeking over his shoulder to check that they weren't being followed. At long last with nearly held breaths, they made it into the castle and back to Max's room.

"You all right?" Cormac asked.

"No," Max said. "Not even here is safe. If Aubric can just make my mother hand me over, I'm as good as—"

Cormac brought Max into his arms. "He can't. He can't make that seem reasonable. And I will not let him."

Max's face sank into Cormac's shoulder, and he let himself cry.

Chapter Eighteen
Machinations

Max paced outside the throne room, his father and Cormac both close at hand. Eren frowned deeply. "You signed a *contract?*"

"It seemed the safest way to engage with the Guild," Max said, folding his arms to his chest. "I read it, reread it…it seemed sound."

"I don't think the Director has intentions of honoring it," Cormac said, glancing at the large doors.

"If that's the case, we have legal recourse," Eren said.

"After the harm is already done," Max interjected. "The contract was supposed to be a way of *dissuading* harm. That's failed."

"I wouldn't say it's completely failed," his father mused. "He had to come here himself."

"After his assassins failed."

The doors opened, and the guard said, "The Queen will see you now."

Max took a breath. His father put his hand to his shoulder. "We'll be here on the other side. Good luck, son."

Max nodded once and headed into the throne room, where Aubric and the Director stood to one side. Max stepped in toward the center of the dais and bowed to his mother, who smiled at him. "My son, Maximillian," she explained to the Director.

"We've met," Max said, barely disguising his distaste.

"Oh," she said in some surprise. "I knew you spent some time in Clockbridge, but I hadn't realized that you had become acquainted."

"I'll be brief," Max said. "The Director ordered an experiment on me against written authorization and failed to respect the contractually obligated end of that experiment, sending agents after my partner, Lady Nythera, and me both in Clockbridge and here on our own soil."

The Director spoke up. "I'm terribly sorry, Your Highness. There's been a grave misunderstanding. Any contract composed without the seal of an Auditor of the Guild is invalid."

"Oh, is that the rule you just made up?"

"*Maximillian*," his mother said sharply. "You will keep your head level."

"Apologies, Your Majesty," he said.

"There is the matter of the incursion," she told the Director.

"Another dire misunderstanding," he said, bowing. "I'm afraid some of our enforcers may have gotten ahead of themselves."

"You name them the instigators?"

"I do. Yet I am here to negotiate for the terms of our reparations and their hopeful release."

She considered deeply. "I do not like to hear that you have performed any sort of experimentation on my son, but as it appears," she said, fixing Max with a look, "that undertaking was done in error, I will look past it. For now. However, we will need to discuss further the attacks perpetrated against the prince and citizens of Saltrush. To that end, you may stay."

"Thank you, Your Majesty," the Director oozed.

The Queen continued, "Join us for dinner this evening. We will discuss further. Maximillian, won't you and your partner join us as well?"

Max felt like his soul was draining out of his body. This was not something he could say no to. "Yes, of course."

"Good. Now, Aubric, if you could show Director Fein to accommodations, I would be grateful."

"Majesty." Aubric bowed. "Come, let me show you to your room."

The Queen said, "Maximillian. Come here."

As he'd done so often, Max went to the dais and sat down. This time, though, he didn't just silently boil in his resentment. It out. The second the doors shut behind Aubric, he turned to his mother. "Can there never be a moment where you're just my mother?"

Taken aback, she said, "What?"

"I have to come in here and beg you to keep the man who abused me and tried to kill the people I love out of your kingdom. And you don't."

Tenderly, she reached forward and stroked his hair. "Maximillian. I understand your disappointment—"

"Disappointment!" He laughed bitterly. "Disappointment is when we have a disagreement. Right now I am utterly defeated."

"You will understand when it is your time to sit here."

"No, I won't," he said, standing. "I won't repeat your mistakes."

"Maximillian—"

"It's just Max," he snapped, and he stalked from the room.

He sagged against the door and breathed hard. Hopefully, the King asked, "How did it go?"

Max just shook his head.

Cormac took his hand. "Let's go for a walk."

He nodded, leaving the grand foyer with Cormac. Cormac let him brood in silence for a while until they reached the central courtyard, where the grand fountain stood frozen by winter. Max paced in front of it.

"She makes me feel so small," he fumed. "I'm old enough to marry, but young enough to still be lectured like a child. Old enough to learn her craft, but so young that I must be reined in. And honestly, being treated like this drives me back into behaviors I left behind with everyone else. Including my father. I do not like who I am with her when she is like this."

Cormac let him ramble, keeping him from stepping into the deep snow. At length, he stopped him, put his hand to his face. "Have you ever told her this?"

Max scoffed. "As if she would hear me. As if she even *can* right now."

"I think she is listening, Max. Or trying to."

"Weren't you the one who said you didn't like her?"

Cormac lifted his shoulders. "I said that before I saw her. Now I think she's flawed. Maybe deeply. But not irreconcilably."

Max kicked at a chunk of ice. "There's a five gold word."

"Thank you. All I'm saying is I wish—I wish I had felt a fraction of the warmth she feels for you from mine. It's clear she cares for you."

"But is it enough? Is it enough to care if she doesn't try to meet me anywhere I am?"

"I don't know," he said honestly. "That's for you to decide."

Max nodded, slowly breathing out a hot puff of steam. "I'll… get there eventually. For now, I have to separate what's Aubric from her."

Cormac nodded, then looked out across the way. "Someone's running towards us."

Max stepped around the side of the fountain. "It's Flora."

Flora finally made it across the wide courtyard, breathing out hard. Her eyes wide, she asked, "What—is—the Director—doing here?"

"A personal guest of my least favorite person," Max sighed. "Did you run into him?"

"Run into him? They put him right next to me in the guest chambers."

Max's fist clenched. Of course he did. "I'm sorry, Flora. I can have you moved."

"No, it's okay—actually, yes, please do. But what are we going to do?"

Max wished he knew.

This dinner was not in the Rose Garden, where the Queen most liked to sit with her family. It was in the formal dining room, which Max disliked. High, straight-backed chairs marked every place around a large, burnished oak table, and depending on how many guests there were, sometimes a person might have to shout to be heard across the echoing distance. Today they were all grouped at the end, Anora presiding over the head of the table; Max, Cormac, and Eren to one side; and Aubric and the Director to the other. Aubric took the seat directly across from Max and pretended not to look at him. Max shot him the occasional glare.

Cormac put his hand to Max's knee under the table and patted it. "Steady," he said under his breath.

Anora was watching, and she wouldn't have any pettiness—just as long as it was her son's. Aubric's went apparently unnoticed. Max knew it was probably whatever hold he had over her, but it still galled him. He wasn't sure if it was pure ex-partner jealousy or if it had to do with Max not handing himself over to be examined, but either way, he was doing a good job of seeming overly attentive to the Queen and his guest.

Eren watched the Director with mild interest. "Tell me, Director. What is your area of expertise?"

"I am a government official. One of the executives."

"I meant your craft. I heard that everyone there must have

one."

"Oh, yes," he said. "I'm an alchemist."

"Fascinating."

"Of course, it's been many years since I've practiced the art. But I wager I still know my way around a kit."

And he was here to test that, most likely. "And how do the pair of you know each other?" Max asked suspiciously.

"Oh, we're old schoolmates. Didn't Aubric tell you?"

"No," he said flatly. And frankly, if that was true, he questioned how old Aubric actually was. The Director seemed so much older, but it was hard to tell sometimes with elves, especially mages.

"Yes, well, I knew right away when I was informed of the incident that I needed to come personally to make amends."

"Yes, and how are you planning to do that, exactly?"

"Research sharing," he said. "We have a wealth of information in our annals. I know that Saltrush is a studied country; it values knowledge and learning."

Max sat forward. "And you think that makes up for—?"

"Son," his mother said. "There may be some room for discussion."

Max looked immediately at Aubric, who politely dabbed at his mouth with his napkin. No sign that he'd cast anything, but if Max concentrated hard enough, he could hear the faintest hum of ether passing between him and his mother. "And will my data be part of that sharing?"

"No, I'm afraid it's far too valuable." Max waited for him to laugh or some sort, but he stayed completely serious.

Max leaned forward. "I feel you owe me this much. What are you going to use it for?"

"I cannot divulge—"

"You can and you will," Anora said sharply. Max looked at her, surprised. "If you wish to see these talks proceed peaceably."

The Director set down his napkin and held his hands up. "Very well, Your Majesty. I—and others—are interested in replicating portions of your…condition. Consensually, of course."

For the first time, Cormac spoke up. "The way you *consensually* attract your agents?"

The Director squinted at Cormac until realization relaxed his face. "Now I recognize you," he said. "You're the enforcer."

Cormac's face flushed, and he looked to the Queen. So did Max. Her mouth turned down. "Enforcer?"

"I was employed by the Guild for a number of years to intimidate people, yes," he said. "It was ugly work. I'm not proud of it. But it wasn't my choice. I was a scared kid who was told that this was all he could do to take care of himself and his sister. It wasn't until Max came along that I realized I deserved better, too."

"Saltrush also highly prizes recognizance and redemption," Max informed the Director. "Something I don't feel research accomplishes. Especially, let's not overlook—you're trying to *make* cursed people?"

"Surely you've realized by now," the Director said.

"What are you getting at?"

"You aren't cursed. You're enchanted. Whether we call it a

curse or a hex or a benevolent spell—that's all societal. You've been brought up to think of this as a bad thing. It is a boon."

"Not so," Aubric said. "I have said and I maintain that the prince's curse presents a danger."

"My dear fellow, you'll have to convince me. Because I have only seen evidence of a person who can shift forms. With some strain, but all the same."

This was interesting. They didn't agree. But why? Was Aubric lying to keep the Queen around his finger, or was there something underlying?

"I don't *feel* cursed," Max said. "Not with my medicine. I have never felt anything that wasn't…me."

Aubric tented his fingers. "Let me put it this way. There is no way that a curse or enchantment or whatever you want to call it would leave your desires, your feelings, your thoughts untouched. Any amount of transformation implies change. And whether society thinks it's a bad thing or not, the giver intended it to be thus. Therefore, it is my assertion that for your safety and others', it is best you are supervised until you break this curse."

"My safety and others'?" Max retorted. "I have never once done something unsafe for anyone."

"Not yet. But you are a well-trained mage. Skilled with blades. If an impulse turns deadly—why, I would say *when*—"

"You're wrong," Cormac blurted out. Everyone turned to look at him, and he flushed dark gray-purple. "You're all wrong. Max is the gentlest person I have ever met. I have never once, even when he was faced with his deepest fears, seen him turn to violence first. And you." He shot a look at the Director. "You look at him and see opportunity. Max isn't cursed, but not because of the way we look at it. It's what he made of it himself." The room stayed silent. He cleared his throat and he said, "So. You're wrong."

The Queen cut in gently and said, "The matter of Maximillian—Max—being accompanied is settled." Max looked at her abruptly, and she continued, "He has Cormac. Would you tell us, if you felt his weal was affected?"

"Of—of course, Your Majesty."

Aubric started to speak, but she put her hand up. "Your opinion is well noted, Master Aubric. As for you, Director—I will not look kindly on your using my son's condition to *augment* other people. You may consider any trade between Saltrush and Clockbridge ceased should I catch wind of it."

He looked at Aubric, shocked, then stammered, "A-as you wish, Your Majesty."

"We can speak privately on your prisoner situation. Aubric, Cormac, Max, you are dismissed. Eren...."

He bowed his head deferentially. "I'll leave you to handle this one, my dear. Come along, boys. Much to discuss."

They went into the hallway and Max pressed Cormac against the wall and kissed him hard. Eren flushed and looked away. "Oh, my."

"Sorry, Father," Max said, breathless. "I just felt that ought not to go unrewarded."

"You certainly struck them silent," his father agreed, still looking away. "But we should go. Walk me to my chambers."

Max fell in next to his father, still holding Cormac's hand. Cormac looked up guiltily. "About…my work."

"Do you intend to leave it in the past?" the King inquired.

"Gods, yes," he said, then went subdued. "Sorry."

"Then I am happy to leave it in the past. As far as I am concerned, you are very much welcomed and appreciated."

"That—" Cormac's breath caught. "I don't think I've ever been welcome anywhere but once before."

"That wears on a person." Eren clapped him on the shoulder. "No more." He glanced behind them, and once he was convinced no one was following, he said, "Aubric wants those plans. Whatever the Director has cooking, he's desperate for."

"How did you—?"

"Aubric twitched when the Director mentioned it, and when your mother declared they were not to use you, he frowned. Just a little. For a man who has very few tells, that's significant."

Max had thought he felt the ether concentrate in that moment. And she'd still defied him? There was something of her there. "Any idea what he could want with that? I mean, I know you can't know everything, but have you found anything about him?"

"I looked briefly—and gently. All I found was his schooling records."

"That's the second time his schooling has come up, though. Maybe there's something there."

"I can press it. After all, what are spymasters for?"

"Thank you, Father."

"Is that a real thing?" Cormac said.

"A—spymaster?" the King said, puzzled. "Unofficially, of course. Saltrush has no spies." He winked. "Why?"

"Just—hells of a title. Respectfully."

He chuckled before growing serious again. He stopped and took Max by the shoulders. "Whatever he's after, we'll find it. Don't give in."

Max nodded, dropping his head forward. Cormac set his hand to his back and made a comforting circle. Eren squeezed Max's shoulders once. "I'll carry on from here. Think I know the way."

"Father, I really appreciate—"

"I know, son." He smiled. "It's my job." And he set off down the hall.

Max folded his arms and leaned against the wall. He turned to Cormac and began to speak, but a strangled cry down the hall caught his attention. He said, "Call the guards! Something's wrong."

Cormac nodded, and Max dashed down the hall, listening for magic as he went. Something loud swirled in the air, and he couldn't quite place it, but it flowed to and from the direction of the King's chambers. "Father!"

The King lay on the ground, wheezing, clutching his hand to his side. Max dropped to his knee next to him and pulled his hand back. It came away red. His head snapped up as the assassin came back, his knife readied and bloody. Max threw out his hand and brought his ether to bear, blocking it in midair with the left hand while drawing his own blade with his right. He stepped over his father and slashed at the newcomer across the chest, holding the knife to his neck. "Drop it. Drop. It."

The knife clattered to the floor, and the man backed up to the wall. Max went with him, bearing down with the blade. "Who sent you?"

"The—the League," he eked out.

"Give me one reason I shouldn't have done with you right now," he snarled.

The man's head lolled backwards, his eyes rolling. At length, he picked his head back up and blinked. "Where am I?"

"Don't play with me."

"Who—aren't you the prince?!"

Max frowned deeply. "What are you…?"

"There," Cormac shouted, and in rushed six guards and the Queen. Max held the assassin there until the guards took him from him. On a whim, he listened to the magic again. It was still present, hovering around the man's head, but fading, no longer coursing through the hallway.

He could puzzle that through later. "Father." He dropped his knife and returned to his side.

Eren held out his bloodied hand, and Max took it. It was trembling, cold. Max tried to warm it in both of his. "You're going to be all right, Father," he said, his words shaking in his chest.

"The physician, get the physician," the Queen told a guard. "Hurry."

Cormac got to his hands and knees and looked over the wound. He smiled a little gently, pressing a handkerchief firmly into his side. "It's a good one, aye, Your Highness, but Max has the right of it."

The Queen approached warily, as though unsure her presence would help or harm. At length she dropped to the floor in her silk dinner dress, pulling Eren's head off the floor and resting it in her lap. She smoothed back his hair, matted to his forehead with sweat. "Have you—have you seen many wounds like this?" she asked Cormac.

"I have, more than a few," he said. "Talks gone wrong. Taken one myself. But it's important to stop the bleeding as much as we can and keep him till the doctor can have a look."

She bit her lip and nodded. Max kept hold of his father's hand. Eren looked up at him. "My brave son," he wheezed, pride in his face mixed in with pain.

"Don't talk," Max urged him. "Just keep holding my hands."

He tried to firm his grip even as his father's faltered. Cormac looked up as the doctor and two assistants entered with a stretcher loaded the King onto it. Only then did Max let go. He offered his mother a hand up, and she pulled him into a hug. He stiffened at first, uncertain where this was going, but at length, he sagged against her. She swept his hair over his head and kissed his forehead. "Come," she said. "Let's follow."

The doctor worked long into the night, and Max fell asleep against the wall. Once he'd cleaned the blood from his hands,

Cormac scooped him up and carried him back to his bedroom. Max awoke with a jolt just before dawn, considered grasping the stone, and, weary, ultimately let the change wash over him. Cormac held him until a knock sounded at the door. He said, "I'll get it," and tossed on his shirt over the breeches he'd not changed out of last night.

Max heard their voices, muffled by distance, and pulled the pillow over his head. It was news on his father, he was sure, and he wasn't sure he was prepared for it—in either direction. Once Cormac shut the door and made his way back, Max uncovered his head and sat up. It wasn't until now that he realized which form he'd changed into. Number six.

"Your mother wants to see us," Cormac said.

It was the only thing worse than direct news. News he had to wait for. If he never received anything, he could hover in that space where things were all right, tentatively. If he received word he had to wait for, he knew there was something that he didn't know. He wound his arm around his stomach and tried to pull it together. At last, he nodded and rose to put on number six's clothes and wrapped the blue scarf around his neck. He wasn't sure his mother would recognize six. Cormac put himself together quickly, and he walked hand in hand with Max down the halls.

The guards in front of his mother's door froze at first at their approach, but Max watched their eyes snap to the blue at his throat. At length, they nodded and opened the door.

Anora was in her pale blue dressing gown over her nightdress. Max's heart sank. His mother was never unkempt in front of others, not once. He was relatively certain that she'd been fully dressed at his own birth.

He crossed the room quickly and took her hands. "What is it? Is Father—"

It took her a moment to realize who stood before her. She visibly tried to wipe the shocked expression from her face as she subtly shook her head and blinked. "Son," she laughed weakly. "This is…new."

Just to you, he wanted to say. Moreover, he kept himself from outright screaming, "What's going on?"

"I've had word from the doctor. He expects Father to be all right."

Max slumped, still holding onto her hands. His heart pounded against his chest still, and he felt like he could burst into tears at any moment, but it was…relief.

Anora looked over at Cormac. "I'm told this news could be very different had you not taken action." She held out a hand to him, and he came over and took it. "Thank you." He bowed his head, and she lifted his chin. "Not today," she said softly.

He smiled a little. "How is His Majesty?"

She smiled too, a little fondly, a lot tiredly. "He tells me that he is grateful for the excuse to stay in bed and read all day. Not that he should be holding a book up, but you try convincing him of that."

Max let his head drop forward, and he smiled. "I shan't be trying that. I know better. Is he in much pain?"

"Some," she said with a small sigh. "He won't say how

much."

"I…I have someone who may be able to help that."

She gave him a strange look. "Who, exactly?"

"The man who gave me the means to control the curse."

"He is in Clockbridge, is he not?"

"He's been here, helping me," Max admitted.

"And you haven't introduced us? I would certainly like to thank him myself."

"He and the Director of the Guild are not on the best of terms."

The Queen lifted an eyebrow. "I am not the Director. Yes, please send for him to your father's room, and I will meet with him later."

"As you wish." The chance of Aubric knowing about Molas seemed so much less important than bringing his father rest at the moment, Max couldn't bring himself to argue about it. He hadn't seen Aubric anywhere, last night or today. Hesitantly, he asked, "What's become of the assassin?"

"In the dungeon, though he speaks oddly. He claims not to know where he is."

"I believe there's a chance he might be right. I sensed some magic in the hallway that diminished as soon as he was caught."

She frowned. "Aubric mentioned nothing."

He wouldn't, if he was behind it. Max said, "It was over very quickly. But still, I would ask that you put a mage guard in front of the prisoner's cell. It could very well be they intend to eliminate him, putting the truth out of reach."

He didn't have to identify *they* to her. She'd fill it in on her own. She thought for a moment, then nodded. "This I will do. I would have the truth. I owe it to your father."

Max smiled a little. She meant it, but it wouldn't come to pass. Not without intervention. "Thank you, Mother."

"He assures me you were quite heroic in detaining the prisoner."

He hadn't felt heroic. He'd felt desperate. He just smiled demurely. "Kind of him to say, especially given how busy he was at the moment."

"We will have to acknowledge the both of you at court, once the welcoming is done and Father feels better."

The welcoming. She was still planning for the welcoming? "All things considered, Mother, neither of us will mind if we need to postpone."

Cormac nodded. Anora said, "We must not give the people cause for concern. Father also has no compunctions about missing social events."

"No, that's true," Max conceded. Usually he and his father avoided them together. "There won't be talk?"

"Of course there will, but that can't be avoided. No, it will have to carry on the day after tomorrow if we want the focus to remain the pair of you."

Max simply nodded. "I should go see to Father and Master Molas," he said.

His mother nodded and set her hand to his face as though this one weren't completely foreign to her. "Darling," she said hesitantly. "With the League able to breach our walls, I think it's safest if you…returned to your first self."

Max looked down at himself, at the willowy frame and freckled skin. "I can't do it midday," he said. "I only have a very brief window of time in which the change can take place at dawn."

"But tomorrow," she said anxiously.

"Mother, the League doesn't care what I look like; they just want me dead."

"And they'll find any excuse, any way to do it. If they were to turn the people against you—" She pressed her lips together, unable to finish the thought. "Please, darling. For me."

He looked at the ground a moment and nodded. She lifted his face again. "This one is pretty," she said quietly.

Max met her eyes and she smiled, though he could see a bit of sadness in her eyes. He wondered who that was for.

Outside, Cormac asked, "Are you all right?"

"She's just frightened," Max said. "Father was just stabbed in the safest wing of the palace. Of course she's frightened."

"That doesn't mean you'll be comfortable changing into number one all of the time."

No, he supposed not. But it made it easier to be asked.

Max knocked on his father's door, Molas and Cormac in tow. "Enter," a thin voice called. Eren sat propped up in bed, in his nightshirt with a book spread across his knees. He look ashy, tired, but he smiled. "Cormac, my boy," he said. "And who's this?"

"Father, it's me," Max said. "Max."

"Oh! Of course. Scarf. And Master Molas, too. It's a busy moment. What are both my heroes doing visiting an old man with little to do but read and moan?"

Max pulled a chair over to the bedside and sat. "We thought we'd come listen to my old man moan. Unless you'd rather us go?"

Eren carefully marked his page in his book and shut it. "No, no, stay!"

Molas came to the other side of the bed. "Tell me, how is your pain?"

"Be honest," Max warned.

Eren squirmed a little. "It's not good," he said.

"I figured. A stab to your abdomen hits several nerves, among many important other things. If you'll permit me, I'll brew and administer something that will dull it."

The King squinted. "Will it also dull my mind?"

"It may put you to sleep, yes."

"Father," Max said. "You should be resting."

"I am, I am. But you think I should take the draught."

"I do."

"All right," he conceded. "I trust you, Davitt. If you were going to poison me, you'd have done so already."

"And with great subtlety," Molas said, eyebrows lifted.

Max said, "This is really concerning, both of you."

"Permit old men their humor." He patted Eren's shoulder gently and went to work, pulling a portable burner from his bag and setting up in the corner.

Eren looked from Cormac to Max. "I haven't yet said it, so I shall say it now—thank you. Both of you. Without you, my proverbial goose would have been, shall we say, spatchcocked."

Cormac laughed. "That one's a five gold word I don't know, but you are very welcome, Your Highness."

"Careful," Max said. "If you tell him you don't know a word, he'll make you go to the dictionary and look it up."

"Oh, now now," his father said. "That's reserved for you and any children you might have."

"I suppose that's fair."

"Thank you, son. Or is it daughter today?"

Max squirmed on his hard wooden seat and smiled a little shyly. "It's both. But you don't need to worry about it."

"No, no, I happen to like being exact," he said. "In all things, but especially in what matters to you."

Max fidgeted a piece of his long red hair behind his ear. "It's not too strange?"

Eren sat back against his pillows, a pleased expression on his face. "I've always wanted a daughter. I've always been proud of my son. Both are true, and in the same person! I'm very fortunate."

"You don't have to say that just because you think I need to hear it," Max said, looking down. "Besides, it's son from here on out. Mother has requested it."

"Has she?" He frowned slightly.

"For my safety," he clarified.

"Hmm. We'll see about that."

Max wasn't sure his father would get very far in arguing that, but he appreciated him trying. Cormac gave him a little smile, and Molas busied himself pouring something into a glass. He brought it over carefully. "Drink it while it's still warm."

Max held it for his father, who tried and failed a few times to get his arm up high enough to drink. He drained it, and Max set the glass aside on the nightstand.

"How do you feel?" he asked.

"Hmm. Warm. I think it'll take a second…to…." His head sank against his pillows, and immediately he began to doze. Max set his hand to Eren's forehead for a minute, then took his book and set it beside the glass. Cormac helped him get his legs laid flat, and the King mumbled something and woke up a little. "Who's the father here?" he mumbled.

"Yeah, well, it's my turn to take care of you."

"I love you, my child."

Max stopped. His parents rarely said that. He could count the times on one hand. Perhaps it was the draught, or perhaps it was everything that happened. Either way, his eyes went wet. "I love you too, Father."

He smiled to himself as he fell asleep again.

Chapter Nineteen
The Party

Cormac ranged the room, nervous in his new clothes. Once again, Max had found him something that he said he didn't feel ridiculous in, but he still moved stiffly, seemingly afraid of wrinkling himself. Max found the ignored, dusty box and set it on his desk. Out of it he lifted the circle of silver leaves and sighed. He never felt right wearing the crown. Cormac came and stood at his shoulder. "That's a pretty thing," he murmured.

"Want to see it?" Max asked.

Cormac tentatively held his hands out and accepted the crown. "It's heavier than I thought," he said with a nervous laugh.

"You're not kidding. Try putting it on."

"No, no thank you," he said. "I'm happy leaving that one on your head."

"It's just a hat," Max told him. "A weighty, somewhat silly hat."

He reached out and placed it on Max's head and stepped

back, smiling. "You wear it well. I know few who would."

Max closed the distance between them and placed a kiss on Cormac's lips, soft at first, then decidedly firmer. For the first time that day, Cormac relaxed. Max set his arms around his neck and looked into his pale eyes. "It's going to be all right."

Cormac looked petrified for a moment, then melted in Max's gaze. "I'm not—I'm not like these people, Max."

"Which people?"

"These nobles."

"No, you're right. You're better than they are." Cormac looked down, and Max persisted, "When I was cursed, it was you I could tell. It was you who never once judged me, never thought less of me. When Flora was in trouble, it was you I could come to. When things were dire for your sister and you, it was you who stepped up and took care of things, even at your own expense. You know what it is to struggle. To work. You deserve the world, Cormac. The least I can give you is me."

"You are my world," he answered, putting his hand to his face.

Max felt the ring box heavy in his pocket and swallowed hard. Now. It was time now. He slipped his hand into his pocket and pulled out the box. "Cormac—"

A knock at the door split his sentence. "Your Highness?" A guard called. "It's time."

Cormac pulled at his collar and headed for the door. Max let his head lower and tucked the box back into his pocket. He caught Cormac's hand. "Hey." He lifted the enchanted cloak from the hook where it stayed, swept it around Cormac's shoulders, and clasped it. "For courage. I love you."

Cormac's chest raised. "I love you too."

"It's going to be good," he promised, opening the door.

This wasn't Max's first receiving line, nor would it be his last, assuming all went well and his mother didn't kill him. This one was unusual: instead of solely being comprised of the same nobility that attended party after party, there were everyday citizens craning their necks to get a look at the prince's beloved in the castle, ordinarily unattainable. Cormac chatted easily with these folk, getting down on a knee to speak to the children, shaking hands with the adults. The nobles came less easily. He wasn't exactly sure what to do with his hands, and he bowed frequently, which wasn't an unsafe thing to do when uncertain.

At long last, the line ran out. The guests milled around as refreshments started going, until the dancing began. "I'm surprised," Cormac said, his voice low. "No one took us to task for both being men."

"Oh, never to our faces," Max told him, taking his arm. "That's for scathing whispers under their breath when they think no one is listening."

"Well, at least they're quiet about it. Where I'm from, that would fully be done in our faces."

"We're nothing if not superficially polite here." He looked across the room. "The common folk have had the right to choose their partners for years now. It's only we nobles who cling to backwards thoughts about tradition and heirs. It's not a *shock* that I've taken up with a man, it's just shameful that I'd eschew the trappings of an arranged marriage with a woman."

Cormac surveyed the ballroom full of people, chattering and laughing. It was hard for Max not to wonder how much of the laughter was at their expense. He was sure Cormac was thinking something similar.

"And the fact that I'm a commoner?"

"Not as much of a gossip-worthy thing," Max assured him. "You aren't the first."

"And that I'm part underkin?"

"That's probably got a few tongues wagging."

"I'm used to that, at least. It's strange being the only ones, Brenna and me."

"There are very few underkin in this part of the world. That doesn't excuse ignorance."

"Well, it's nice to hear someone say so," Cormac remarked. "I didn't get any off the regular folk."

"No, there are quite a few people in the city with part-elf heritage."

A servant approached and bowed. "Your Highness, the musicians are about to begin."

Max nodded. "Very good. Thank you. We should get to the front."

Cormac's shoulders tightened. "I've never been a dancer."

"It's all right," Max said. "Just follow my lead."

"Always," he said nervously.

Max found himself with a case of the jitters of his own as the the string quartet acknowledged him and began. His heart hammered at his chest with the first strains of the song he'd tucked in that box so long ago in Clockbridge. He took up Cormac's hand and set his other hand to his shoulder.

"You're trembling," Cormac noted quietly as they began to whirl. "What is it?"

"It's the song," he said.

"What's wrong?"

"Nothing. Nothing. Just the first time I'm hearing it out loud."

Cormac tilted his head with a smile. "You wrote this, didn't you?"

"You were always pushing me to give someone my music," he said, smiling anxiously.

"And you did. That's phenomenal."

"And that's a five gold word."

"You've earned it," he said in wonderment, listening to the music and letting Max lead him around and around in time to all the others who'd joined them on the floor. "It's beautiful. Warm, and gentle, and just the littlest bit sad."

Max flushed. "I wrote it for you," he said softly. "All those days in Clockbridge."

"Max," he breathed, "*thank you*. Thank you for letting me hear it."

That was the whole reason he'd given it to the musicians in the first place. Unbearably embarrassing for him was necessary if he wanted to gift it. But as he looked into Cormac's shining light eyes, he found that he *could* bear it after all. Cormac had recognized himself in it. That was worth everything. "I love you," Max told him, reaching for his pocket.

In that instant, Max's entire body seized in Cormac's arms. The stretching, pulling feeling began at his core. Involuntarily, his eyes went to the ballroom's great windows. How? It was mid-afternoon, not even dusk. Cormac's eyes went wide, and he whisked him from the dance floor into the wings, behind one of the great marble pillars.

From across the room, Flora came running. "Max!"

Cormac held him close. Max watched Cormac's eyes darting between Max and the light areas past the dim pillared corridor. He felt the urgency, too. Any moment now, someone else could come rushing over. Cormac picked him up in his arms and ran for the nearest door, which led into the hallway outside the ballroom.

He dashed until he found an empty stretch of hall. He paused, cradling Max in his arms. "What's happening?" he demanded.

"I don't know," Max groaned. "Something's—something's wrong."

"Molas," he said.

Flora grabbed fistfuls of her lavender skirts. "I'll go for him. You get him in his room."

Max put his hand to Cormac's chest. "You can't be gone long. People will ask questions."

"And they won't ask them if you're not with me?"

"Tell them—I went to—speak with the Queen," he eked out.

"Can you even make it—? Fuck it, I'm not letting you do this alone." He hurdled over a few stairs down and continued barreling down the colonnades. A few guards started, jarred out of the fugue of boredom, but Cormac dodged them until they made it into Max's room. Max tore off his crown and let it fall to the seat of the chair near the door and yanked his collar loose as he let go of the painful restraint and let the change come. Number five's wings ripped through his shirt, tangling in the jacket over it. Cormac hurried to help free him, placing him in bed on his stomach. Max got to his forearm, gritted his teeth, and loosened his pants as five's ample hips came in. He breathed out of what felt like barbed lungs and let his head sink forward to the bed, his back arching.

In between waves of pain, he wondered how on earth this could have happened. It was as though the tonic didn't mean anything and the crystal's resonance had backfired. He was certain he'd have felt if someone nullified the tonic again—wouldn't he?

The door opened, and Molas and Flora rushed into the room. Molas knelt next to the bed, his hand to Max's shoulder. He frowned deeply. "Someone has sabotaged you," he said darkly. "Where is the crystal?"

"Nightstand," he got out.

Molas went for it and held it in his hands, muttering something under his breath. "It's been tampered with. Someone has cast a spell into it and poisoned the well of magic."

"Can it be undone?"

"I'm unsure," he said. "We will need to see if it can be puri-fied; else you may need to start anew."

Max finally felt the tension go out of his muscles, and he sank onto the bed and breathed out. He turned to Flora. "Please take Cormac back to the party. Help him."

Cormac grasped Max's hand. "I don't want to leave you."

"I'll be fine," he said. "The people are going to talk, and that can be as vicious as anything. The best thing you can do to help is to mitigate that somewhat."

Cormac set his mouth to the side, but nodded. He touched Max's face briefly, then went to the door. Flora hurried to follow after him. Max let his head settle against the pillows and regarded Molas. "What does this mean?"

"If we are unable to rectify what has been done, I fear outside forces may be able to impose the transmutation upon you." He held up a hand. "I have not given up yet. It may take some time, but I believe we can cleanse it. In the meantime: do not leave the crystal unattended. I think someone must have snuck in and tam-pered with it while you were away."

"I guess locks don't mean anything to wizards," he grumbled.

"Not a good one. And I fear you are dealing with a good one."

"Depends on your definition of *good*," he said.

"Certainly a talented one, then."

"That is very true."

Molas held the crystal up and observed it. "I will try to cast into it. There is only so much magic it can hold; perhaps whatever was added will bleed out of it, like diluting water."

Max watched him hold his hand over the crystal and try to connect his will to it via the ethereal strings they all shared with the world. He unfocused his eyes and watched the golden threads pull taut around Molas. All at once, they snapped, and Max jerked forward as a new transformation began.

Molas whipped his head around, scowling. "That shouldn't be."

No, none of it should.

Molas took the crystal to Max's desk and took a vial from his bag. He spilled something from the container onto the surface of the crystal, which started bubbling furiously. "No, this can't be," he said.

Max wrapped an arm around his stomach and tried to sit up. Number four's webbing started growing in between his fingers. Barely a few seconds later, it retracted and the blue to his skin faded in favor of number two's gray. "What is going on?" he gasped.

"It's been alchemically treated. There's a *barrier* keeping new magic from passing in. But to do that would take a mage and an alchemist working together."

"Bad news. I happen to have a pair like that down the hall." He groaned, his body writhing in total discomfort. "Can you make it stop? I don't even care which form."

"I'll try," he said. "Are you in pain?"

"Just a bit," he answered testily.

"I can give you something for that. Your heart is under much strain; we need to reduce that strain by any means." He flew over to his bag and found a flask. "Drink."

Max took it and downed the contents. They burned much like the tonic did. Slowly, he felt everything warm and the pain subside. He could feel the draught trying to soothe him to sleep, but the next jolt kept him from fading. Number three came into the world the way he always did—with stress on his muscles and his bones.

Molas mumbled an incantation under his breath and sent it in Max's direction. The strain eased a little, but Max couldn't quite hold his head up.

If they couldn't get this figured out, it was going to be a long night.

Max was half-asleep when Cormac slipped back into the room. His shirt had burst at nearly every seam by now with all of the expanding and contracting. Molas worked feverishly, moving back and forth from boiling things on Max's desk and treating the crystal repeatedly and checking on Max. Cormac sat on the bed and gathered Max into his arms, absently stroking his hair while the shudders carried on. Flora came too and assisted Molas with basic alchemy, watching at his elbow.

Max was utterly miserable, but even in the depths of that, felt well-cared for.

If only he could catch a breath. The changes came and kept coming. At midnight when Molas was rubbing at his eyes, Max fell into an uneasy sort of slumber, dozing through several more revolutions through his cadre of forms. Cormac nodded off, too, still holding Max until Molas shook Max's shoulder gently.

Max blinked into the soft candlelight, and Molas pressed the crystal into his hands. "I've stripped off the binding," he said softly, "and cast spells into it until it no longer radiated the malevolent energy. You'll need to re-familiarize yourself with it, but it should work for you come dawn."

"Am I done?" he slurred.

"Until dawn, yes. You should be done."

"Thank you," he said blearily. "What—do I look like right now?"

"Can't you tell?"

Max held up his hands and observed them, delicate and lightly shimmering in the low light. "Back to number five," he mumbled.

"It seemed prudent."

"You controlled it?"

"It was not easy. A complex combination of triggering the change in you on purpose—in essence, making your body believe it is dawn—and utilizing the crystal to adjust the change. I believe this is what our rogue wizard was doing."

"Which means it could be done again."

"Yes, but fear not. Most wizards cannot be subtle when using this much magic. In the meantime, I will look into a binding of our own, to protect the stone from future tampering. For now, rest. You need it. Undergoing that much transmutation is hard on the body."

"Thank you, Master Molas. Truly."

He put his hand to his shoulder. "I'm glad to be of help. Your friend—" He inched out of the way to reveal Flora, asleep in a chair alongside the desk. "Is she going to be all right there, or should I wake her?"

"Let her sleep," Max said.

"She was a capable assistant. I'd happily work with her again. Let us hope in less urgent times." Molas gathered up his bag. "Good night, Your Highness."

Max drifted off again almost immediately. Cormac got up and locked the door after Molas, taking the crystal from Max and setting it gently on the nightstand. "I need to magic that," Max mumbled.

"In the morning," he whispered. "Sleep now."

He did.

He barely fumbled awake early enough to cast into the stone, and once he felt it attach to him, dawn arrived. At the last possible moment, he managed to control the transmutation and change into number one. He felt himself shrink and grow back into his clothes, and he relaxed back into sleep.

It was split by an authoritative knock on his door. Cormac smoothed down Max's hair. "I'll get it. You go back to sleep."

"She wants me," he said in dread.

"Your mother?"

"That's what that knock means. She's sent a guard."

Flora stirred. "Hmm…wha?"

Cormac stood determinedly. "Back to sleep, both of you. I'll take care of this."

He went to the door. Loudly, the guard on the other side pronounced, "Her Majesty requires the presence of Prince Maximillian in the throne room immediately."

"His Highness is not feeling well," he said firmly.

"That is the subject of her order. She says he is to join her or accept High Wizard Aubric's presence in his room."

He frowned deeply. "Listen—"

"Cormac," Max said tiredly, sitting up and clutching his arm around himself to keep his tattered shirt together. "It's all right. I'll go."

"Max."

"It's okay. I'll be all right."

Cormac gave the guard a look. "He's coming," he said in what must have been his 'talking to people' voice. "Give him a moment."

"As you wish."

He shut the door. Flora looked to Max. "What are you going to tell her?"

Max sat on the edge of the bed, struggling to hold his head up. "The truth."

Cormac looked at him. "Do you think she can hear it?"

"I don't know. All I know is she seems to have been resisting the compulsion. And it's about bloody time."

He grabbed the crystal and stuffed it into his pocket and cast about for a new shirt. Cormac helped him on with it while Max attempted to tame his hair somewhat. Cormac watched him dubiously. "Let me help you to the throne room, at least."

Max nodded. Cormac held out his hand to brace him, and Flora took up the other side. "I'm sorry," he said as they stumbled along. "You shouldn't have to be minding me."

"Everyone needs to be minded sometimes," Flora told him.

"Yes, but I feel like it's me so very often."

Cormac leaned over and gave his cheek a kiss. "You have enough going on without worrying about that. Let us worry about you."

Max rested his head on Cormac's shoulder for a spell, glad of the bolstering. The throne room loomed closer, and his dread built along with his utter fatigue. Before reaching it, he stopped Flora and Cormac. "I'll be all right from here," he said.

"Do you want us to wait?" she asked.

"Thank you, but no," he said, anxious. "I get the feeling that this will take some time."

"We don't mind—"

He took her face in his hands and leaned down to see at eye level with her. "You are too wonderful. Go have a rest. I will see you later."

"Max," she said, her cheeks squooshed against her face, "you're really sick."

"And I'll still be really sick later."

"That's not making me feel better."

"I just mean," he said, patting her hand within his, "that you ought to use a little of the care you show me on yourself, too.

There'll be plenty of opportunity to help later."

"All right," she said, dubiousness radiating from her face and voice. "But I'm checking on you later."

He bowed. "I look forward to it. In the meantime—" He kissed Cormac and squared his shoulders. "—Off I go."

The guards let him in, and he found himself staring down Aubric and the Director both, to the side of the dais. He looked to his mother. "What are they doing here?"

His mother did not answer. Instead, she looked him over with an exacting eye that so often spelled trouble in his younger years. "Maximillian. Where *were* you yesterday? The guests say they saw you nearly collapse, and then you did not return."

"I would really prefer to have this conversation somewhere private."

"Private?" She waved her hand, encompassing the whole of the throne room. "The whole kingdom was witness to your fallibility yesterday."

Max shut his eyes against the sharpness of her words and tuned them out, listening instead of the crackle or hum of ether. There was magic passing back and forth between her and Aubric at an intensity he hadn't encountered before. He was going to have to be very compelling in order to break through. "Mother, I can explain."

"Explain, then. Because by your own word, this curse is meant to be under control."

"It *was*," he answered a little hotly. He took a breath. "But yesterday, someone infiltrated my room with malicious intent and tampered with my means of controlling it, I think likely so I would have a slip in public. I was then subjected to hours of repeated transmutations—an experience I assure you is more unpleasant than answering for it later."

Her expression changed. "Are you well?"

"No," he answered frankly. "I am still feeling very ill today. It was only through the intervention of Master Molas that I settled on a single form again. It will likely take me some time to recover from the strain."

Distressed, she looked between him and Aubric. "You could have stayed in your room, my sweet. I'd have sent Aubric right away—"

"Why would I want you to do that? Who could be behind the tampering but him?"

He spluttered, laughed. "That is *preposterous*, Your Majesty. How would I have even known where to find his crystal?"

Max's eyes narrowed. "I never told you it was a crystal."

For the first time, Max saw Aubric's face fall—the briefest of moments, before he put that perfect mask of placidity back on. "I simply assumed, based on what I know of transmutation magic. But now you have confirmed that, finally, so thank you."

"You didn't assume anything. You saw the crystal yourself when you activated that charm you put on my door to let yourself in. And then you gave it to him—" He pointed to the Director. "—to work his alchemy on it. A powerful wizard and a powerful alchemist. Quite the coincidence to have both under our roof at the same time."

The Queen eyes creased subtly in distress. "Aubric—are these allegations true?"

"Certainly not," he said, sounding affronted. "Perhaps it has escaped our young prince's notice that there is another in our midst with the capability to do such a thing."

The Director spoke up. "Master Molas is both a learned scholar of the arcane and a purveyor of alchemical goods."

"Both expertises in one person. I think that's far more likely than some grand conspiracy."

Max glowered. "Don't you dare. Don't you dare wriggle out of this by pinning this on the one person who has ever made this better for me."

"What pinning? All we are doing is stating the facts of the matter. Something your flights of fancy seem to be neglecting. Furthermore, I maintain there was no need for any charm on your door. Your room has a second inhabitant. A second inhabitant with a curious amount of access to the King and a prior connection to our mage-alchemist. Didn't you say there was a faint hint of magic when His Highness was attacked?"

"*Enough,*" Max burst out. "Baseless accusation to try to distract from the truth. Mother." He looked at the Queen pleadingly. "I have done much in my time to cause you grief. But you know I would never bring *anyone* to this household who would harm my father. You know I would never stand in this room and lie. I am standing here on the verge of falling apart, begging you to see clearly. The people who harmed me are *here*. I know it."

Reserved, she said, "Perhaps we might test the truth of these accusations.”

Aubric’s confidence wilted just briefly before Max felt him push a wave of ether at the Queen. “And how would we do that?” Aubric said. “Magic does not leave fingerprints.”

“It does,” Max said. “There are ethereal signatures.”

“And what will you do?” He sneered. “The last one to touch your stone was your Master Molas. I can tell you that. How will you prove to a non-mage that I was anywhere near your belongings?”

“I won’t,” he said squarely, turning to look at his mother. “I will just ask the Queen to believe her son.”

Conflict in her eyes, conflict in her face, conflict in her heart as his words clashed against the waves of magic being sent to her mind. Max said softly, “I know how confused you feel. Something is wrong, and you know it, don’t you? But he doesn’t quite let you see. So I ask you to trust what you’ve always known.”

Hesitantly, she opened her mouth. Max met her eyes and nodded. She put her hand to her head.

“Her Majesty is feeling unwell,” Aubric snarled. “I think it’s best we put this to rest for now and let her retire.”

“Her Majesty can speak for herself.”

“Max,” she said slowly.

“Yes, Mother. We’re listening.”

She fixed him with a long look, then smiled.

Pain tore through the center of him as another transformation took hold. He gasped, buckled, braced a hand on the marble floor. As best as he could, he turned his head to look. Aubric was staring murder into him, and he felt it. With every new burst of pain, he felt Aubric drive the magic into the crystal and back into him. No incantations, no hand movements, nothing. Not even in sight of the crystal. Molas had promised it wouldn't be subtle, but here it was, barely requiring Aubric's full attention.

The Queen abandoned the throne and rushed forward to grasp Max's shoulder. "Darling! What's wrong?"

He gasped, "It's—happening again. He's—"

Aubric stepped forward and took Max's other shoulder. He felt a fresh pulse of ether leave Aubric and hit his mother. "Your Majesty, this curse is unstable. I said as much before, and now we see its fruition. For his own safety, I ask that Prince Maximillian be remanded into my care."

Max looked at his mother, his eyes wide. "No. You can't give me to him. Mother. He will tear me apart."

She looked into his eyes, her expression torn. "My love, you need help."

"Not from him. Please. Can't you see I am begging you?" He doubled over as his spine lengthened and took the wind right from him. "Get Cormac. Get Flora. Anybody but him. Please. Anybody but him."

Soothingly, Aubric said, "We will take good care of Prince Maximillian. He's with experts. That's right where he needs to be."

Max picked up his head again, sending a look of sheer terror at his mother. She stared back at him in her own horror. "Take him," she said, her voice thin, frayed.

The doors burst open and two of Aubric's assistants entered with a stretcher. Max clawed for purchase, fought against being rolled onto it, but his strength was gone. From so many transformations, from this one, he just couldn't find the force. "No, no, no," he cried out. "You can't take me. You can't—Mother, *please!*"

The assistants pulled leather straps across the stretcher, pinning his head and chest and legs down. His eyes traveled for the brief moment he could see to his mother, who stood with her hand clamped over her mouth, tears rolling down her face. The stretcher lurched, and soon enough the doors shut behind them.

"Now," Aubric said, stepping into Max's view. "Now our own little party can begin."

Chapter Twenty
The Undercroft

Max wasn't sure where he was. He only knew he was under the castle by the smell. It was dank, cold, moldy-smelling. It wasn't the dungeon, but it was close. The small room was lit by torches. His straps had changed—his wrists, his strangely bent ankles were held to the cold metal examination table. His tail was belted in around his hips. It was all a little much for a man who could barely move. Aubric and the Director talked in some adjacent room—he could hear the strains of their voices, exclamatory and loud, but indistinct. The assistants were in the room with Max. They bustled about outside his field of vision, occasionally crossing it to the other side. Young men, both, barely out of university, if that. Revulsion filled Max even as he plotted his escape. "You. You there."

The nearest young man started. An elf, with long golden hair tied back and the sort of mouth that looked wrong not smiling. "I'm sorry, Your Highness—but I'm not permitted to talk to the subjects."

"Subjects," he persisted. "There's more than one?"

The assistant suddenly turned his head, petrified. "I—I didn't say that. You said that."

"It's all right," he said slowly, hoping it sounded soothing. Number three wasn't the best at soothing strangers. "Listen. Whatever he's promised you, whatever he's said to you, if he told you he loves you, he's lying. He lies like he breathes."

The assistant hesitated, hovering in Max's vision.

"Jonas," the other assistant said. "Keep your head about you."

Jonas turned away. Max pressed, "If you take me out of here, I can protect you from him."

Jonas laughed dully, setting tools out on a tray. Max didn't like how heavily they clanked. "That's a big promise, Your Highness."

He supposed his performance in the throne room didn't much say heroic protector as it did pathetic mewling child. "Is he threatening you?"

"No! No."

The second assistant snapped, "Jonas."

He fell silent, arranging the tools in some order that would make sense to their wielder. Max looked up at the ceiling. He couldn't let those tools be used on him. He tugged on the straps around his wrists. The right was looser. If he could work that open somehow....

The second assistant was watching too closely. He'd need to make some kind of distraction. It was hard to do magic restrained, but as Aubric himself had so handily demonstrated, not impossible. Max gathered what little energy he could muster and focused past the room. A clattering noise sounded in the hallway. The second assistant turned his head and went down the hall. Max moved quickly, easing the buckle on the strap open and freeing his hand. He moved to undo the left strap while Jonas' back was turned. His heart pounded. What next, what next…?

He wasn't likely to be able to dash out of here. He was still weak. His hand trembled as he fumbled with the buckle. But with his hands free, he could cast. It was a different reserve of energy, one he still had access to.

A hand caught his wrist, and he looked up to see Aubric standing over him. "You thought you could use magic here? In my domain? Oh, Max." His fingers clenched around his wrist, and with preternatural strength, he slammed it back to the table. "Did you really think that would work? Did you really think I wouldn't notice your ether changing? I *know* you, Max."

"You did, once," Max said, grimacing through the pain.

"Oh, please," Aubric laughed. "As though you could change enough I wouldn't recognize you. Who taught you? Who nurtured your talents? Who paved the way for your becoming something more?"

"What?"

"Don't tell me you haven't figured it out. You—really didn't. Who do you think invited the fey? Do I have to tell you who sent the assassin to your father, too?"

Max's eyebrows lowered. "*You.* You did this to me. All of it, you."

"Being fair, I had no idea what she would actually do. I just know that enchanters tend to be drawn to the powerful and the uncharitable, so thus—you were a perfect target."

"Why?"

"Because *I can*," he said, buckling Max's wrist down, tight this time. He reached behind him and retrieved a pair of scissors. Max flinched, but Aubric didn't take up any body parts this time. Instead, he said, "Look at these tired clothes. You're practically bulging out of them. Let's put them out of their misery, shall we?"

He sliced through Max's clothes, removing the top layer, leaving him lying on the bottom. Max realized too late that the crystal and the ring box were still in his pockets. Aubric weighed the front of his trousers in his hands. "What does the prince carry in his pockets?" Max flinched. Aubric drew them out one at a time. "The much vaunted crystal, and—what's this?" He opened the ring box and a smirk crept up his face. "No! The Prince's Folly?! Was our poor prince planning on *proposing? You*, the happy-go-lucky royal man-about-town with his heart on his sleeve? Oh, it's too much to bear!"

Max's face burned. Steps sounded from behind, and the Director said coldly, "Stop playing with your food, wizard, and make good on our deal."

Aubric tossed the ring box to the tray next to the examination table. "Very well, Director. If you're so impatient, we'll begin."

"Can you get results or can't you?"

"I can, and I will, if you can be patient." Aubric located a brown bottle on the table parallel to Max. He emptied it onto a cloth that had previously been covering the tools and balled it into a fist. "I don't doubt that the answer to what you seek is somewhere in his biological makeup. We just need to isolate it."

"You won't get away with this," Max told him. "The King knows what you did last time. You won't be able to slice me up with impunity."

"For *your own good*? I'll do whatever I wish." He took the cloth and clamped it over Max's nose and mouth. "Don't worry, my pet. You won't feel a thing—yet."

Max struggled for air around the overwhelming chemical scent wafting off the cloth. Panicked, he tried to pull his hands free, jerked his head back, anything to free himself from the oppressive fumes. It didn't work. Aubric held fast, and within instants, Max faded.

Cormac wandered around, swinging his arms. He hadn't had the heart to go back to Max's room, but neither did he defy him and stand directly outside the throne room doors. Instead, he hovered somewhere between the two, watching in the *direction* of the throne room. That was how he heard the scream from deep inside the chamber. By the time it reached him, it was just the hint of something audible, but it set his very soul on edge. "Max?" he asked nothing in particular. Of course, there was no answer, so he went running.

The doors opened, and two men bearing a stretcher came out. A slowly lengthening red tail that he knew *very* well indeed dangled off the edge. Shortly behind came Aubric, that smug prick, and the Director, somehow even smugger. Cormac ducked behind a pillar and didn't even breathe. They passed him without so much as a glance. He edged around the other side of the pillar and fell in behind them, keeping to the outer edge of the hallway, ready to duck away at any moment.

He only had to hide when Aubric stopped abruptly, the way someone does when they've gotten where they're going, and looked around. There was no door, but there was a conspicuously large tapestry. Aubric lifted it and pressed on a series of stones. The wall began to retract and slide away. Cormac squinted, trying to see what he'd touched, but he couldn't.

Aubric, the Director, and the two men—boys, practically—moving the stretcher proceeded through the opening and into the tunnel the wall revealed. Cormac waited for them to be out of sight, then ran as the wall began to slide back into position. He cast about and saw a crate left outside the kitchen. He dashed for it, nabbed it, then back to cram it into the narrowing gap. The wall groaned to a stop, and he breathed out—just for a moment. Then he ran for the guest wing, holding the cloak Max had given him to keep it from flying off.

Flora was finally out of her formal gown when she answered the door. "Cormac," she said. "What's—?"

"Max," he panted. "He's in trouble."

Her face darkened. "Hold on." She backed out of view then returned with her sword. "Show me."

They ran back to the tapestry, which Cormac pulled back and

thanked all the gods he could remember at that moment that the crate was still jammed in there. Cormac held out his hand to help Flora slip past the box. Easy for her, she was tiny. He followed after, straining against the narrow gap. Finally he fought his way to the other side. Flora started feeling around the walls of the dark tunnel, likely for a torch or whatnot, but he grabbed her hand to guide her through the shadows. His eyes could see fine, and they didn't need to let Aubric know they were coming with the light of a torch.

The tunnel seemed to slope downward forever. Cormac was starting to wonder where in the hells they were when he spotted the very edge of light from a torch moving along the floor. Someone was pacing. He told Flora, "Easy does it. I'm going to let go and take a look at what we're dealing with."

She nodded, biting her lip, her hand at the hilt of her sword. Cormac crept forward and, as the light started moving away again, peeked around the corner.

A little room full of six people he knew well enough to greet in the halls of the Guild. He'd worked with some of them. Others he knew by reputation. All of them could get shit done, some without leaving a trace behind. They stood guard at a single, unassuming thick wooden door.

The Director was behind that door.

He retreated. "There are six," he whispered. "Think we can take them?"

"Probably not," she said. "We could get some guards."

He shook his head. "If Max is here, it's because the Queen let him be. The guards aren't going to help us. So, are we doing this?"

She fidgeted. At length, she nodded and drew her sword, and Cormac turned back toward the doorway. He burst through with his fists raised, and looked around at the room's occupants. They reached for weapons and readied themselves. Cormac swallowed hard and lowered his hands. "I don't want to fight you," he said, lowering his head. "You're all here because the same fuckstick that roped me into fighting and busting my ass for the Guild did the same to you."

The enforcers looked at each other, confused. Cormac knew this was not usually how their jobs went. Flora was equally confused, but seemed to sense this was something that he needed to say.

He looked earnestly at the other enforcers. "Did any of you want to fight people for him? Do you now? Honestly, how many of you would take a punch in the face for that bloke?"

Quiet reigned as the enforcers shuffled about, eying one another. Cormac swung his arms. "Listen. I know I'm the last fellow you'd expect to say this, but this doesn't have to come to blows. You're in someone else's city. Not his. If anyone takes a fall, it's going to be you before him. And even if that weren't true...you're more than what they've made you."

More silent eye contact. At length, one of the enforcers near the door stepped out of the way and turned his back. One by one, the others followed. "Thank you," Cormac said, and rushed for the door.

Flora followed him into a narrow passage. "Good for you, future prince," she said.

"Oh, gods, don't call me that."

"Max is rubbing off."

He smiled a little in spite of everything. "Yeah, suppose he is. How'd they even *get* him down this hallway?"

"Don't know, but heads up. I hear Aubric."

Cormac tensed. "Now *him* I want to fight."

"Be careful. He is a powerful wizard."

"I know how to handle those," he said, rolling out his neck. "His friend made sure I knew."

"He's just very subtle. I don't even think he uses his hands."

"Unfortunately for him, I do." Even if Aubric didn't need his hands, Cormac knew that restraining him would make the fight or flight response kick in, which tended to mess people up trying to do magic. That, and mages—especially fancy ones like this prissbritches—didn't like pain. "Stay low and hard to hit."

Flora nodded, and they rounded the end of the passage. A pair of young men—the ones who'd borne the stretcher—stood pumping water through a pair of troughs, washing instruments. The water ran red. Cormac seized one of the men and pressed him up against the wall, bearing his forearm down against his throat. Flora pointed her sword at the other, who put his hands up.

"You're going to tell me what he's done to the prince," Cormac said, his voice low.

"E-exploratory surgery, tissue collection," the assistant answered, his face paling. "He's not that far in—you can still stop him."

Cormac looked into his face for a moment. He had been right. Barely older than a boy. The other one, too. He dropped him to his feet and jerked his head to the door. "Get out of here. Both of you."

The one he'd held scrambled away. The second one lingered, but Flora stepped forward with her sword, and he hurried after the other.

Cormac threw open the door, thoroughly unprepared for what he found on the other side. A small operating room in a basement cell, and in the center was Max, laid out on a table with his clothes discarded. A large incision ran from his navel to his chest, and Aubric leaned over, ready with a pair of forceps. He startled as Cormac and Flora entered. Flora ran forward and raised her sword to his throat.

"Step—away—now," Cormac growled. "Hands where we can see them."

Aubric slowly, dutifully backed away from the examination table. Blood covered his hands. Max's blood. Cormac swallowed hard on fear and fury and regarded Aubric coldly. "I should let her run you through," he said.

"Do it, then," Aubric answered, his voice thin but defiant. "Ah, but you won't. It's not the kind of thing he would approve of."

And that was the only reason he continued to draw breath. Cormac stepped forward and grabbed him by the throat, hoisting him into the air. "He's not the one dealing with you. You've got me."

Aubric struggled, clawing at Cormac's hand. "You—can't," he rasped. "Only I know—the enchantment—I have used on him."

Cormac whirled and slammed him into the wall. "Bet we could figure it out."

His face reddened, veins sticking out of his forehead. "Not… if he's…dead." Cormac's hand unclenched, and Aubric dropped, sucking in air. "That's right," he gasped. "Even a great lout…like you understands…that repeated transmutations—can kill. That's why I've taken—the liberty of safeguarding…his heart. If you kill me—he loses that. I can also end it— at a moment's notice. Choose carefully your next moves."

Flora looked to Cormac, terror in her eyes. "Cormac."

Cormac glared into Aubric's face. His deep green eyes held steady, didn't blink. In fact, had he blinked even once? And why weren't there any marks on him where he'd smacked into the walls?

"This isn't real," he said slowly.

"So you're not as intellectually indolent as you look," Aubric said, his lips curling up into a smile. He removed one of Max's blades from his stained white coat pocket. "Are you willing to bet on that?"

"At the very least, you're not real."

"Cormac, what are you talking about?" Flora said.

Aubric strode past Cormac and went to Max on the table.

Cormac reached for his arm and his hand passed straight through. Flora cried, "No, don't—!"

Aubric raised the knife above Max, and Cormac's mind raced. Could an illusion person harm a real person? Flora charged Aubric with her sword held high and slashed. The knife clattered to the floor and Aubric, Max, and the surroundings disappeared, leaving Cormac and Flora in a dark, empty room with two doors, one of them open. Cormac seized the handle of the shut door and yanked. Locked. He squared up against the door and threw his shoulder into it. Even if it was a good lock, the wood was old and fragile. Too late he realized that this was a split door—the top half swung inward while the bottom stayed firmly latched.

On the other side of this door was the same scene—Max spread across an operating table in the center of a small room, Aubric standing over him—but this one was much more detailed. The tables were lined with specimen jars and beakers, some housing things, others waiting to be filled. The copper smell of blood filled the air, and the true extent of Max's injuries was much greater. Two incisions ran across his belly, another down his forearm. One of his horns had been sawn off, his hair roughly chopped short. Aubric hastily worked near Max's eye.

Cormac vaulted over the half-door, ran forward, and grabbed the jackass by the edges of his coat. Rage and grief shook his voice. "Enough," he said. "You're done here."

"Oh, I beg to differ."

He lifted a hand, and Flora shuddered. Cormac looked over

his shoulder. "Flora?"

She looked up at Cormac with a deep fury in her eyes. "Look at my friend! You let this happen!"

"Flora, he's manipulating you. We have to help Max."

"I think the lady is beyond talking," Aubric said.

Flora raised her sword and charged at Cormac. Cormac swung Aubric into the path of the blade, but instead of running him through, the sword was deflected like it had hit an invisible shield. Cormac tightened his grip on Aubric and yanked his arm behind his back. "Let her go," he growled.

"I'm afraid I can't do that. If I release the magic on her, I have to release the magic on Max. That's what's keeping him alive while I work."

"You're bluffing."

"Am I?"

Flora took another swipe, and Cormac dodged, dragging Aubric with him. "You're dodgy as all hells. You used Max, you used those kids out there—" he shot the briefest of looks at the Director, who stood stock still, wedged into the corner. Not a fighter, apparently. "Bet you're using him, too."

Aubric's expression remained amused as Flora shook off the change in direction and started towards him again. "You think that will shake him?"

"Tenseré," the Director said nervously, looking out of place in a bloodied white smock instead of his usual impeccable suit. "If you plan on turning this around, don't draw it out any longer."

Aubrie sighed and rolled out his head dramatically. "*No one* appreciates timing." He shot Cormac the snidest of grins. "Max would have."

Cormac gritted his teeth and jerked Aubric's body as he darted past Flora's extended blade, her expert strike carrying her just a touch too far to turn and adjust for his new position—but she managed to follow through on the backswing and swipe toward his face.

He saw it coming, and for a fraction of a moment, everything seemed to move slowly. He twisted sharply. The point glanced off—barely even stung. He probably wouldn't have even noticed it if it weren't for the warmth running down his face.

Flora held her hands up to her mouth, dropping her sword. "Cormac, I'm so sorry," she gasped.

Aubric's smug expression fell. Cormac slammed him up against the wall, his face finally starting to smart with the wound across his cheek. "You can't just control people," he snarled. "They have their own wills."

"I can and I will," Aubric snapped. "In case it's escaped your notice, I have permission from the Queen to do this."

Flora reached down for the sword again and brought it up to Aubric's throat. "We know what you've been doing to her."

"And what will you do about it? What *can* you do about it? Her mind is mine, her boy is mine, this kingdom is mine!"

The far wall opened abruptly, and they all turned to face it. Queen Anora appeared in the gap, her face incandescent with rage. "That is enough!"

The smugness returned to Aubric's face. "Your Majesty, I was simply performing my duties in service to the Prince when these *interlopers* arrived—"

"I wanted to believe you," she said, her voice deadly. "I gave you this space. I gave you unprecedented freedom to work. I gave you my trust. And this is what you've done to my son."

"All in the name of *helping*—"

"Look at him!" she shouted. "You've mutilated him!"

Aubric's gaze on the Queen intensified deeply. Cormac yanked his arm back harder to try to break the connection, but even he could feel the crackle of building energy. He couldn't stop it. "Heel, you royal bitch," he said through clenched teeth.

Anora's eyes unfocused. Cormac looked to Flora. "We have to drop him."

"If we do, he'll lose the spell on Max," she said.

"He could drop it at any moment anyway. Look at her."

Flora bit her lip. She closed her eyes just briefly, then jammed the sword in between Aubric's ribs—or she tried. With inhuman strength, he ripped his arm free from Cormac and waved the sword away as though it were nothing.

Anora blinked hard, staggered. She reached out to a nearby table for support. "I'm such a fool," she said. "I should have listened to him. I should have heard him."

"Well. Now it's too late," Aubric snapped. "You've done this every bit as much as I have." He swiped up a hand, and a chill wind picked up from nowhere.

Cormac blinked and found himself standing outside somewhere, high up—on the battlements—facing Aubric in the swirling snow. He held onto his cloak.

"I will not have it," Aubric shouted over the wind. "I spent too long building my place here, too long cultivating trust with the Queen, for it all to be ruined now by some common prat."

"Max saw you for what you are," Cormac said vehemently. "He knew you were a viper. It was only a matter of time before she saw the truth."

"Oh, but he didn't," he laughed. "For the longest time, he was in love with me."

Cormac's fists clenched at his sides. "And you squandered it."

"Please. It's hardly like he was serious. He's never been serious. He plays at it from time to time, then runs from it."

"You don't know him."

"And you do? Some matter of weeks or months and you think you're ready?" Cormac stepped forward, and Aubric put his hands up. "Uh uh. Get any closer and I will end the spell on him and he'll start bleeding out on my table. Awake. Killing me will have the same effect."

Cormac gritted his teeth and cursed him silently. "What is it you want? Why did you bring me here?"

"Because if I'm going to lose everything, so will he. It's only fair."

Aubric raised his arm and sent a blast of force at Cormac. Cormac dropped and let it pass over him. A twist of his hands and Aubric sent a warbling sphere of energy rolling at him, gathering snow as it gathered speed. Just like before, everything except Cormac seemed to slow, just for a moment. He felt something like humming around his shoulders. He dove out of the way and rolled to a stop near the edge of the battlements. Whatever had just been coming at him struck the wall on the other side, cracking the stone.

No matter what he did, Cormac knew Aubric would drop the spell on Max. As his head rang, he tried to think of what Max would want him to do—beautiful, selfless Max—and it was obvious.

Aubric advanced on him, holding a spell crackling in the palm of his hand. Arrogant fool. "It's so easy," he said. "Bodies are so fragile. One gesture, and you fall over the edge."

Cormac shook himself, tried to reorient himself. Next to his elbow was a worn ballista. Slowly, he reached for it as he stood to face him again. Aubric's eye caught it, and he smirked. "What do you think you'll do with that?"

"Distract you," he said. He took one step and punched Aubric square in the face harder than he'd ever punched anything before. The force sent Aubric staggering backward. Cormac hooked Aubric's leg and sent him tumbling over the side.

He wiped at his mouth and peered over. Instead of the mess he expected, he saw nothing. No disturbed snow, broken roof tiles, nothing. He must have vanished again.

Cormac's chest clenched. Max. He ran.

It took him far longer than he'd like to figure out how to get off of the battlements and back below, but eventually he found his way back to the tapestry and took off down the hall. It was filled with guards, interrogating the enforcers and the Director. Cormac couldn't even stop to look at them. He ran back into the operating room. Max's eyes were shut, but his eyelids fluttered, and he jerked in restlessness. Flora paced the room relentlessly, and when Cormac walked in, she changed direction so that she could come fuss over the slash across his cheek.

"Are you all right? What happened?"

"I'm fine," he said. "He got away, that son of a—" He caught himself, noting that the Queen was still standing there holding Max's hand.

"He won't have gone far," Flora said.

"How do you know?"

"Teleportation only works short range unless he has a key in hand. Did he have anything in his hands? I—"

Max jerked upright and screamed, pain and horror mixed in his groggy expression. Cormac hurried to his side and laid him back down. "It's okay, it's okay," he said, trying to sound soothing. "He's gone."

"I'm *open*," he gasped, looking down at his bleeding incisions.

"Yes, can we do something about that?" Cormac asked Flora.

"We've sent for Master Molas," she said, her voice just a little too anxious to be calming. "I'd close them myself, but I don't know what was done internally…"

"Oh, gods, it hurts," Max got out.

"Just hang on, darling," Cormac said, stroking what was left of his hair. "It's going to be all right. I promise."

Flora gathered up a cloth from a stack folded on the side table and began to staunch at the incisions. "That rat dropped the spell."

"He was always going to," Cormac said tersely. "Whenever it suited him."

"I don't understand. Did he want him alive or not?"

Cormac looked to Max, who was starting to shake, his gaze hazy. He simply shook his head. Anora's eyes shut around tears and she pressed Max's hand to her lips.

A shuffling sound from the hallway and a deep voice boomed, "Let me pass!"

Cormac went to the door and told the guards, "Please, let him through." Molas was shuffled into the room, and Cormac intended fully to tell him everything that had happened, but instead, what came out was, "Help. Please."

Molas' eyes lit in horror and disgust on Max's injuries. "We must work quickly. Lady Nythera. Aid me."

She steeled herself and nodded, rolling her sleeves back. Molas produced a draught for Max to drink, and shortly, his eyes fell shut again. He cast about the operating theater. "Thankfully, it doesn't look like they got far along, but they were ready to receive all kinds of samples. I will need to check that there is not internal damage before we move to close him up."

Cormac took the hint, but Anora was lost, holding her son's hand. He held out an arm to her. "Your Majesty," he said. "We should let them work."

She couldn't pry her gaze from Max's face—not easily. In the end, she took Cormac's arm and let him lead her from the tunnels. They walked in silence all the way to the magically-warmed rose garden, where they'd had dinner all those days ago. Anora sank to a seat.

"He is not wrong," she said. "I did this to him."

Cormac sat down across from her. "He had you under his control. Max knew that."

"He begged me. Pleaded with me not to let them take him. And I did."

She buried her face in her hands, her shoulders shaking. Cormac sat quietly, unsure of how to handle this. It wasn't as though one generally pulled the Queen into a hug. At length, he looked up. "Why did you come down to the experimentation chamber?"

She lowered her hands just slightly, a little perplexed by the question. "I suppose my heart wasn't set. I just—he was so shaken, so *desperate*. I couldn't leave it."

Cormac smiled just slightly. "So you believed him in the end."

"I would say, *of course I did*, but I've given him no reason to trust that." Her head hung forward. "I truly believed him. Aubric. I thought he would help my boy. I thought he was helping me. Instead, I've acted a fool, and an imperious one at that. Please, can you forgive me?"

"Me?" he asked in surprise. "There's nothing for me to forgive."

"That is…kind, but untrue. I did not make you feel welcome. I forced you to speak on your family. Put you through the trial of a welcoming to legitimize your relationship when it needed no such thing."

Cormac folded his hands on top of the metal table. "Truth be told, Your Majesty, we knew you were under his control. We expected some tension."

She persisted, "But it was not complete control. Some of that was me."

"How much do you remember?"

Anora pressed her hand to her forehead. "All of it, now. At the time, everything was foggy. As though I could only see what was close at hand. And he made sure to stay close. My poor boy…he tried so hard to reach me. And this is how I repaid him."

"He did reach you. You came for him."

"Too late."

Cormac looked at her shrewdly. "No. Not too late. Too late would have been after Aubric was done with him."

"You really think…he'd have disposed of…?"

"He told me. He wanted Max to lose everything."

"But why—?"

Cormac started to break out into a cold sweat when he remembered that Max's mother knew nothing about Max's history with Aubric. He hoped it was okay to say no to the Queen and said, "It's not my story to tell, ma'am. I'm sure Max will tell you now. But the way I see it, it's our job to make sure he loses as little as possible. All the time, really, but especially right now."

She smiled faintly and reached out to set her hand on top of Cormac's, just briefly. "I think I see what it is my son sees in you. He is very lucky. As is this nation."

"Thank you," he said, a little stunned.

She looked him in the eyes. "Are you all right?"

"If I am being honest, this is all very new to me. I come from a village where relationships like Max's and mine are *at best* a laughingstock. And I know I'm not…any parent's dream for their child."

"Oh, Cormac," Anora sighed. "That is not true. Now that we know you, I can say that is far from true."

He smiled down at the ground. "I'm a poor man with three jobs, no social training, and a tendency to solve problems with my hands."

"And you are learning. You are caring and sweet and you love my son enough to learn. That is all I could hope for."

Cormac smiled a little bigger. "Thank you. Sincerely."

"No. Thank *you*. You stood by Max while all of this happened around you. I am proud of you both. I simply…I hope I get the chance to tell him."

"You will," he promised. "He's strong."

He told himself almost as much as he needed to tell her.

Chapter Twenty-One
The Promise

Max floated in the darkness, vaguely aware that things were happening to his body, but mostly blissfully unheeding. It was a pleasant change from the drugging Aubric had given him, where he was always on the edge of consciousness and the pain wasn't far away. Both had been largely dreamless—until now.

He blinked and found himself in a room that wasn't his, but one that he knew well. He lay between purple satin sheets while soft music played from somewhere—a favorite trick of Aubric's. A hand found his bare chest. "Rest," Aubric told him.

Max's eyelids were heavy, and he *was* tired, but this was wrong. He sat up slowly. Aubric sat on the edge of the bed, fully dressed. "Shh," he said. "Just let this be nice."

"It can't be," Max insisted. "I'm not in love with you any-more."

"Well." He looked off into the darkness. "You're not one to pull the bandage off gently, are you?"

"Apparently it needs to be said. I'm not in love with you, and had I known the truth about you, I never would have been."

"The truth. And what truth is that?"

"You used me. Just like you used that kid I found you with." He clamped his arms around himself. "Hells, *I* was a kid when you started—I was lonely, I wasn't out, and you told me what I wanted to hear—that an older man thought I was mature and intelligent beyond my years."

"I waited," Aubric said tersely.

"You waited until it was legal. But ethical? It was never ethical."

"You act as though you had no part in it."

He laughed darkly. "You were the teacher. I was the student. What part had I in my own use?"

"You seemed more than happy to participate."

"I didn't know what I was doing!"

"And I was happy to show you."

Max shook his head, holding the sheets to himself. "And then you couldn't have me anymore, so you used me in a different way. As though you still had a claim on my body."

Aubric turned just slightly to look over his shoulder. "No one knows it the way I do. Certainly not that meat-headed, hamfisted git—"

"You will not speak about Cormac that way."

"You need an intellectual equal. Someone who challenges you."

"Is that what you were doing?"

"It was all a puzzle. For you."

"I didn't ask for it. I didn't want it."

Aubric turned sharply on him. "Nor did you solve it. All these pieces, collected for you, and I have had to hand you the solutions time after time. *Why* do I want you, Max?"

"I can't honestly fathom."

"That's just lazy. Try. Think it through."

"You don't like losing. You never have."

"Yes, but *why*, Max? Why your parents? Why did I come up with the threat of the Assassin's League? Why am I bothering to corner you now?"

"The League—that was you?"

Impatiently, Aubric said, "Yes, yes. Fear is a more potent means of control than any spell I could cast. Why do you think I had those mercenaries take your friend?"

"Because you have no interest whatsoever in being a decent person," Max said.

"Will you take this seriously?"

"I will not," Max said. "I've had enough. I don't want to dance to your tune anymore."

"You have no choice. I have you trapped in your own mind."

Yes, that was somewhat panic-inducing, but Max forced himself to retain an air of calm. Likely Aubric was just using the fact that he was asleep to his own advantage. If that was true, he would wake when Molas was done with him. If it was something more sinister, they would figure it out when he didn't come around. He just had to keep him from doing something drastic in the meantime.

"Truth be told, Aubric, I don't know. I've tried to understand from the beginning. You took control of my mother, only to not avail yourself of the power having control of the queen gave you. Instead you focused on the research your old school chum was doing on transmutation."

Aubric pressed his lips together. "The power I would receive from one is greater than the other."

"No, you're flat out desperate for what the Director has. Something you haven't been able to achieve for yourself. You want an army of secret soldiers."

"Silly boy. With access to your mother, I have that."

"Not shapeshifting ones. Not ones willing to jettison their forms for you. And in Saltrush, you're unlikely to find that. So you're riding the Director's coattails."

"It...is remarkable to have such a wide sample set of willing participants."

"Willing. That's a funny word for *trapped, with no choice.*"

"It depends on how you look at it."

"You would claim it's subjective. But it doesn't matter. You've already been experimenting on them."

"How did you—?" His eyes narrowed. "The laboratory boys."

"Don't take it out on them. It was obvious. Such an elaborate setup only for me? Doubtful."

"Oh, don't be so modest. You are the key to all those little soldiers."

"And I will be their undoing," he said. "I swear it."

"Not if you never leave this place."

Max's heart pounded. So that's what he had planned. Keep him suspended in twilight while dawns rolled by him in real time. But that was easier said than done. It was difficult magic to sustain when in the same room, and as far as he knew, that wasn't true. He had to wake up.

The draught was keeping him asleep. His eyelids felt heavy and his limbs weighted and warm. Even the tail, which moved reflexively, was still. Max willed himself to move something, anything. His tail twitched. Good. He tried to will his breaths to come shallower. Aubric looked over. "No—"

Max smiled lopsidedly. "See you around, Aubric."

He felt the magic swell, try to press him down again, but he felt himself rise above the oppressive layer of enchantment and his consciousness float to the surface again. His eyes snapped open, and Molas looked up in alarm. "Your Highness! You should be asleep—"

"He's trying to keep me in a forced slumber," Max said quickly.

Molas looked to Flora, then the guards. "That means he's nearby," he said.

Flora ordered, "Quick, search whatever is immediately upstairs. He's not getting away."

The guards immediately trooped out. Cormac entered against the tide of guards and looked around. "What's going on?"

"He tipped his hand," Molas said. "He has to be in one of the nearby rooms."

"I'm on it," Cormac said, immediately turning on his heel.

Max longed to call out for him to stay, to come back, but his head was thick and swimming with the magic assailing it and the draught still trying to do its work. Molas followed his gaze. "He will come back," he assured him.

Anora stepped forward tentatively, and Max turned his bleary eyes on her. "Mama," he managed.

She put her hand to the unbandaged side of his face. "Max," she said. "I am—so—"

"I know," he said with a little smile.

"All this time talking about your curse, and it turns out it was me who wasn't myself." He lifted his hand to her, and she took it, trembling, unable to look him quite in the face. He caught her eyes, and she froze. "I was wrong," she said. "About so much, but I see you now."

He kissed her hand. "Thank you."

"Can you ever forgive me?"

"Already done. As long as you're done taking…advice from Aubric." She nodded profusely. Max didn't dare close his eyes, but they creased in pain. "I should tell you—"

"Not now, darling," she said. "Whatever it is, it can wait until you're better."

Molas nodded. "We weren't quite done with the bandaging, Your Highness."

Anora stepped back and folded her hands in front of her, giving Molas and Flora the room they needed to maneuver around the table. Max tried not to think too hard about the pain in his midsection as they coaxed him into sitting up enough to wind yards of clean white bandage around him. Flora slung Max's arm over her shoulder while she worked, and despite how cold and terrifying this room was, he felt a little warmth. Now if only Cormac could return.

The guards charged through the adjacent rooms, leaving sub-tlety to the wind, and cleared all the downstairs rooms quickly— all that was left was the room above, and that was the one Cor-mac made straight for.

Aubric's room.

Cormac listened at the door and heard movement behind it. The guards tried the knob, which didn't budge, then immediately moved to kick in the door. Cormac gave them space, but as soon as the door was open, he barreled inside. Empty. The guards looked dejected, but Cormac wasn't done yet.

There were tables and cupboards and shelves all over, and there were things all over them. It only took him a second to find something suitable. In a dish on the bedside table was a deep black powder. He idly grabbed a handful then scattered it into the air. Most of it fell back to the ground, but some of it clung to something invisible.

Cormac reached out and grabbed a fistful of clothing. "I have him."

Aubric dropped the invisibility. "Not terrible, for someone with a substandard education."

"Give it up," Cormac advised. "You're surrounded."

Aubric lifted a wooden token with a circle burned into it, and

Cormac froze. This had to be one of those teleportation keys. Aubric could get far from this place—anywhere. And Cormac bet that if he didn't let go, he'd be transported to gods knew where with him.

He had one chance to take the key from him. Cormac reeled back and sent a fist straight into Aubric's face. His nose exploded in a spray of red, to go with the badly split lip he'd gotten from Cormac's last punch.

Aubric tilted his head back, cradling his face in his hand. "A *very* good try," he said, and he disappeared.

Cormac slumped. How was he going to tell Max and the Queen that he'd lost him? After everything he'd done, the bastard had whisked himself off to parts unknown. For all they knew, he'd be seeing to his beat-to-shit face on a tropical island. He stared at the floor, at the fresh droplets of blood. After everything, it wasn't enough.

Defeated, he returned downstairs. Max laid back on the table again while Molas wrapped his arm. Cormac approached the table, and Max's unbandaged eye opened. He eased into a tired smile, and despite everything, Cormac found himself smiling, too. "Hi."

Max took his hand, observed some blood on it. "Yours or his?"

"His," he said, wiping it off. "Wasn't enough. He teleported."

Max swallowed. "Well. That's…all right. I don't think we could have held him."

Anora spoke up. "Every protection we have against a mage in

the prison is one he put there. I don't think he would have been there five minutes."

Still. Cormac didn't feel particularly good with him loose in the world, and he bet Max felt the same.

Molas said gently, "I can place wards against his return."

"I do seem to have a vacant position for an arcane advisor," the Queen said. "I would be honored if you would consider the prospect."

"I will have to think on it, Your Majesty. My city is not the most hospitable to mages at the moment, and I heard the Director asserting that he has broken no laws."

Cormac would have liked very much to break something of his, but he kept his peace. Anora said, "We will have to see about that at his upcoming trial. In the meantime—we should leave this dismal place."

"Yes, please," Max said.

Cormac positioned himself to lift Max from the table, when he saw Max quickly grab the crystal and something else that he didn't quite catch. He handed both things to Flora, who pocketed them so that Max could hang on around Cormac's neck. Cormac gripped tightly as though if he let go, he might get whisked away again. Hells, he hoped that fear would go away soon.

When they arrived at Max's bedroom, Cormac laid him down. Carrying number three was much harder than any others, but he didn't want Max to think he was straining. He was heavy, but not a burden.

Cormac knelt at the edge of the bed and gently set his hand

to Max's forehead. While Flora and the Queen were asked to stand a short distance away, Molas did not shoo him. "We are lucky," he said, his voice low. "The opening incisions were as far as your captor got in most cases. There were a few more cuts made near your eye, but nothing that will not heal on its own. Your horn, I'm afraid, is unlikely to grow back."

"My tail did," Max said.

"Good heavens, he cut off your tail?"

"It was in a jar down there."

Cormac heard Molas uttering things that sounded dark and vile under his breath. "If that's the case, it may come back the next time you change into this form. Your body has a template that it follows when making changes. Injuries will transfer—that's written in the flesh. But modifications should not. I expect you will be weak for some time. Between the rapid transformations of the last day or so and now this—do not expect much of yourself."

Max nodded. Cormac held his hand close to his chest and stroked it. "Can you make sure that no one can tamper with the stone again?"

"Yes, I think that is of utmost priority. Lady Nythera?"

"Yes, I have it," she said. "I'll go with you in just a second." She bent at the waist to give Max a gentle hug, and Cormac clocked her slip an object into his hand. "You'll need this back."

"Thank you," he told her, putting his hand to her arm.

"What are friends for?" she asked cheerfully.

"No, Flora," he said seriously. "*Thank you.* You keep saving me."

"Well, you keep returning the favor." She smiled and patted his cheek softly. "Love you, Max. Rest well."

She and Molas slipped from the room. Anora looked around. "I should let you rest."

"Mother, wait," Max got out.

She paused in the doorway, uncertain of herself in space. She didn't often leave her set of chambers, the paths between well-worn and familiar. "What is it, my darling?"

He extended his other hand to her, and she swallowed and crossed the room again to take it up. "You don't have to say anything. There is no simple script for this, no polite fiction," he told her, his voice low. Her lip trembled, and he leaned his head forward and tried to make eye contact. "I know. This is what he does."

"I owe you…much more than this," she said wretchedly.

"I hope you know that I will not hold you to that debt."

Her eyes shut. "You are gracious, my love. You did not get that from me. And I will see it paid, should it take the rest of my days. I only—"

"Mother, I don't expect you to have everything sorted," he said with a lopsided smile. "You've only just now regained yourself. Take some time. I'll be here."

Anora held his hand in both of hers tightly for a space, then pressed the back of it to her lips.

Without another word, she left them to their quiet, and Cormac sat on the edge of the bed with Max's head rested against his hip. They didn't speak much, but in their touches they said everything. Max's seeking, insecure reaches, Cormac's reassurances of them both.

Max still clutched something in his left hand, the thing Flora had slipped to him. "Cormac?" he ventured at last.

"Yes, my heart?"

He clawed his way up to a sitting position to face Cormac. "I've been waiting. Searching for the perfect moment. And there were some good ones, but then I waited too long. I don't want to ass this up."

Cormac tilted his head. "You? Impossible."

"That's kind of you, but it's really very possible. I've run through it again and again, and there are so many ways I could just completely screw this up." He looked up at him. "I'm only asking you to share forever with me."

"Oh," Cormac said, realization setting in. He knew he should say more than that, but that's all that came out.

"But I realized today that if I wait—the future is not guaranteed. I don't want to have waited for the perfect moment only to miss a half-dozen near-perfect ones." Cormac nodded. Max took his hand and placed what he'd been cradling in it. A small velvet box, warm with the heat of his hand. "I won't ask if you don't want me to. I can wait until I'm better, or for just the right moment. But I don't want to miss any more time. I didn't know what was going to happen to me back there, and all I could think of was that I hadn't managed to ask you."

Cormac closed Max's hands around the box. "Ask me."

Max opened the box. "Assholes call this ring the Prince's Folly.

Whether it's yours or mine, I'm not sure." He removed the ring from its box at last and set it aside. Max lifted his uncovered eye to Cormac. "Will you marry me?"

Cormac kissed Max. "Yes."

He slipped the ring on. "Its real name is The Prince's Promise," he said. "I think it's a little more apt, as what you get is no more and no less than one prince engaged to you."

"I don't think I could handle more than the one," he said, grinning.

Max held his hands in his. "I can't ever repay you for what you've given me," he said softly. "But I figure giving you the rest of my life might be a good start."

Cormac kissed him again. "A very good start."

Max had been instructed to refresh number three the next day, and indeed every day after that as he healed. Cormac made no objections. Molas was fairly certain the stress of his body remaking itself would delay the process if not thwart it, and he was happy enough to listen to the closest thing there was to an expert on his condition.

He wasn't quite prepared for how remaining the same every day would leave him restless after a time. Max found himself bumping his head into the wall as though he had forgotten he wasn't shorter, resenting his bulk in Cormac's arms, surprised by his own tail. Part of it was almost certainly being constrained to bed, but even as Molas unwound his bandages and told him he was free to move about again, he felt nervous, trapped.

In service of trying to ease this feeling, Max left his room one afternoon when Cormac had gone to town to post a letter to Brenna, pulling a far-too-short cloak to himself for the chill and ranging the colonnades for a time. At length, he found himself following the snow-bound path to the warmed rose garden so he could doff the irritating, ineffective cloak. The furl of the fabric startled someone along the back wall where the roses mingled with green hedges.

"Max," his mother said, standing quickly and placing her hand to her chest.

He smiled lopsidedly. "Still not a fan of number three, I see."

"No, no, I simply wasn't expecting anyone—ordinarily it's only me and the flowers at this time of day."

"Am I unwelcome?"

"Never." She brushed off her hands, folding them in front of her and approaching cautiously. She reached up with a hesitant hand to his uncovered eye, still swollen from the incision from the brow to the top of his cheekbone. She pulled away and folded her hands again. "Are you well?"

"Getting there," he said with a little laugh. "Bit at a time. That is usually how these things work."

"You never could stay down," she said, a touch of fondness pulling at her lips. "When you were ill with the ague it took your father, two governesses, *and* me to keep you from running through the halls."

"How old was I? I have no memory of this."

She waved him off. "Oh, four. You also refused clothing much of the time. Most of my cabinet has seen your backside."

If only she knew. He pushed at his forehead. "That…wondrous."

She cleared her throat. "I apologize. That may not have been what you were hoping to hear."

He laughed a little tentatively. "No, actually, it was rather surprising."

Anora set her mouth to the side. "It it really?" she asked softly. "That I might have memories of my only son as he was?"

Max found himself at a loss. Part of him wanted to break into a smile and tell her *of course not*, that he felt fondness too when he thought back. But there was a part of him that remembered that fondness with no small amount of chafing. He settled his number one-sized cloak over his arm and thought carefully.

He felt her hand touch his forearm, and he looked up. His mother looked pained. "You've never held back before. Tell me."

He found himself laughing darkly. "Oh, if only that were true." She arced a single silver eyebrow, and Max caught himself, tried to rearrange his words. "You don't know how intimidating it is, being in my position. My mother, the Queen. Beloved by many, feared by some. And then there's me, at the corner of both."

She stepped back a little. "Feared? When have I—?"

Max entreated, "Please, just—listen. All my life you told me who I was." He turned toward the tall white spires and gestured loosely to them. "The Crown Prince of Saltrush, only heir to your throne. And I tried. I tried to just *be that*. But there are pieces of me that made you angry. And you brought the Queen to bear on them, when all I wanted was my—" His voice went thick, and he looked away.

Stricken into silence, Anora barely breathed. "That's what you thought?" she asked, her voice barely audible. "That I was angry with you?"

"It was hard to think anything but," he said a bit bitterly. "The edicts, the ever-increasing rules, the—contempt for my bids for my peace."

"Max," she said, and his name in her voice sounded so sorrowful that he couldn't help but look at her now. "I was never angry."

"Then why?" He asked, unable to keep his eyes from stinging. "Why did you try to change me? Why couldn't you see me for all I was?"

"I...." She pressed her lips together. "I feared. I feared what would be done to you, said to you. I feared the scheming in the dark. The arrow—" Her throat caught. "It was never about *you,* who you were. Only your position in this place. And that version of you is all most will ever know. I feared letting them see more."

Max knew. He'd known since the day in her chambers after his father was attacked. Even still. Barely able to bring his voice above audible, he said, "But you had to know what it would do, forcing myself small for people who could never love me regardless. What it would do to me, to you."

"You would survive."

"But would I live?" he asked, trembling.

Anora pressed her hand to her mouth, unable to look his way. He let go of a held breath, his shoulders coming down. He fished a handkerchief from his pocket, crossed the space they'd held between them, and handed it to her. "I'm alive," he told her. "You don't need to mourn me."

She blotted at her eyes and looked up at the pale layer of clouds spanning the sky. "Forgive me, darling. I have yet to assure myself of this."

It felt awful, but it needed to be done. "Mother, there's something you should know."

"What is it, my love?"

"All of this—the curse, the Assassin's League, the control Aubric took over you—it started a long time ago."

"I don't understand. Those are all different things."

He shook his head. "They were all woven by Aubric. He invited the enchantress here. He falsified the League. And it's all because...." He trailed off. "He pursued me. When I was his student. Barely of age. I never told you, because I was ashamed to have been so taken in. When I saw him for what he was, I ended it. And I don't think he's ever gotten over that."

Anora's eyes flashed, and she drew herself up, but something she saw in his face softened her. "That could never be your fault, my darling. *He* was the adult. *He* was the teacher. It was his responsibility to comport himself appropriately. And he did not. Had I known—"

"I know, I should have told you."

"I doubt he encouraged you to."

"No. But I just—at the time, I thought it was my indiscretion."

"He taught you well." Disgust radiated from her features. "If I see him again, I will make him long for prison." She looked down. "My love—there are no apologies I can give that will ever suffice."

"You came for me," he said. "Even with him in your head. You heard me and you came. That's more than enough for me."

Anora shut her eyes and smiled, though trails of wetness streamed down her cheeks. "Then let it be for me, too. It may take some time."

Time. He looked down at the green blades of grass around his hooves. Time had been gnawing at him these past days. Time lost to a veneer of sameness, despite knowing better now. He chewed on his words, tried to start, realized he didn't know where to begin. He looked up and saw her looking back, pensive. "What?" he asked insecurely.

She stepped up to him and reached up to put her hand to the uninjured side of his face. "My boy—my child. I have done too much pronouncement. My debt grows." He started to shake his head, but she stopped him. "I hope you will allow me this."

Crunching footsteps sounded from behind them, and Cormac puffed into view. "There you are—" He pulled up short and awkwardly sank into a bow. "I—er, sorry, Your Majesty."

She smiled and touched his shoulder to straighten him, then took his hand and placed it in Max's, clasping hers around them. "Live," she exhorted. "Together. Yourselves, always." She turned to Max. "For everything that you are, for all."

Cormac blinked, looking kind of dazed. Max blinked too, much harder, against tears. Anora swept them from his cheeks and bowed his head for a kiss, touched both of their arms, and left them to the garden.

Cormac looked to Max immediately. "Are you all right?"

Max cautiously wiped at his eyes with the edge of his thumb, trying to avoid irritating his incision. "I'm not convinced I woke up," he said with a wet laugh.

Cormac placed his other hand over Max's and held on in quiet for a moment. "I couldn't find you," he said clumsily, "so I came."

"I'm sorry. I should've left a note. I just couldn't lie there anymore."

He nodded, eyeing him carefully. "Did this help, or…?"

"It helped. Or started to. It's an old hurt with new edges. I think…she just gave her blessing. Without any sort of magic at work. Though I guess I could have fetched a toad to be sure."

"That is what it sounded like. What will you do with it?"

Max looked around at the garden, the reds and oranges of the roses, the green of the grass against the white snow. The spires didn't seem to loom anymore. He was home, and he was himself. He laughed a little disbelievingly. "Live."

Thank you!

Please consider giving the book a rating or leaving a review, they really mean a lot to us indie authors. If you want to know the latest that's going on and everything that's coming up for me and Elyssia Books, the best thing to do is sign up for my newsletter. It has news, musings, insights into my process, and my adorable pets.

amazon.com/author/anna-holmes

-

elyssiabooks.com

Acknowledgements

Without Jason, Max wouldn't exist. Giving the character space to exist first in the context of a two-person D&D campaign and then as a novel meant the world to me. Max was an attempt to keep me cheered up during my convalescence with long COVID. As it turned from medical leave to long term disability, keeping morale up was a challenge, and sometimes, telling Max's story was one of very few reasons to keep on. Jason's patient indulgence of my need to tell stories even when the energy for everything else was gone is the reason I can do this. He agreed that not only could I write Max's story, but that I *should*.

This was the first book I wrote from scratch since my diagnosis- everything else existed in draft form beforehand. And Jason was here every step of the way, from lending me the version of Cormac he played in the game (I promise to take care of him and only put him in peril sometimes) to providing the voice of Max's mother to talking through the plot holes I write for myself to editing to the incredible art on the cover. There would be no books and very little me without Jason.

Dana calls me every week. We talk about anything and everything, but oftentimes we talk about queerness, media, and queerness in the media. When I said I wanted to write about a genderqueer prince who doesn't exactly know what his answer is by the end of the book, I believe she said "good fucking luck", which I choose to believe was encouragement. In reality, she's been showing people my cover like a proud aunt and yelling at the weird trolls vicariously. "OF COURSE IT'S A GAY BOOK, YOU'RE GAY." The validation is everything for me, a bi ace genderqueer whatever who is perceived as a woman. Sometimes everyone needs a Dana to cut through the crap.

A million thanks to Amanda, Scott, Mike, and Stephanie for keeping my head on these last few months and sensitivity work, whichever you contributed to (Scott wasn't the sensitivity guy. I feel compelled to note that). Thanks to pocket friends on Bluesky for the times my head fell off. And thank you for letting me share Max. It means everything.